"... she writes with great power, and the prose is exhilarating
... Mlle Blais is sustained by her sense of life, her native
humanity, her eloquence, her feelings for the possibilities; we
may say, paraphrasing Yeats, that she sets her chisel to the
hardest stone."

– *The New York
Review of Books*

Born in Quebec City in 1939, Marie-Claire Blais has become one of this generation's most well-known French-Canadian writers. The eldest of five children, Blais had to curtail her early convent education in order to help support her family. Later, however, she was able to attend Laval University, and it was here that a priest encouraged her interest in writing. Her first novel appeared when she was eighteen.

Widely respected in the U.S. and France, as well as in her native Canada, Blais has won the Prix Medicis (for her novel *A Season in the Life of Emmanuel*), and a Guggenheim Fellowship. Although, for a time, she made her home in the U.S., she currently lives in Quebec.

Marie-Claire Blais

St. Lawrence Blues

Translated from the French by Ralph Manheim

Introduction by Margaret Atwood

New Canadian Library No. 183

McClelland and Stewart

ISBN 0-7710-9337-3

McClelland and Stewart Limited
The Canadian Publishers
25 Hollinger Road
Toronto, Ontario
M4B 3G2

Printed and bound in Canada

To the
Memory of
EDMUND WILSON

Introduction

1

Marie-Claire Blais is undoubtedly the Quebec writer best known outside Quebec. In fact, it is perhaps through her work, especially the much-praised *A Season in the Life of Emmanuel* and *The Manuscripts of Pauline Archange,* that Quebec itself is best known outside Quebec, at least as a country of the imagination. She is almost unique among Quebec writers in that her work has been translated into twelve languages. She has won France's most coveted literary prize, the Prix Medicis, as well as several other awards, and she's drawn the attention of numerous critics, most importantly the late Edmund Wilson, who singled her out for special praise in his book *O Canada.*

Her reputation has been fairly earned. The dozen or so novels, the several volumes of poetry, the seven plays for stage or radio she's written during her brief but incandescent career display an astonishing range of style and subject, from the experimental and dream-like to the grimly realistic, from the bleak lives of impoverished children on Quebec's back streets to the convoluted philosophical musings of Baudelarian social outcasts who choose crime or suicide as their only means of protest. Although sometimes intimidated by the uncompromising nature of her books, critics have always been dazzled by their brilliance of execution.

This brilliance was apparent early. Blais made her literary debut in 1959 at the age of nineteen, with *La Belle Bete (Mad Shadows),* an hallucinatory tale of jealousy, hatred, mutilation and incest set in a lurid and only semi-real rural Quebec. The contrast between her age and her subject matter was sensational, and she was treated as a "discovery," both in Quebec and in English Canada. Much was made of her background of comparative poverty, her shoeboxes full of novels, her lack of formal education—she'd dropped out of school at fifteen and taken secretarial jobs in order to support herself—and the precocious intensity of her writing. Some critics saw her as a young genius, others as a child prodigy who would burn out early. It took her several years and as many novels to recover from her initial notoriety and prove herself as a serious writer.

It's paradoxical that a person whose name has been so closely associated with the Quebec cultural renaissance, the "quiet revolution" of the early sixties, one who was recognized abroad as its major and sometimes as its only literary voice, should have spent these important years outside the country. But her exile was not intentional. She went where her fortunes took her: first to Paris on a Canada Council grant, where she underwent the painful experience of being treated as a hopeless provincial in the city regarded at that time as the French cultural Mecca; then to New England, where she mingled with the Cape Cod artistic community and taught herself English by reading the novels of Jane Austen; later to Brittany, where she lived and wrote on a communal seven-acre farm. But although she was not physically present in Quebec, she was certainly there in spirit, and no one who has read the work of Jacques Ferron, Roch Carrier or Réjean Ducharme, to name a few, can doubt her right to membership in the Quebec literary community. In the past fifteen years, Quebec has evolved a manner as well as a matter which is unique and unmistakable, and Marie-Claire Blais has been central to that evolution.

She has recently moved back to Quebec, where she is currently re-establishing her roots and becoming acquainted with the new Quebec which came into being during her absence. For her there are two Quebecs. The old one was characterized by brutality, suffering and repression, symbolized by those sadistic nuns and slightly mad priests, those hulking, child-beating farmers and the tubercular urban poor that haunt her books. This was, at least in part, the Quebec of her own convent-educated childhood. For her it was a society that specialized in judging, condemning and punishing, and, although as a novelist she might be expected to feel some regret at the disappearance of a society that has provided so much of her own subject matter, she is not sorry to see it go. The new Quebec, she thinks, is a far different place: vibrant, alive, with a new confidence and freedom. But although she is enthusiastic about the changes, she is less certain about the intense political activity and awareness that brought at least some of them into being. Writers, she feels, should observe and record; they cross the line into political involvement at their own peril. "A writer is a *témoin*, a witness," she has said. "Dogmatism closes a writer off."

2

In some ways, *St. Lawrence Blues* is the first book in which Blais has attempted to bridge the gap between the old Quebec and the new one, to show representatives of both encountering each other, disputing, reacting. As such it's a very ambitious work, wide in scope, swarming with characters, aiming for breadth as well as depth. Blais has done many detailed studies of single characters, but *St. Lawrence Blues* is populous and many-faceted.

It's a fresh departure for her in other ways as well. She has always been amazingly versatile, switching with ease from romantic fantasy to novels of ideas to psychological studies to carefully-drawn social chronicles. But *St. Lawrence Blues* is none of these. The predominant note is satire. It's not a totally new element for Blais, as her previous work has often contained satirical and even humorous interludes; but these were asides, whereas in *St. Lawrence Blues* the tone is constant.

The book takes the reader on a tour through the seamy lower layers of present-day Quebec. The narrator is a Quebecois Everyman, an amiable minor rascal and self-proclaimed nonentity nicknamed Ti-Pit, "little nobody." Ti-Pit is an orphan who feels he belongs nowhere. Earlier in his life he's been put through one of those repressive nun-run orphanages so familiar to readers of Blais; later, he's been hired out to a brutal farmer. Now he's a drifter, living in rooming houses, working at degrading jobs until he can no longer stand them, getting by however he can. Everything interests him but he trusts nobody; consequently he is close-mouthed with his friends and associates, but carries on a constant silent conversation with himself. *St. Lawrence Blues* is the transcription of this oral diary, and it's evident from its verbal richness, astute commentary and improvised fantasies that despite his stunting and dehumanizing background Ti-Pit has somehow been able to retain both his mother-wit and his humanity.

Through his shrewd yet innocent eyes we are allowed to view a wide assortment of Quebecois, some sinister, some grotesque, some pathetic: Baptiste, an old-style working class drudge who is finally rewarded for his years of slavery at the Rubber Company by being fired so the boss won't have to give him a pension; his son Ti-Guy, an incurable addict, despised and neglected by his conservative father just as the father has been despised by society; Vincent, the worker-priest, constantly defrauded by those he tries to help; Mère Fontaine, the motherly, sentimental owner of Ti-Pit's boardinghouse, who steeps herself in police and murder literature and lives vicariously through her tenants, who include Mimi, a babyfaced female impersonator, Lison, a pregnant nymphomaniac, and two fifteen-year-old lesbian prostitutes, Josée and Monique. Through a chance encounter in a tavern, Ti-Pit is introduced to a side of Quebec life new to him: he meets Papillon, a verbose, self-aggrandizing poet who wants Ti-Pit to teach him *joual*, the language of the people, so he can use it to further his own literary ambitions. Papillon's friends include a shady lawyer from Quebec City who is writing a pornographic novel, Corneille the publisher, and Papineau, named ironically for a nineteenth century Quebec patriot, a phoney Marxist ascetic who demom trates his own ideological purity by attacking that of his friends, and forces his wife to live on rice while he himself is having a secret affair with a lush rich-living Westmount matron. Papillon's wife is involved in a peculiar brand of Quebec feminism: she and her friends storm the *Men Only* section of Ti-Pit's tavern, disrupting a few old alcoholics and proclaiming their right to drink Molson's on an equal footing. Papillon himself is annoyed by this because he feels she's stolen his own political cause, becoming even more *joualonese* than he himself has been able to. The bourgeoise intelligentsia in *St. Lawrence Blues* treat po-

litical ideas as if they are dog bones, squabbling over
sole possession; a situation familiar to anyone who has
watched the ultra-nationalist fringes in the rest of Canada during the past few years.

These people are all diversions for Ti-Pit: fascinating
and amusing, but not central to his real life. His own
past reappears in the form of Ti-Cul, his best friend from
orphanage days. Whereas Ti-Pit has adjusted to his half-
life by trying to stay out of trouble, Ti-Cul is a savage
pessimist who has embraced it. He writes violent, bitter
letters to Ti-Pit from prison, and when he gets out he
butchers the farmer who once victimized them both. Instead of applauding, Ti-Pit finds the crime sickening and
rejects Ti-Cul's efforts to involve him. He too has hated
the farmer for his brutality, but he does not see greater
brutality as the proper response. He is not interested in
the role of romantic rebel, or indeed in any of the roles
being played out by those around him.

Blais brings all the elements of her broad canvas together at the end of the book in a giant demonstration
against social injustice, which is supposed to be heroic
but instead turns into a combination of farce and tragedy. The groups of demonstrators, including nuns, prostitutes, students, fishermen, homosexuals, and even some
disgruntled policemen who feel the public is not grate-
ful enough, wallow about in the ever-present snow,
exchange insults, scuffle and shout each other down
until the police break up the march with needless viciousness, killing a student in the process. Only then can
the bewildered and injured treat each other with anything resembling kindness and humanity. For Blais,
ideology separates, suffering unites.

Reading *St. Lawrence Blues* is like listening to the
many voices of Quebec arguing among themselves. It's
a domestic argument, and as such, parts of it are not
totally comprehensible to an outsider. There are private
grudges, puns on names and titles, snide references, in-
nuendoes and complicated in-group jokes. But like all
domestic arguments, it provides more intimate and in
many ways more accurate insights into the personalities

of those concerned than their polished official facades
would ever give away. This is the book of a culture
laughing at itself; though as befits a colonized culture,
the laughter is not totally lighthearted, not without bitterness and a characteristic Quebecois sense of macabre
irony.

It's important to remember that *St. Lawrence Blues*
was originally called *Un Joualonais, Sa Joualonie,* a title
whose virtual untranslateability underlines not only the
courage of the translator but the nature of the special
situation the book deals with. Ti-Pit's kingdom, his
joualonie, is a colony within a colony within a colony:
the lower classes oppressed by the rich French within
Quebec and by the English who control both of them,
oppressed in their turn by their economic position *vis-a-
vis* the United States. *Maitres Chez Nous,* the rallying-
cry of the early separatist movement, indicates what was
lacking: a sense of control over one's own cultural and
economic destiny. *Joual* is the language spoken in
joualonie (the term comes from a dialect form of the
French word *cheval*), the language of the man on the
street, the "little guy," the "assholes" who demonstrate
at the end of the book.

And here there's a joke within a joke, for Blais herself has been criticized by certain ultra-*joualonist* Quebec literary figures for her early work and its lack of
purity according to their standards. For them *joual* is a
shibboleth: those who speak it pass, those who don't
fail. But in *St. Lawrence Blues* Blais out-*jouals* the
most ardent *joualonists,* thereby proving that she can do
it too, while at the same time jumping these pretensions
through hoops of her own construction.

Every character in the book is defined by his or her
relationship to this language. Ti-Pit himself is a natural
inhabitant of *joualonie,* and its logical product. Papillon
the poet, on the other hand, has had to learn it—his
own language would have been more Parisian middle-
class French—and like all converts he overdoes it: he
speaks it self-consciously, proclaiming its virtues at
every turn and sprinkling his conversation with oaths

such as "holy pyx" and "bleeding veronica" in a way
that makes the strictly-trained Ti-Pit blink. Papillon is
a linguistic purist; at one point he picks a fight over an
English-language restaurant, declaring, "Revolution, the
dignity of our people, is a matter of details, of bacon
and eggs." He longs to be accepted as one of the people
and writes in what he considers to be "pure" *joual*; yet
he is constantly being attacked by those further to the
left. One of his most crushing humiliations comes when
he has an affair with a Parisienne, who has trouble understanding his accent, calls him a "noble savage," and
patronizes him in much the same way that he himself
patronizes Ti-Pit.

The irony of the Quebec situation as depicted in *St.
Lawrence Blues* is that the real *joualonese,* the natives,
don't care about their language. If they think about it
at all, it's as a sign of their lack of education, their op-
pression, their inability to make themselves understood.
The most poignant example of this is Ti-Foin ("little
hay" or "hayseed"), a poor farmer's son who has come
to Montreal because he couldn't stand the wretchedness
of life at home. "I want to talk to you like a man," he
says; then he bursts into tears, declaring that he has no
words because nobody has given him any. It is only the
petit-intelligentsia who idealize *joual,* while at the same
time using it to score points against one another and
exploiting it for their own ideological or artistic ends.
Their world is permeated with an inverse snobbery
which Ti-Pit himself cannot understand. He admires the
big cars and plush apartments of the intelligentsia, as
well as the contents of their overstocked refrigerators,
but he has little use for their slogans.

However, *St. Lawrence Blues* is far from being simply
a political allegory. Ti-Pit is a fully developed character
in his own right, and it's against his very human per-
sonality that the frivolity, viciousness and bloodless
idealism of the others are measured. His motives are
simple: he wants to be happy, to get as much as he can
from his life, despite its limited prospects. Behind his
protective cynicism and his taciturn exterior, he has a

love of words and of what they can describe, and a practical charity most of the other characters lack. As he is a bastard and an orphan himself, he sympathizes with underdogs of all kinds; he even defends Ti-Cul the murderer. He dislikes the death, violence and squalor which surround him, and resists the despair of Ti-Guy, the hatred and destructiveness of Ti-Cul and the nihilism of his co-worker the ambulance driver, for whom all human life is worthless and expendable. Despite much evidence that would refute him, he believes that "life is better than limbo."

The novel's loosely-constructed, frenetic and sometimes wandering narrative is held together by one single thread: Ti-Pit's search for a sense of self-worth, for an identity. His real name is not Ti-Pit at all: it is Abraham Lemieux, and someone calls him by this name for the first time in his life at the beginning of the novel. "Ti-Pit" means "nobody"; Abraham Lemieux, however, has quite a different connotation. Abraham was the father of a people, and Lemieux means "the best." "Come to think of it," Ti-Pit remarks, "Lemieux has a noble, cheerful ring. . . ." Throughout his wanderings and encounters, Ti-Pit is looking for some element in his society which will recognize him, and implicitly all those like him, as something more than a bastard and orphan, something more than a nobody. But those of his own class are too helpless, too twisted by cruelty, or too hardpressed by practical necessities, and the bourgeoise intelligentsia are presented as clowns or absurdities who have lost touch with human realities in their worship of abstractions. Perhaps, Blais may be suggesting, it is Abraham Lemieux and the qualities he represents— hard-won experience, charity, practical wisdom and a tolerant love of life—who will "father" the emerging society of Quebec. But it's a vague and tenuous hope. At the end of the book, Ti-Pit dreams of meeting Papillon, as he did in the opening chapter. Papillon calls him by his *joual* nickname, and Ti-Pit replies, "Ti-Pit, never heard of him . . . my name is Abraham, Abraham Lemieux." But as Ti-Pit himself remarks, it is only a dream.

Blais may be hinting that *joual* and the impoverished kingdom of *joualonie* will have to be changed, renounced, even obliterated, before its inhabitants can attain the human dignity for which they seek. But that event is a long way off, even in imagination, for men like Ti-Pit, who must experience the social conditions which have formed *joualonie,* who can react to them as one reacts to a kick, but who, lacking credible leaders, do not have the power to change them. On this level, *St. Lawrence Blues* is more than an amusing satire. Hidden beneath its surface, as Abraham Lemieux is hidden beneath the surface of Ti-Pit, is the threat of revolution.

1.

WHEN I was a kid at the orphanage, they called me Ti-Pit, when it wasn't Ti-Père, Ti-Cul, or Ti-Noir, and you know what that means in French? It means "little nothing" or "big hole in the ground"; I'm not like other people, no education at all, not a speck, but I catch words like the measles, I have these highfalutin confabs with myself, that's my secret, words seem to pick you up when you haven't anybody else. But the other day fate spinned its wheel and Ti-Pit pretty near dropped dead. It happened in a tavern I go to after the Rubber Company, tires, good winter tires they turn out as fast as a hen can lay Easter eggs, so I sashay into this tavern and I see this scribbleroo, the gentry would call him a poet, he looked it, but he could just as well have been in business, he's got a little pot under his white shirt and a smiling moon face with a fringe of dark hair around it, you could say he looked like a friendly dog that wouldn't hurt a fly, and he panted like a dog that's been running a long ways, yes, that's the picture. He's got a big sheaf of papers, he's reading and turning them over, the beer bottles are standing in front of him like a row of queens, and his face was grave, like he'd worn himself out from thinking so hard, that's it, that's how I want to describe him. He had at least seven beers under his belt, and that was only the beginning. "You may sit down," he says. "I won't eat you. My name is Papillon, Eloi Papillon, remember that name, Papillon, it murmurs, it sings, it makes you think of the autumn wind. Papillon. But what is your name?"

"Ti-Pit."

Christ, take your real name out of your pocket, honor it, you're not nobody, a French Canadian and citizen of Montreal isn't nobody!"

"My real name is Abraham Lemieux."

"Abraham Lemieux, I salute you! Stand up and give me your hand."

That's how, at the Dancing Cat Tavern, Abraham Lemieux, for the first time in his life, had his ears tickled by his real name. Come to think of it, Lemieux has a noble, cheerful ring, even if Abraham Lemieux has been unlucky all his life. So we batted the breeze, you'd have thought this Papillon was the same class of people as me, a bum dressed up for Sunday, but it wasn't true, he was only trying to put himself on a level with my britches, and the Christs and holy pyxes and bleeding veronicas poured from his lips like three dozen rosaries, and I thought, Hell, this guy curses too much! but I didn't say it, you know why? Because when my chum Vincent the curé, a second St. Vincent de Paul, no two ways about it, came to see me in jail when I was only a kid practically, I promised him that before I was thirty, middle-aged like, dammit, I'd stop cursing, and that's the way it is, except when I'm ripping mad I don't never curse. Papillon, this guy with the papers, went all out, he said he said Christ all the time so's to understand me better, he lectured and I listened with my tongue hanging out. I was in a dither because in addition right over this free-for-gratis word machine's head the television was howling, and television twists my heartstrings. The characters around us, with and without beards, fathers of five and fathers of nothing, are sipping their beers or running out to piss so fast they knock each other over, or watching the boxing match spellbounded, but when there's real punishment, when the human blood flows for real, they make faces or close their eyes. When television gets into my bones, I feel like a worm; there I was with the world before my eyes, I saw it losing its blood and I wanted to go out in the gutter with all its corpses and martyrs. "What's wrong with you? What are you making that long face for? Got a funeral on in the morning?"

"I wanted to be a boxer. Sometimes it makes me sad."

"You've still got the build, but your muscles have

softened with age;" says Papillon. "You can't have everything, you can't have hunger and muscle at the same time, as my father used to say. Take me, I wanted a bicycle when I was young, I never got it, I'm still waiting. It was a big disappointment in my life, bitter, bitter, ah, Christ!"

While he was dreaming like that with his two elbows dug into his pile of poems, thinking about his bicycle (a spoiled brat if there ever was one, some people haven't even got a hoop to play with in the back yard, and this guy moans and groans like a woman in labor), I'm thinking about the dream I'd had last night, an old pal, died long ago, but there he was. I don't even remember his name. Anyway, this guy had tried to escape, they'd caught him in the field and beaten him up good, never heard from him after that, but last night he comes up all bloody and lies down in the middle of rue Sainte-Catherine, he's not screaming, just a faint moan, his head is open on top like a box, a lot of blood coming out and his whole body's streaked with red, one thing I remember, he's wearing sky-blue jeans, clean like they'd just been washed, he's calling somebody but I didn't know who, a cop comes up and sticks a baby's bottle in his mouth and says, "Drink, you bastard, drink . . ." It wasn't vinegar, it was a baby's bottle, you got to be nuts to dream stuff like that, and my pal, all he could do was make this faint moan, the blood and saliva were flowing down his neck.

"You know what, Lemieux? I'm in love with your language, head over heels. I've always given a lot of thought to words, the word is my cult, are you listening to me or not, bleeding veronica?"

"I'm listening, monsieur."

"Stop calling me monsieur. My name is Eloi. I'm not an asshole, as they say in Joual. You know what I mean, Joual, your language?"*

"I understand fine, but what's the good of talking to me? I'm not inneresting."

"Abraham, you have things to tell me."

*[Joual: the French-Canadian dialect.—Ed.]

"Most of the time, when I come here, I watch TV. I never say a word."

He thought I was going to tell him the story of my life just like that, but he didn't get a peep out of me.

"I look at you, Lemieux, and holy pyx, I can't help wondering if you're not a fucking conservative. You don't seem to have very advanced ideas. I'm not a nobody, you know, I've got culture to give away. Want some? Take it, but I want you to teach me Joual. Is it a deal?"

I was wondering if Papillon was a schoolteacher or maybe even a professor, anyway I was getting the fidgets and I wanted to get out of there, Papillon was torturing me with his questions, I've never liked nosy people. I was thinking I should have gone to see my friend Vincent the curé, because sometimes when he'd finished with his sacristy bugs and his prison school he taught me to write French like eddicated people, sentences like:

> Do I pity my fellow men?
> Yes, I pity my fellow men.

He gave me these dictations like I was some backward kid, he didn't know that words spout from my head every second, but it's no use asking for strawberries in January.

"You know, Lemieux, it's the same with me. I invent images too, and velvety sounds, I invent at least ten words every day. What do you think of this? 'The dazzling plectrum of my word'? Or how about this? 'The austere steppes of my silence' . . . Does that appeal to you?"

"Don't mean a thing to me."

"Christ, that's because your head's a vacuum. But come home with me anyway, my wife's not there, we'll make ourselves a feast."

Me too, my stomach was grumbling and I was pitching pretty bad when we left the Cat, it was only the beginning of November but winter was coming on hard, it was drizzling sleet.

Papillon stretches and says, "Snow, O snow, my beloved country!" He only saw the bright side, he didn't see that cold kills, it shrivels you up like a little old man. He didn't have to wait for the bus every morning, he had his car, he told me so. He didn't need to steal now and then.

"What kind of a car you got?"

"You're all alike, dregs of la Maine, all´you care about is dough and American cars!"

So the two of us step into Papillon's navy-blue Cadillac, a regular grandfather's rocking chair with seats as soft as cotton or clouds. The first snow swept across the windshield like little white peas, and leaning back in that hearse with the radio mooing songs, I could easily have slept. But Papillon was as wide awake as a firecracker, he slaps me on the knee and says, "I suppose you want to know how much I make a year?"

"It's none of my damned business."

"Ten thousand smackers, it's ridiculous, starvation wages on this great North American continent, my wife eats up half, the government leaves me the bare bones. It's not even enough for a daily club sandwich! A very shitty business, my friend. As you'll say one of these days in your expressive language: "It's a *chiar*. I hope you agree."

"Seems to me you're plenty lucky!"

"You're out of your mind, Abraham Whozis, all the kids in my class, kids not half as brilliant as me, little Jesuit bastards, you know what I mean, Latin, Greek, genuflections in front of the honor roll, the ones that had an ounce of gray matter are all making at least twenty-five thousand, and I know a lawyer from Quebec who harvests fifty thousand, and do you know how, all he does is fix parking tickets, his vineyard's growing fast! Christ, he's just bought himself a hotel. Wait till you see my pad, you'll understand my desolation."

So we climb up in an elevator that's as quiet as a wheelchair, with buttons that light up all by themselves, Papillon's wheezing, on account of his asthma, he says, he's still got his papers under his arm, he never lets his creations out of his sight, he tells me. His apartment was lit up like a new Frigidaire, we go in through the portal, and Papillon says, "We're going to cook up a great feast, what do you say? Christ, where are those cheeses I bought three days ago, usually the perfume hits you at the door, but what are you looking so pale about, Lemieux, is it the pinch of hunger? Take off your cloak and bonnet, make yourself at home. We're going to rejoice our palates and refresh our gullets with a seven-dollar Bordeaux!". It was like the days of the kings, I was looking around like a jerk, rubbing my nose against the blinds, they came from Venice it seems, I could see all upper Montreal, the whole place was jiggling, looked like I wasn't the only one celebrating that night. "You could give me a hand with the grub," says Papillon, "get out the sausage, while I grace your ears with the strains of my record player. Listen to this heavenly Bach and shut your trap!" The guy seemed to know music inside and out, he was humming sharps and flats and beating time with his flipper.

When the record made a mistake, he'd get mad and say, "That's no good, Bach wouldn't have liked it. Christ, some people play the flute like they were playing the bellows! Come on, Lemieux, go get the salt instead of gazing at the belly button of your vest!"

"How much did this furniture cost?"

"The furniture? You're a damned materialist, Abraham Lemieux! I spawned this furniture myself, it was fifteen years ago, we'd just got married. We were dead broke, nothing to do but try our hand at furniture making. In three months we'd turned out two tables, a bed, and three chairs. But, like Balzac in the triumph of his mature years, I've put on weight, I can't squeeze into my chair any more! But my dear ignoramus, you haven't asked me about those two illustrious individuals on the wall. The one on the left is Flaubert, the one on the right is Cézanne, it's all the same to you, you barbarian, I know! But they're my life companions, grown from the same swaddling clothes! And those paintings, frescoes, I should say, were created by yours truly, Papillon, master painter on top of everything else, the bastard. What talents, dear Lord, and so little admiration in return!"

"You must be pretty smart."

"Smart, Abraham, is no word for it. You've heard of Minute rice, I'm Minute genius, instantaneous and automatically transformed into steam, heaven help us!"

The wine glittered in the goblets, my head wasn't acting quite right, but I didn't care, we piled in the salami and the rest of brother Papillon's delicacies, he even had pastry that had come from Paris the day before on a plane. "I adore France when it comes to food," says Papillon, licking his chops and smearing his face with chocolate cake.

"So your wife is gallivanting around?"

"Christ, what's the good of being faithful for fifteen years if she's going to do this to me on the ninety-ninth day and the eleventh hour. She's gone, I wasn't going to chain her up. You don't chain a monkey when you see him getting restless in his cage."

There was a tear or two in his eyes. "Christ Almighty," he muttered. "I don't understand, I don't get it, I thought women were like the Catholic Church, that they only changed on the surface."

"Sometimes they're like raindrops, they slip through your fingers."

"What do you know about it, you yokel, shut up!"

He was good and mad, so I buttoned up. Then all of a sudden the doorbell rings. Papillon goes rolling out like a ball to open it, and then I hear him exclaiming, all cheerful again, "Why, if it isn't the lawyer from Quebec putting into port!"

"They told me you needed someone to play chess with. I didn't hestitate for one moment, and here I am."

"Psychoanalyst's advice, *mon cher,* the healing powers of chess, the cuckold's balm. Come in and take your boots off. I've just polished the floor with Johnson's wax, *mon cher.*"

The lawyer from Quebec shakes hands with me, he wasn't wearing a suit or robes, just a polo shirt like it was hot summer and corduroy pants with holes in them. He takes off his boots very carefully, Papillon bends over to examine them.

"Why, Augustin, fur-lined boots, that's sheer debauchery, you must be rich as Croesus, you stinker."

"All from parking tickets," says the lawyer from Quebec.

"You nauseate and frighten me, when I think that the Jesuits nursed us on the same milk!"

"It's what I tell my clients, no use expecting much justice on this earth."

"Christ, you have no honor!"

"That's the way it is," says the lawyer from Quebec. "Sail into the grub before Lemieux eats up all the crumbs and the tablecloth, even the humble and lowly have appetites, as you can see. How about your hotel? Still raking in the profits?"

"One little drawback, I shouldn't have built it across the street from a hospital."

"You see, I was right when I told you not to confuse your private bourgeois instincts, your ambitious idleness, with the spectacle of sickness and death. If I were you, I'd seal the windows on that side and put in different ones on the inside with a view of a little garden swarming with birds."

"I'll think about it," says the lawyer in a bleak voice. So they go on talking the way that kind of people talk to each other, and the lawyer from Quebec starts complaining that even if he did pocket his fifty thousand smackers a year he wasn't happy. He kept saying, "Yes, but there's one drawback . . ." It made his guts turn over to think that the poor slobs, the little jerks like me with their empty pocketbooks, had to bow and scrape to the judges and call them "Your Lordship," "Your Reverence," and suchlike applesauce, and that he, Augustin, even if he had a weakness for lucre because he had small fry to look after, so he said, and a wife who liked gadgets, supersonic potato peelers, etc., a modern woman, don't you know, she was filling the house with hardware and organization, "like a Boeing, *mon cher,* you can't imagine how women go for technological progress!"

"Ah, Augustin, you can talk, you at least have a wife, the rest is poppycock," said Papillon, still in his bath of sentiment, his nose in his wine, on the brink of tears. Augustin went on about the goddamn judges; if he had his way, he said, he'd plead the cause of the bums, it wrang his heart to see the lines of bums at daybreak, hanging around the Carré Saint-Louis and every place else; he wanted to gather them to his bosom and defend them like sparrows.

"Don't tell me you're going ascetic, Augustin," said Papillon. "You've got too much money in the bank."

"Can't a man love money and stand up for the poor?"

"That's bad dialectics; Christ, if it isn't!"

The longer those two went on caucusing, the more I wanted to hit the feathers at my Jeanne Mance boardinghouse, especially the way the snow was prickling the windowpanes and the wine singing and chanting in my noodle. So finally I says to Papillon, "I'd better be setting my sails for home."

"What's this, Lemieux, you talk of leaving when I've just feasted you like an old college chum? You can't mean it. Are you going to walk out on your pals when their minds are flushed with fever? Don't worry, my boy, we can go on like this all night."

"I know, but I'm sleepy."

"That's not a rational argument, dammit. Where's the fire? You going to early Mass?"

"No—it's my job."

"At the Rubber Company? That's no job. If I were you, I'd go to work in a gas station. I know some boys your age that are getting good tips."

"No tips for me. I'd sooner take it straight out of people's pockets."

"You mean you're a lousy rotten thief? Get a load of that, Lordship of Quebec, here's a case for you . . ."

"I know," says the lawyer from Quebec calmly, in a voice like he'd been asleep, "the flaws in our young friend's character have not escaped me, but you see, Papillon, at the moment it's three o'clock in the morning and I'm not chained to my professional life."

"Lordship, you're nothing but a Pharisee. A Pharisee. You wanted a future bum, well, you've got one right here. Am I right or wrong, Lemieux? Sooner or later you'll be panhandling on the sidewalks of la Maine. Picking pockets at your age!"

Go on, I wanted to say, the way the world is today,

it's not so easy to reach into people's pockets; and besides maybe they've got their troubles too when they come home from their money mills at night, but all I said was, "You just shut up, Papillon, or I'll tie your ears around your face!"

Papillon fondles his mustache and answers with a funny smile, "So you really won't tell us what it was like when you were a cunning little fellow at the nursery with the sisters? Tell us in Joual: all about the sisters, and later on, the little monks with their straight-faced cocks. See what I mean?"

"To tell the truth," says the lawyer from Quebec, "there's very little difference between your childhood and ours. Haven't we all had a priest in our lives at some time or other? In bed or in the pulpit, it comes to the same thing."

These two guys were so smart they thought they could outsmart me; they thought I'd tell them my biography, but I didn't say a word, I gave them a chilling silence.

"Do you know, my boy, you're a stubborn son-of-a-bitch, an uncooperative mule."

Papillon grabbed the bottle by the neck and poured himself a healthy drink. Then he told us about this little sister he'd known who'd worked for the monks, she washed their underwear in Spic and Span, and when she did their sheets she was always surprised, the way Papillon told it, to find "prodigious quantities of semen, enough to populate the whole country." She wasn't very bright. "Ignorant of the nature of this nocturnal and diurnal production," she notifies the head monk, the colonel of the monastery, that she wouldn't do their washing any more, because the little brothers had "a most deplorable habit, they blow their noses in their sheets!" That's the kind of story those two foulmouths told, and more of the same, sticky-spicy, but I don't remember them. They asked me if the little brothers had done the handkerchief trick with me and if they'd given me beans to eat.

"Plenty of beans," I said, "but that's not so bad. If it wasn't for the little brothers I'd have taken a short-cut to purgatory, maybe I'd have died before I was born."

"That's a fact," said Lordship of Quebec. "We forget that in spite of it all, they've performed certain services for humanity, for ours at least."

"And the little sisters too," said Papillon, "but, Christ, are they prosperous! It's a wonder they don't own the Sky Plaza—you know, Abraham, that thirty-story hotel they've just built right near your Jeanne Mance. And you, poor bastard, rotting away down below in your six-dollar-a-week boardinghouse!"

"No, seven dollars, Madame Fontaine has just raised her prices."

"Ah, the rising prices, an abomination! You can put me on your list of paupers, Augustin, you can do it right now without a qualm . . ."

I'd put on my coat, ready to beat it. Papillon throws his arm over my shoulder and says, "Christ, you're my guest, you're going to take a taxi, you're my diplomat, you're my buddy, I want you to come back into my humble dwelling, we'll do Joual together. Right now, I'm in a bad way, that sharpens the wits, the intelligence, so my psychoanalyst says, and those shrinks are never wrong, so while I'm waiting for my wife, me and Lordship while away the time like this, but you've got to come back, understand? Don't be a dope, don't forget the hand that fed you, but as for the hand that blessed you, don't hesitate to chuck it in the fire. Call a cab, Augustin, we wouldn't want our young vagabond to walk home; he's got to report to the Rubber Company at 8 a.m. Holy pyx, an outrage, a man like you in the jailhouse!"

I said I wouldn't forget, I went downstairs and the taxi carried me away like a bundle. It was only the beginning of November, and already, Christ, as Papillon would have said, it was snowing, man, was it snowing!

At four in the morning, Mère Fontaine was on her feet like a standing army, with her hair in curlers and her bedtime finery, even her dressing gown with lavender flowers. She's holding a pair of my pants with a respectful air. "Just throw them on the bed, Madame Fontaine," I say.

"No, Monsieur Ti-Pit, no, you know me, I like to keep my men nicely pressed."

"I know, but they're all right. No use knocking yourself out."

"I can't sleep, Monsieur Ti-Pit. Monsieur Ti-Paul has been playing his rock music so loud, men are selfish creatures. So I might as well think; I think on my feet, and while I'm at it I do my fine ironing and read my yellow scandal sheets. Did you know that an Italian girl was murdered last night right here in the neighborhood? Another jealous husband!"

"And all for a piece of tail, Madame Fontaine!"

"Hush, Monsieur Ti-Pit, you ought to be ashamed. I'm a respectable woman! Which reminds me, Monsieur Ti-Pit, did you get paid today?"

"Yes. Here's my seven bucks."

"You smell terrible, Monsieur Ti-Pit. I bet you've been hanging around the Dancing Cat again . . . It's no good spending your substance on drink, take it from an honest woman, the whole neighborhood knows I'm honest, beware of drink, your own mother wouldn't tell you different. And where did you go after that?"

"I was with some bums."

"Do I know them?"

"No, Mère Fontaine, not these bums."

"Why wouldn't you talk to me a bit?"

"Too tired. Good night, Mère Fontaine."

There she was with her finger in the fly of my pants, the ones she was holding, I mean, making goo-goo eyes and ready to swoon, so I make a dash for my cubbyhole. It smelled of cooking, there was a Greek restaurant next door, but that was my pad, it was good enough for me, the partition was cardboard, there were gashes in the wallpaper, which came from Kredgie's, but what's the odds? I nested in with my coat on top of the blanket and memories hummed in my ears. I heard Papillon with his "Christ, Christ, Christ," and me who'd sworn not to swear. I was just about snoozing off when Nicole starts gasping on the other side of the partition, "More, Pierrot, more, my little Pierrot," banging her hysterical toes against the wall.

I could have killed her. In all the time I've shared

that girl's body and soul, I've never shown any jealousy, I've never made a scene, but I sure felt like it that night. Then she calmed down, but an hour later Pierrot got his second wind and they started up again. It's incredible all the misery people put you through, absolutely incredible. But in spite of Ti-Paul's rock music in room 3 I toppled into sleepy creek. And there I was back at Jos Langlois's farm, that was where the monks sent us out-of-wedlock kids when we hit thirteen, and sure enough, there was Jos Langlois himself, parading his cows in the twilight, it was only eight o'clock, but it was dark in the woods, you couldn't see the cows, only the tip of Jos's cap and the cows' backs like a wave flowing down into the valley as quietly as a flock of pilgrims, I was behind Jos, guiding the cows with a stick. Then all of a sudden my little movie is over, Mademoiselle Mimi is tugging at my feet and my blanket falls off. "I only want you to hook me up in back, Ti-Pit."

"What's the idea of waking me up like this, Mimi? That's a mean thing to do."

"Quick! It's almost time for my act. Nobody else but you can tie my bows in back. Tell me, Ti-Pit, am I pretty this evening?"

"Sure, sure, but get out, I'm tired."

Mimi's a twittery kind of kid with a face like a baby moon and eyes that shine like two lakes, and he always wants me to hook him up and help him on with his nylon stockings, etc., before he goes out to show off his glad rags at the Dear Boy nightclub. The place is pretty well known and the yokels go into ecstasies when they see Mimi, as tender as a newborn kitten with velvet paws, a cherub of the slums, you'd say, especially when he frames his cheeks in his blond wig, but he's got his nerve, he thinks Ti-Pit's room is open at all hours like the men's room in the subway, he comes in and tells me that even with his act at the Dear Boy and tangoing with the citizens he doesn't make enough to keep him in bras and bikinis. Fagging and queening is hard work nowadays, and when he gets back into his jeans and sweater at six in the morning he hasn't even got time to wash before cruising down the St.

Lawrence, peddling his meat to anything that comes along. "Ah, Ti-Pit, it's shitty standing up against a slimy wall, sucking or buggering, you never know what to expect from those yokels, but sometimes I'm lucky, sometimes I make enough for a ten-cent hot dog."

"You've got to admit you're kind of provoking," I tell him. "You paint, you powder, that doesn't appeal to everybody, but someday, you never can tell, maybe the right Betty will come along and keep you fancy, in caviar and chocolates, and two ain't as shitty as one."

"That reminds me of my Betty," he says, sitting on the corner of my bed rouging the hollows of his cheeks, while I helped him hook up his jewelry. "She was sweet, a singer in the theater. Yes, Ti-Pit, I often think it might be better, she was the cutest thing, you should have seen her, we spent a night once in Quebec on the Plains of Abraham, ah, what a night, you should have been there. Afterward we drank gin, and I don't need to tell you that we ended up squinting at each other through the bars of the Quebec jailhouse, some fun! Jean-François was his name, did he know how to bugger! But I never saw that queenie again."

"Haven't you ever thought of going into the theater yourself, Mimi?"

"They can't use me, you see, I'm too far out. Jean-François was different, he was the manly type, he only came to see me at night, never in the daytime. He was a respectable queen, a fag with a future. He doesn't go in for fruits like me, he likes the kind he doesn't need to be ashamed of, 'gents' he calls them, 'my social equals.' Oh well, that's his business. Can you see him in my cubbyhole at Mère Fonfon's between the bed and the washstand? No, he'd pine away, he's a grande dame!"

"Maybe he'll meet the right faggot himself one of these days."

"Don't say that, Ti-Pit, you break my heart. I've got plenty of faggots, I'm up to my neck in them! We're always tearing each other's hair out at the Dear Boy, they're jealous of my precocity, my beauty. Sometimes it drives me crazy."

"Had any news from Matane, from your folks?"

"No, not a thing. They haven't written for months. They're respectable people, you know. They don't know about the Dear Boy and all that, they still think I'm studying philosophy; well, got to be going, Ti-Pit, thanks for my bows, you're my chum, so long."

The cherub set sail in the snow, Ti-Paul, who works in a butcher shop, was still running his rock, next door Pierrot was melting away inside his Nicolette. My night had been cut kind of short, it was time for me to get up and hightail it to the Rubber.

2.

AT THE Rubber it was a bad day for old Père Baptiste, because Jerry Faber, the boss, was putting us all through the X-rays; they do it once a year in the factories, so Jerry can say to the oldtimers, "You've got spots on your lungs, you'll have to quit." Baptiste is going on sixty, that's just what he didn't want. "Just keep your mouth shut, Ti-Pit," he says to me, "I'll go hide in the crapper while the rest of you are getting your lungs looked through." But Jerry Faber's no dope, he'd counted all his men and one was missing. That's how Baptiste lost his job 'cause he was no good for anything any more, too old, sent home to sit with his old lady. "But we'll give you a bonus all the same," says Sir Jerry. "Sure thing. A splendid bonus, a hundred dollars, aren't you glad, Baptiste, at last you'll have a chance to rest."

And Baptiste answered, "Go take a shit, Faber. Go shit in the flowers!"

And out he runs like a fury. It gave me the blues to think that Baptiste, worn out before his time, wouldn't be sticking his fingers into my lunch box any more. "Your Mère Fontaine's sandwiches are a dream, you no-good, looks like she's taken a shine to your curly hair." "Sure," I say. "Mère Fonfon knows her business,

but she's got one fault, she sticks to me like glue."
"That's nothing," says Baptiste, "that's a woman's instinct, they're all alike, even the nurses at Sacré-Coeur hospital, so they say, practically rape their patients on the operating table . . ." So I tell Baptiste about Mère Fontaine, how nosy she is, how she rummages around in my drawers and looks through the keyhole when Mademoiselle Mimi is entertaining his sweetheart.

I grab her by the apron and say, "Get back to your kitchen, Mère Fontaine, it's none of your business what goes on in Mimi's room."

"It's that little girl's future I'm worried about," says Mère Fontaine, "you know I love him like my own son; you know how it is with the maternal instinct, Monsieur Ti-Pit, it burns like passion fire. When Mademoiselle Mimi gets married, I'll be at the wedding, I'll hold the train of her dress. Don't you think Mademoiselle Mimi ought to be a little more careful who he hobnobs with, guttersnipes and princesses, it's all one to him, it's worrisome for a mother, Monsieur Ti-Pit."

"Mimi's bed isn't yours, Mère Fontaine. Go see who's cooing in your own bed."

"Exactly!" says Mère Fontaine. "My bed is pure, Monsieur Ti-Pit. Nobody ever crawls in, not even you, Monsieur Ti-Pit."

Yawning over his peanut-butter sandwich and Coke, Baptiste would listen. Then he'd say, "I've never been unfaithful to Mère Baptiste, she'd have crowned me with her rolling pin. I wouldn't have minded a kiss and a toss now and then, there was a little minx that made spaghetti at the Erect, you know the place, on rue Sainte-Catherine, with the sign SPAGHETTI NIGHT AND DAY, I'd give her a little pinch now and then, but it never went any further than spaghetti, I couldn't get my mind off Mère Baptiste and her rolling pin. Never get married, Ti-Pit, when the brats start coming, one two three . . . four, bawling and pissing all over the place, you've had it!"

When the snow came down and the thermometer zigzagged around zero, Jerry, our boss, would say, "How about doing me a little favor, Ti-Pit? Suppose you and Baptiste go shovel a bit of snow around my residence, I'll pay you two dollars an hour." You couldn't turn down that kind of a deal, me and Baptiste would tag on out to Upper-Nose Town with our shovels over our shoulder. Mrs. Faber and Co. would scratch the ice off the windowpane to see us, but the snow was head-high, Old Baptiste was feeling chipper that day. "Don't worry, Mrs. Faber," he said. "We'll get you out of that shit." "Shut up, Baptiste," I tell him. "That's practically the Immaculate Conception you're talking to. You've got to speak respectful to the boss's wife." He took a little nip from his pocket flask and we started shoveling. Yeah, but where do we start? That's what he wanted to know. It was a regular apocalypse. We could practically hear Mrs. Faber behind the door, up on her tiptoes crying "Help! Help!" "Do we start with the steps or the chimney, Ti-Pit? With the entrance or the middle? What do you think?"

"Let's just dig, Baptiste. Then we'll see."

It was like digging into the womb of the universe, as Papillon would have said. The more we dug the less we were getting anywhere, our faces were covered with snot and the white stuff was squizzling into our ears. "You that's supposed to have bronchitis, Baptiste, you should have put something over your face, in two minutes you'll start coughing, you'll be ready for the hospital."

"I'm spitting red already," says Baptiste, "it's those spots on my lungs, but dammit, we've got to snag those two bucks. I ain't come up to Upper-Nose to pick daisies."

So Père Baptiste went on excavating and I couldn't get the shovel away from him. By the time we'd broken our backs for three hours, the steps were done and Lady Faber was able to open her door. "How lovely! How lovely!" she says, "I can see the mountains." "Good for you," say I, "but now you'll have to pay us off. Old man Baptiste isn't feeling so good, he's got the wobbles."

"But come in, my friends, dear fellows," she says. "Come in and get warm. The maid will make you some coffee."

So we sloshed down our Upper-Nose coffee. There

were six of us, the maid, us two slobs, the chauffeur, and a dog by the name of Puss-Puss that the lady cootchy-cooed at and called pussy darling.

The lady told us not to soil her carpet with our muddy feet. She was sitting on the edge of a seventeenth-century chair, nibbling at a piece of lemon, to refresh her, she said, after all the worry and excitement. "You've got beautiful paintings on your walls, Madame Faber," I said. "And these chairs, the kings of England could have sat on them, and, say, you've got a fine fireplace too."

"My husband has taste," she said.

So we took our money and started back to Lower-Nose. "That lady's got education," says Baptiste. "Did you notice, she didn't call me Frenchie." "Sure," I said. "But I didn't care for that routine about the carpet, only her puss-puss has a right to shit on it. Did you catch the sneaky way she looked at the soles of our boots?"

"All the same, she's got education," said Baptiste.

"You're not proud," I tell him. "You sure ain't proud, Christ, I wouldn't put it past you to get down on all fours to thank your benefactors. You got no backbone, chum."

That's the way it was with me and Père Baptiste, always arguing. Now that he was staying home with his old lady, there was nobody to jaw with at lunchtime and I went to the Erect by myself. I thought maybe I'd get a look at Baptiste's spaghetti madonna, but the waitress told me Lison had gone to the hospital on account of a brat, and plunks down a big plate of macaroni in front of me. "It's the fault of you men if we're always sick," she says, "you're all a lot of perverts. A kind friend of mine tried to operate on her, we ran into trouble, the baby didn't want to be rubbed out, he hung on, they always do, he didn't want to be cut loose, stubborn little bastard . . ."

"It must be pretty rough on her," I said to the waitress.

"It's hell. I've been through it, and it's all on account of you men, you ought to take precautions."

She went on grumbling while washing the dishes, a

hefty bighearted kid with her sleeves rolled up and the sweat pouring down her neck. How do I know, maybe Ti-Pit's mother was just that kind of a girl. "Don't you think she'd have been better off keeping the brat?" I ask her. "I had a blonde that had a little accident with a guy, we lived together at my Jeanne Mance boardinghouse, it was fun, Mère Fontaine used to feed the baby. We raised that little pooch for a year, then I ran out of bread and my girl found somebody else to support her, but the brat's still alive. They say that life is better than limbo."

"You talk like a dope," she says. "Eat your macaroni and shut up. What do you know about life, you're an idealist, all you sex fiends are idealists. Lison should have done like me, I got rid of mine by throwing myself downstairs. That's the best way."

She kept going on about men and their nasty little balls. There was one guy that came to see her quick quick and they'd disappear behind her spaghetti stove. His name was Max and his job was drooling on the radio, he did commercials, Lux washes whiter, that kind of crap, you never saw anybody in such a hurry, he did all the radio stations, he told me, morning, noon, and night, he was all over the place like an ambulance.

Once in a while this Max would say to me, "C'mon outside for a man-to-man talk."

He never had time to sleep, he told me, the chicks took big chunks out of his pocketbook, etc. "Women are bloodsuckers," he said, "I've got four on my hands, the spaghetti girl, as you've probably noticed, two young mistresses, and my divorced wife, every week she sends me bills for the children's dancing school or some such rot, I haven't even got a pillow to lay my head on, sometimes I have to sleep standing up at my waitress's counter." A sad story, but luckily this Max had a Chevy with TUNE IN ON CKBB, YOUR FAVORITE STATION written on it. This Chevy was his pad, he kept his TV set in it and all his clothes, and the spaghetti girl washed his socks on Saturday. "But, my dear fellow, it's not a life," he'd say. "Can a man live forever in a Chevrolet, summer and winter, spring and

fall, without a roof over his head, just because none of
the women in his life lets him sleep in her bed for more
than one night? No, it's not a life, it's a creeping
death."

When Max got his pay on Friday night, he'd blow
me to a chicken leg and a glass of white wine at the
Rotisserie of the Golden-Brown Turkey. He was so
worn out from purring and gassing night and day on
the radio that he wasn't hungry, he'd always pass me his
plate. "Like many a poor wretch," this lunatic would
say, "I live on love and fresh air." Then he'd say, "But
you, my dear fellow, I hope you've had some joy out
of the creatures and not just hard luck like me."

"It hasn't been so bad. I take it as it comes."

Then he was off on his eloquence again, griping
about how he hadn't seen his little three-year-old
daughter in more than a year, and so forth and so on,
the sorrows and heartbreaks of a family man, his first-
born seed and all that. It's the serpent of pride, I said
to myself, but all the same, it wasn't so bad when
Céline and her pooch lived with me at my Jeanne
Mance, I'd even call it good times, the duckling had
only two or three feathers on his noodle, he was pale,
I've got to admit, hanging on Céline's neck like a me-
dallion. It was me that warmed up the water for his
bottle on Mère Fontaine's little stove. "The water has to
be lukewarm," says Mère Fontaine, "we mustn't burn
our little angel's tongue. Now watch the way I do it,
you squeeze the nipple with your fingertips and pour
out a few drops on the back of your hand. You get the
idea, Monsieur Ti-Pit?" Mère Fontaine was more stick-
ative than ever, she was always in my room, but only
on account of the baby, so she said. "You're a charitable soul, Monsieur Ti-Pit, you love bastards," she
said, rolling her eyes and sticking her pointed fingernails into the opening of my shirt. "My, what a build
you've got, Monsieur Ti-Pit, I only wish you were a
boxer or a wrestler, then we could admire you in tights
on national TV." That was the kind of thing Mère Fontaine used to say while Céline was rocking her pooch,
sitting on the floor of my cubbyhole at Jeanne Mance,
next door to the Greek restaurant that made us feel

like eating olives and seeing the world. "Ah, Ti-Pit," said Céline, "couldn't we go away some place, to some island, up here we'll be snowbound till June, don't you feel like jumping off Mount Royal sometimes, or wrapping the baby up in newspapers and chucking him in the garbage can, nobody'd know . . . don't you feel like it sometimes, Ti-Pit?"

"You mustn't let your thoughts run away with you like that," I said. "It's a cute baby you've got here, he hasn't got much hair, but that will come."

"It's the vitamin shortage, he'll always be bald, the little shitface, he's not cute at all, he looks like an old man, all wrinkled and bald. Oh, he's so ugly, Ti-Pit!"

She was feeling pretty low, there was nothing I could do about it, she was always getting these black thoughts. "And besides," she'd whisper into my ear at night, "I don't even know who his father is; wouldn't it be better for both of us to stick our heads into Mère Fontaine's gas stove? I often think of it . . ."

"You're nuts," I'd say, and then we'd fall asleep with the little snotnose between us, it was nice and warm, it wasn't so bad to be three. But one day I suddenly noticed that the cash box had a hollow ring, there wasn't a cent left. Mère Fontaine knitted our pooch's wardrobe, he'd be pretty near taking his first steps by spring. Céline was sobbing.

"Don't take on like a widow," I told her. "I'll get the kid something to eat. There's art in my fingertips and I know my way around the stores. I'll just run along to Stringbird's and kidnap a few cans of 'Baby's Bliss.' "

"Dog food or cat food would be just as good, Ti-Pit, he's too young to know the difference. The little shit-face don't know which way is up!"

"Don't talk that way, Céline, don't talk that way."

So I went to Stringbird's like a regular husband with money in his pocket, I'd put on my tie that Mère Fontaine had ironed for me. "Look like an honest thief at least," she said. "Honesty is the best policy." So I wheel my pushcart around, trying to act like everybody else, I had to buy a big pile of salad to look honest, but that doesn't cost much. There were cans of dog and cat food, Kitty Kat and Pretty Pup, and there was one called "I Am a Happy Dog," pure mare's meat, they told me. But they had other stuff that looked even more tempting, big rows of baby food with an overfed baby on the label, he was grinning without any teeth and his mouth was whiter than snow; seems it was strained vegetables, and I thought to myself, Won't this make our little shitface happy! Quick, I slip a dozen cans in my pockets, nobody saw me. Christ, was I scared! I paid for my salad and split. I get back to Jeanne Mance and I'm so happy and excited I drop all my canned goods in the doorway, but nobody's there, no pooch, no Céline, they're gone, that was the end. There was a note on the bed:

I guess I'd better be going, Ti-Pit, don't worry, Sainte-Catherine is a long street, between one end and the other I'll find a man to help me, I took your brown sweater to wrap the baby in, your Céline who'll never forget you, goodbye.

So that was the end. I went to the little sisters at the Home for Retarded Children and gave them my pile of canned goods. The mother superior said, "Our Saviour will requite you in paradise, amen."

Max gets up, he hasn't had a thing to eat or drink, and pats me on the shoulder. "You're going to make me cry with your Céline story, it's as sad as Good Friday, but now I'll have to leave you, duty calls, I've got a character to interview, a remarkable man who had the courage to kill his wife; eat your fill at my expense, I have a Quick Dinner Club card, farewell, my Chevy's waiting at the door . . . You know, I love my Chevy like a wife."

I did a lot of overtime at the Rubber Company, I didn't mind so much, except not having Baptiste any more to bat the breeze with, so one morning I went in to see Jerry, my boss, and told him what a louse he was for discarding my old Baptiste like a rag and I was fixing to join him on the manure pile. A buddy had told me there was money to be made at the infirmary if your nose wasn't too sensitive, and it seemed to me

I'd like that better than the Rubber because pox and scarlet fever and all those diseases are up my alley, I'm not afraid of them.

So Jerry Faber says to me from the heights of his magnificence, "My dear young man, it's none of my business if you choose to go to the dogs. I wash my hands of you. Here are your wages for the next two weeks. We thank you for your loyal services."

"No hard feelings," I said. "And just say the word when you want me to shovel shit for Mrs. Faber."

"Who knows, Ti-Pit, maybe bedpans really are your future. Still, I had hopes, I even believed that in time the Rubber Company would inspire you to higher things."

My heart felt smooth as silk with the Rubber Company behind me. I amble back to my boardinghouse and there in the hall, passing the time of day with Mère Fontaine, is Papillon, with his corporation out front and a cigar in his face.

"Christ, if it isn't my friend and comrade Abraham Lemieux in person! Normally it's the beggar who knocks discreetly at the poet's door, today it's the opposite, the noble artist comes humbly to take you to a gathering . . ."

"No, Papillon, you people give me the yawns."

"Never mind, we'll try to be a little more sprightly tonight. Come on, don your tunic and follow me, Lemieux, we'll tickle our larynxes with vintage wines, the lawyer from Quebec is waiting for you, and there's a student, my constant reader, he's even written a thesis elucidating the mystery of my *Three Hermetic Poems,* I want you to know my work, brother, it's high time."

"How about your wife? Is she back?"

"Christ, no, it's grim. I've been cleaning the house and beating the carpets all by myself."

Luckily it wasn't snowing that night, but getting into his Cadillac Papillon says, "What an admirable night! Our dear Louis Fréchette was right." And in one breath he declaims:

"The day was cold, I wandered on the moor
Dreaming of times and seasons left behind,

With glitt'ring frost the road was covered o'er,
The branches shook forlornly in the wind."

"The guy was too sensitive," I said.

"You have no intellect," said Papillon. "You'd be wiser to keep your trap shut, because, Christ, that's what poetry is."

"Careful on your left. You're going to hit that truck."

At Papillon's place it was Chaos, Inc. These people that have nothing to do but stand around blatting with a glass in one hand get pretty fuzzy after nightfall. They all shake hands with me, there's the lawyer from Quebec in his corduroy pants, and a little student from Ontario, and another student with a crew cut who'd read all Papillon's works. Quaking from the waist up, he declaims in a piercing voice:

"Avaunt, despoilers of weak innocence!
O autumn, with your gentlest breath caress
This cheek . . ."

But there the lawyer from Quebec protests. "No, Papillon, I'm sorry, but really your muse is too chaste, that stuff will never sell. Nowadays, if you want to be free to concentrate on words like Mallarmé, you'll have to do something a little less appetizing on the side, for instance, you could write a frankly prurient novel, something that would bring in a nice little income; then you'd have time to shut yourself up in your study to work on your exquisite (but insipid, oh, how insipid!) little volumes of poetry; you'll have the same creative inspiration, though of course the Evensongs, the Vapors, Crosses, and Thorns you feed on will lose some of their original fragrance for you . . ."

"Are you crazy?" says Papillon. "You seem to think I have the soul of a banker! Here we've been friends since our Jesuit days, and still you don't know me."

"Talking about the Jesuits," says the lawyer from Quebec, "they have always" (he spoke calmly, "savoring the bouquet of his cognac from afar," as he explained) "known how to conciliate spirituality with necessity and I honor them for it. Why not imitate them, Papillon? You're impractical, *mon cher,* that's why you envy me my fifty thousand a year. I gave deep thought to your problem the other day, when I left you at 5 a.m. after our chess game. I talked it over with my wife (ah, the tedium of conjugal bliss!) and we agreed it was high time for you to write something really bad, something catastrophic, that would sell. That's it, they'd buy your disaster everywhere, in the subway, on the Canadian Pacific and the National Railways, wherever tracks traverse the countryside you'd be read, *mon cher.* Yes, Papillon, what you need is success!"

Papillon was so scalded that he gumped, he couldn't believe that the lawyer from Quebec would flatten him like that. He turns to the goggle-eyed students.

"And what about you, my devoted admirers? What is your opinion?"

"Not a bad idea," says the character from Ontario. "In fact, Monsieur Papillon, I'd be glad to collaborate on the novel . . . I offer you my services. At this moment I feel inspired, I'm high . . ."

But the second student, whose head was shaped like a broom, said, "My friends, you scandalize me, you sully my ideal . . . yes . . . your indecency is such that I wish to leave . . . And leave I will, my friends; in the name of poetry, which I love and honor, I'm leaving . . ." He wasn't fooling, he'd put on his sheepskin gloves and his galoshes, and bam! he was gone. "What a party!" says Papillon, mopping his forehead. "Lucky my wife isn't here, I'm mortified and humiliated in the face of my people."

"I too would be pleased to collaborate," says the lawyer from Quebec, "but under contract of course, with a guaranteed share of the royalties."

"Christ, all you think about is dollars, I'm ashamed of you."

"Let's start right now," says the lawyer from Quebec.

The student from Ontario said he'd come to Quebec to shake the hayseeds out of his hair, it wasn't a bad place for drugs, he was sharing a "den of shadows and delights" on rue Prince Arthur with some pals, not one of them was over twenty, so even if the lawyer from

Quebec did smoke pot he was nothing but an "old biddy" and the dawn of youth was hostile to the "twilight of the biddies." But the lawyer from Quebec wasn't melancholic about his past, what troubled him was his present, and he says to Papillon, "Listen to me, *mon cher*. What would you say to writing the story of a woman, a young girl, a nymphet or a virgin?"

"You're out of your mind. Young girls don't exist any more, much less virgins."

"We could call it *Y, The Story of Y*. That'll give our traveling salesmen something to dream about: Y is mysterious, it's opaque, but at the same time one glimpses the silhouette of a little girl jumping rope. You catch on, Papillon? Y is sexy . . ."

"You're brilliant," says Papillon. "Even in our Jesuit days you outdid me, you stinker."

It's unbelievable, characters like that, educated to the gills, with throbbing brains fit to be nailed on the wall alongside their diplomas and degrees, horsing around like schoolboys, but that's the way it is, the world is full of blabbermouths and hot-air factories. Papillon was in a giddy mood. He says, "You can drown yourself in my liqueurs, Abraham Lemieux, my house is yours. My friends are yours." And then he starts making up stories with his pals:

"My name is Y, little Y, sweet little Y, I've always lived on the banks of the St. Lawrence. I was a good, pious child, they wanted me to become a nun. One day—oh, was it August 4, 1960? I don't remember— as I was walking along, saying my prayers in the garden of the Capuchin Fathers where I used to play as a child, for I was only twelve at the time, I saw coming toward me, white-haired and stately against the background of the darkening sky, the Reverend Father Superior, who filled me with awe because, as I have already told you, I was a good, pious, innocent child. The Reverend Father said to me, 'You are cold, my child, come and warm yourself in our refectory.' I followed the good father, because as everyone knows, I was also an obedient child. 'Come to my room,' said the good father. 'It's more comfortable there.' And indeed, it was a very comfortable room. My eyes fell on the good father's embroidered sheets. 'You may sleep in them,' said the good father, 'but you must first take off your dress.' You will never believe me, but under that Father Superior's soutane there was concealed a passionate young man."

"No, no, Papillon!" said the lawyer from Quebec. "We need some lewd details! You sound as if you were afraid of shocking your mother. Add this: Y languished in the voluptuous arms of the Church, her body prostrate beneath a cloud of sperm and blood. For you see, Y had been raped. The Father Superior said to her, 'Listen to me, little girl. Hold your tongue or I'll cut it out.' Y was only a timid little country girl, she was reduced to silence by the authority and aggressiveness of her religion. 'But it's sacrilege,' she protested, 'it's a great sin.' 'Not at all,' said the Father Superior, 'a man in my position can do no wrong.' The priest was a vigorous, full-blooded man. This was far from the beginning of his amorous career, and it amused him no end to initiate Y into the mysteries. 'I'm light as a feather,' he said, and Y soon discovered that he was as heavy as a buffalo. 'I'm as beautiful as Adonis,' said the priest, and Y thought, The ugly old thing!

"Little by little the worthy father learned to play deftly with words. He said to Y, 'The object you see rising up boldly in the moonlight, that vibrant pillar of fire, never forget it, my child, is the male sex organ; your little grotto is nothing by comparison. That's where a man's dream is situated, on the tip of that formidable sword, I hope I'm not shocking you, little girl, my angel. Ah, how good it is to be a man, what satisfaction there is in perfect virility! For you see, you little slut, your mission in this world is to welcome without hesitation the irresistible wound of this charming and impudent dagger. And by placing your hand here and there, as I am showing you now, little girl, you can transform this fierce, warlike thing into the gentlest of animals, a flaming red cock crowing proudly in the early dawn, yet only too glad to let his wistful head soften beneath the caresses of young fingers and the kisses of your tongue.' "

"You're overdoing it," said Papillon. "That's licentious."

"Not so fast," says the lawyer from Quebec. "The reality of our Quebecan province is cruel, all reality is cruel, as we defenders of human villainy are well aware. We often get paid to defend people who don't deserve it, for they defend themselves only too well with their glaring lies. Now listen to me . . . my idea is that our naïve Lolita was a country girl, maybe her seducer was only her village priest. A village King Solomon, get the drift? He raves, he dreams, he grabs. A little girl passes, he nips her in the bud, her life is blasted."

"You haven't an ounce of poetry in you," says Papillon. "It's obvious that you only want to make a killing. But never mind, go on with your Father Superior, let's see what sink of degradation you have in store for him."

"My Father Superior is a circumspect man, he's not going to compromise his ecclesiastical career for an insignificant child. After thinking it over in the shade of the maple trees in his monastery garden, he decides it might be wiser to take his mistress to a foreign country. He books a sleeping compartment in the Montreal-New York express, heh heh, not a bad idea; little Y packs up her bundle and goes to meet her priest at the station, but not so fast, the worthy father has had the good sense to cover his tracks and put on civilian clothes. When Y sees him, she thinks he looks like an income-tax inspector. The worthy father goes so far as to hide behind his newspaper, and, at that, little Y, even if she is a simple little thing, is rather put out. 'Do you want to jeopardize me and my career?' he says sternly. 'Just go wait for me in compartment No. 8, I'll join you at midnight.' Then of course he frigged her and fondled her all night, as was only natural."

"And at dawn she died like Monsieur Séguin's little goat," said Papillon.

"Not at all," says the lawyer from Quebec. "She simply said, 'I'm afraid of getting a baby.' But her seducer replied, 'You should have thought of that before. And besides, won't it be an honor for you to bear my replica, my royal image?' "

"You nauseate me, Lordship of Quebec," said Papillon. "Your education has marked you too deeply."

"Did little Y like New York?" asked the stoned student. "I was so high there . . ."

"New York or Chicago," says the lawyer from Quebec slowly, "New York or Montreal, it was all the same landscape to the blinded, tormented child. She walked from one high-rise building to another, through the acrid, polluted air and under the leaden gray sky of New York; her wanderings were a nightmare. What was her luxurious room at the Beautiful Sheraton to her? For it was there that she was cruelly deflowered!"

"That'll do for tonight," says Papillon. "I'm getting sick of your little Y."

So the whole crowd went to finish their nocturne at the Open Steak House, where, as everyone knows, topless girls bring you your steak and their boobies on a wooden platter; myself, I wanted to get a little sleep so's to be at the Unemployment Office at eight next morning; you never can tell, maybe there'd be a job open at the infirmary. But back at Jeanne Mance, even at 3 a.m., confusion was rampant. Mademoiselle Mimi was bathed in tears like Mary Magdalene peering at herself in the well. Her blond curls were straggling over her red nose, the kid was really upset, even Ti-Paul the butcher had turned down his rock music and was standing in the corner of his pad, chewing gum. Well, there was poor Mimi, sobbing and sighing, and Mère Fontaine threw her arms around him and said, "Come along, my sweet little Michel, you mustn't spoil your beauty with all those tears."

"What's going on?" I ask. "Did some faggot beat him up?"

"No, the darling got a letter from his brother, the one that's a doctor in Matane," says Mère Fontaine. "They found out that Mademoiselle Mimi was dancing at the Dear Boy and kissing the customers' whiskers during the show. His parents are hardhearted people, Monsieur Ti-Pit, they've disowned their son for a venial sin, ah, Monsieur Ti-Pit, it's a hard life."

"I'll bash their heads in if you say so," says Ti-Paul to Mimi, and Ti-Paul is built like a brick shithouse.

"Massacring is right in my line, cutting meat all day, sometimes I wonder why I don't chop people's carcasses in little pieces and hang them up on the hook!"

"Let's not have any useless violence, Monsieur Ti-Paul," says Mère Fonfon, "remember, this is a respectable house, the main thing now is to comfort Mademoiselle Mimi, he's been insulted by his folks, his own family, fine people, the cream of Matane."

"The stink always comes from up top," says Ti-Paul with his gum bubble between his teeth. "I know all about it, Mère Fontaine. Every day I cut filet mignon for the upper crust."

So they shut Mimi up in my cubbyhole and he plunks himself down on my bed, whimpering worse than ever. So then I ask him, "What's the matter with you? What did your lousy brother write?" Mimi shows me the letter, perfumed blue paper, and here's what it says:

Dear Michel,

We, your parents, brothers, sisters, and cousins, know all. We no longer consider you one of us. Your scandalous activities at the Dear Boy fill us with well-deserved contempt. The disgrace of it, a black sheep like you in our lily-white family, our unblemished household whose reputation had never been sullied . . .

"Oh, oh," Mimi sobbed in his grief, "what have I done, dear Jesus, to have such a brother? We've always been damned, Ti-Pit, we queers, girls or boys, it's all the same. Oh! Oh!"

"Well," says I, "that makes us twins. Both orphans, Christ!"

But Mademoiselle Mimi went on weeping and wailing, he was inconsolable, there was nothing I could do. He took me by the hand and said, "What about you, Ti-Pit? Do you think I'm different from other people? Tell me the truth."

"You're different all right. Like a flea in a flock of elephants!"

"But if I can't go back to Matane, Ti-Pit, you know what? I'll never see Paulo again, my first love. You can't imagine, he looks like the angel Gabriel, and you ought to see him on the beach, he's all sugar and cream, he melts in the sun, he melts in the rain. Oh Paulo, oh! Our kind have always been damned, I tell you, Ti Pit!"

Then Mère Fontaine turns up again and says in her sly way, "Don't be sad, Michel, you have a visitor."

"I don't want to see anybody," says Mimi. "I'm too ugly tonight."

"It's Monsieur Jean-François, what a distinguished lady, she's waiting for you downstairs with a flower in her hand."

Mademoiselle Mimi is over the banister in one jump. "My word," says Jean-François, who was the severe, reserved type, "my word, Michel, a little dignity, if you please." He had practically brushed Mimi off like a speck of dust, but Mimi was beaming through his tears and the blotches on his nose. "Didn't I tell you he'd come back, Madame Fontaine? Oh my darling, oh my love!"

"Don't make a spectacle of yourself," says Jean-François. "You're being very indiscreet."

"You're my sweetheart, my beauty," says Mademoiselle Mimi.

"That'll do," says Jean-François. "Let's go up to your room."

Mademoiselle Mimi was all love and surrender. On the stairs Jean-François gave her a pinch. We could hear him scolding. "You're so indecent, Mimi, so indecent. Everybody'll think I'm a slut like you."

"Do you think it'll end in a marriage?" Mère Fontaine asks me. "Do you think there's a little hope for our Mimi in this liaison?"

"It's none of my business, what I need is some sleep."

"Just a minute, Monsieur Ti-Pit, you'll have all eternity to sleep in, as the saying goes, and eternity always comes too quick. Don't you think our Mimi is asking for unhappiness? This Jean-François is an ambitious actress, proud as a peacock, all he cares about is his career, mark my words it'll be another disappointment in love for Mimi."

"That's about it, sleep well, Mère Fontaine."

Down below my window there was an old bum, I could see he had bottles in all his pockets, he was singing, drunk as a lark.

"I'm going to Quebec to the Carnival,
To see the snowmen, yep, the snowmen.
And one day, yep, I'll see my love in heaven . . ."

"Hey, you!" I yelled. "I gotta sleep. Drag your fleas somewhere else."

"Okay," he says, "I'll sing you a lullaby." And there he goes:

"Lover's sorrow flies away, flies away,
Lover's sorrow lasts but a day . . ."

The best I could do was hide under my blanket. The old-timer had plenty of songs:

"I haven't always been a bum,
I used to be an honest man,
I didn't whore, I didn't kill,
Believe me, friends and neighbors,
I used to be an honest man . . ."

But all the same the night worried along, the EAT GREEK FOOD sign over the restaurant next door kept clicking on and off, and I was tempted by two dreams: in one I kick up my heels and I'm floating in the air, I'm high up above the leafless trees, it was almost like flying except that I wasn't moving; it was pretty nice, I was like a lamp hanging from the ceiling, I could see everything that went on down below, freeways and fields, people that looked like gnats, bridges and mountains, but it took another kick to switch this dream into a different direction before it went haywire, because sometimes that damn dream turned to nightmare even if the sky was blue without a wrinkle. I'd crash-land on a tree trunk, and right next to that tree, a giant oak, there'd be a ten-story apartment house with terrible sounds coming out of it, there didn't seem to be anybody around, there was even washing on the line outside, but those sounds were enough to skin you alive, it was time to veer off into something more cheerful, so I started out for Gaspé with Ti-Cul, my chum from the orphanage. The two of us pinched Jos Langlois's car and beat it away from the farm, we hadn't any license because we were minors. Ti-Cul had said to me, "They say Percé is a nice place, why don't we go there, me and you?" We leave our picks and shovels in the stable with the horses, and off we go. We never did get to see those red cliffs, 'cause the police caught up with us that same day. "You'll see," said Ti-Cul. "Christ, we'll loop around between the sky and the cliffs, when we're hot we'll swim in the cold sea, we'll drink this whole case of Jos Langlois's beer . . ." Sure enough, we drank up the beer and went in swimming, we're floating in the fires of happiness, and then there were three of Quebec's finest hanging over us.

"Hiya, fellas, having a little bath? Take your time, we'll wait for you."

The three of them sit there, warming their asses in the sand and caressing their guns, I guess it gave them a hard-on to think of shooting us in the water. Ti-Cul didn't want to come out, he wanted to chase after the sea gulls, but I grab him by the hair and he follows me to the barred wagon; that put a crimp in our spirits.

"We were on our way to Percé," Ti-Cul told them.

"You'll go to Percé another time, boys, after they let you out . . ."

So we joggle along in their wagon, skidding in the gravel and bouncing on the bumps, heading straight for the bums' improvement school. We were too drunk to feel anything and the landscape was grandioser than Cinerama. Once in a while Cop No. 1 would tickle our chins with the tip of his bayonet and once in a while Cop No. 2 would make us a little speech:

"Well, boys, how do you like joyriding in handcuffs? It's a beautiful country all right, get an eyeful now, you won't be seeing much in the mudhole we're taking you to."

They smacked their thighs and had themselves a good laugh, but so did we in the back seat, Ti-Cul was generous with his memories. "Hey, Ti-Pit, remember the nursery, our cribs were right next to each other, we had blue ribbons on our baby clothes to show we belonged to the 'master sex'; we pissed side by side in our cage until we were four, it was a big room with a glass wall, the future mamas and papas were roaming around, looking us over one by one, 'cause we were for rent and sometimes even for sale. The sister that took care of me didn't like black hair. 'They usually take the towheads first,' she'd say to me. There were always buyers for blond, pink-assed babies, but Ti-Cul and Ti-Pit with their dark complexions were a drug on the market. Everybody was thinking how they'd be coddled in their new homes, the sisters would run their fingers through those blond curls and say, 'Their hair is like silk, little golden-haired princes . . .' The blonds would press their noses to the glass and screech, 'Mama, papa . . .' like lion cubs, while you and me, Ti-Pit, crawled around playing with our blocks and drooling with rage. Say, Ti-Pit, where in hell are we going? Where are these crummy cops taking us?"

"Take it easy, maybe we're going to the jailhouse in Bordeaux!"

In my dream it was better because the cops didn't come into it, they stayed home playing cards, and Ti-Cul and me went all the way to Percé and Jos Langlois's car hovered in silence between sea and sky. Then we went swimming again and it was baking hot like August, you know, the kind of heat that warms your insides . . . heat . . . grass . . . And there's my bum, still bellowing outside:

> "Once there was a captain,
> His ship was broken in two.
> Big Maurice, they called him,
> And stern and proud was he.
> He said, 'My ship is me.'
> And with him all hands sank.
> Someday I'll visit him in heaven

I was just wondering what had become of Ti-Cul when all of a sudden there's a woman's claw on my face, it was Lison, old man Baptiste's little tart, she needs a man, she says just like that, at a time of night when all good Christians are sighing in their sleep. "Hell," I say, "my room isn't a railway station, in and out, in and out, what do you want, Lison, did the spaghetti waitress tell you I'd keep your brat for you?"

"Don't worry about the little marvel I've got in my guts, I'll get rid of him one way or another, all I want in the meantime is a man. It's so cold out my Don Juan didn't show up, there's nobody around but that bum blowing off gas."

"It's no good for your kid to ball right under his nose. Besides, I'm sleepy, you can't turn on love with a button, you gotta have a little ceremony first, you got epilepsy or what?"

"Practically. I'm a nympho, I'm like a mare that's got to have it, see? Some guy told me that nymphos burn themselves out quick."

She'd taken off her hat and scarf. Cool as a cucumber she tells me she's crazy about fucking and if it was 69 or 93 or even 108 I wanted, she was an expert. I touch her belly and ask her, "Say, how old is this kid?" "About two months, it's a mere nothing . . ." "Aren't you afraid he's started to breathe?" "Nah, he's just a fetus, he's asleep, maybe it shakes him up a bit when I do it, that's all."

There was no way to calm that girl down, what she wanted was action. "Now I feel better," she said later. "You have no idea, I was getting so irritable, it's been ages . . ." "Since when?" I ask her. "Since yesterday." "You haven't got much patience . . ." "Why aren't you more violent, more brutal?"

It was eight o'clock and Lison was still there. "I've got to go to the Unemployment Office," I told her, "you'll have to beat it." "Why not keep me? I'll give you what I make on my walks. I know plenty of men who'd accept."

I dressed her ready to go and said, "Look at yourself in the mirror, you've got rings under your eyes, those guys are right, you're headed for the graveyard."

"I know, but I'm a nympho, and that's what it's like to be in heat. Could you lend me a buck?"

I was slipping the lettuce into her bag when Mère Fontaine came in. "I've brought you your scrambled eggs, Monsieur Ti-Pit." Then she smiles to the bottom of her gums. "For you and Madame Ti-Pit, of course. I've just come from Mimi's room, he welcomed me with open arms, the poor little chap, you know what he said when I came in? 'I worship Jean-François, oh, Mère Fontaine, what a sweetheart!' You can't get around it, there's nothing like the fire of passion. His love was still asleep, lying on his side, showing his Greek profile, with one of his lovely hands on the pillow . . ."

"Thanks for the eggs, Mère Fontaine, that'll do."

"You see," says Lison, "we're not the only ones. There's thousands and thousands right here in Montreal, fucking high and low."

After a while Lison blew, and I went out, shaved fresh and clean, to report to the Bureau of Forgotten Men in Lower-Nose. The crowd was as big as the multitude that came to cash in on those fishes that our Saviour split up into a thousand portions, lots of immigrants clutching their unemployment cards, not to mention our native immigrants, grimy and gloomy, from all over the country, from Tadoussac and Abitibi and Golden Valley, where even gold was selling for peanuts, and I was nothing but the odd grape in all those clusters that had been waiting for hours; and there was another line, deadbeats who'd only come for the "Unemployment without Fear" handouts, the kind that sit on their asses summer and winter outside the shithouses they live in, feeding on other people's crumbs. But that didn't bother them, no money no debts. So I'm standing at the end of my line, and next to me is a character by the name of Prunier, an Acadian he told me, and mighty chipper for a guy without a job.

"If the bureaucracy deigns to smile on us, we'll get a job, but don't count on it, Christ, the one thing I care about is freedom, and the only free man in this world is a taxi driver!"

"The infirmary is my ticket."

"Phooey, you're not hard to please, chum!"

Prunier filled me in on taxi driving, you crisscrossed the country, you met people, it was an education. "Some days, chum, you pick up ambassadors, even bishops, not that they interest me very much in themselves, but when it comes to tipping they've got appearances to think about, and you see, I always dress like a dude to impress my fares, I'm not an Acadian for nothing, we Acadians have imagination." But this Prunier was a lousy fanatic. "Would you look at all those foreigners that come here to take the bread out of our mouths, people from God knows where, when you drive a cab you get the lay of the land, those heathens have built themselves whole neighborhoods, you'd think some good Canadian would hitch up his pants and throw them out, them and their filthy merchandise, oh no! It gives me the gripes to see their Greek churches, their movies all in Greek right here under the sky of France in Canada, not to mention the Chinese movies in Chinatown and the Italian movies in Little Italy!"

"Hey there, Prunier, you're a racist!"

"Not at all, I'm just a patriot. Hell, you don't even know your country, you've never gone hunting in Pontiac County, where you can pick up the deer with a shovel, you've never hunted bear, they're not very dangerous, they mind their business, we don't bother them very much, but the wolves, they're wicked, and do you know why, chum? Because they live in gangs and when they attack they're vicious, but with the deer, it's almost too easy, some guys blind them with their headlights and ram them with their cars . . ."

"Number 102," says the clerk.

That was me, so I dropped this Prunier. An ugly old buzzard, the undersecretary of some department, asked me what I "lacked in life."

I told him, "I'm looking for a job at the infirmary."

"We have some choice positions for you in business, monsieur. Have you a degree?"

"Not even the shadow of a grade-school diploma."

"Why wouldn't you consider signing up for our evening courses? They're free, try it, I'll give you a catalogue."

"Too late, monsieur, I'm too old."

"It's never too late, monsieur, ah, the backwardness of our countryside, you're able to write your name, I hope?"

"Oh yes, monsieur. I even have a dictionary in my room."

"That's better than nothing," says the old buzzard, "fill out these forms in triplicate, if you please. But I regret to inform you that the infirmary is falling into disuse. Nurses' helpers' helpers are less and less in demand."

"Then who washes the dying?"

"They die, monsieur. Such is life, the dirtier they are, the quicker they die. Next, please!"

"But what about me? Haven't you got anything for me?"

"We'll let you know, monsieur. Next."

That damn secretary seemed to think that a day or two or three without eating was good for your health; Prunier grabbed me by the collar as I was heading for the revolving door (the kind you're always catching your knee in). "So the Establishment isn't treating you right? Don't you realize that cleaning up shit is no job for a human being. You know, those nurses' helpers, those humble asswipers are good and sick of it. They're all going on strike. Their watchword and countersign is 'Fuck you, goodbye!' Didn't you know that, young fella?"

"Take it from me, Prunier, the pest house is better than the Rubber Company."

"You're nothing but a slave, young fella, why not drive a taxi, I don't say it's beer and skittles every day, there's always a chance of picking up a baddie who'll try to do you in, but that doesn't faze me, I've got my gun in the glove compartment."

"You just want to kill everybody, Prunier!"

"Now don't get mad! Look here, when you're as old as I am you'll wise up. What you need is to be stepped on a little, you're still wet behind the ears. So long, chum, remember Prunier the Acadian. Life is a farce, don't take it too seriously . . ."

I'd had enough of Prunier, I wasn't in the mood. I walked the whole length of the Catherinette, I didn't like myself that morning, it was terrible, it was getting cold again and the sky had buckets of snow up its sleeve. There were lots of sexy posters on the boulevard, but after Lison they didn't mean anything to me, I'd been inoculated, as they say. They were showing *The Two Hundred Positions of Love from the Wheelbarrow to the Four-in-Hand* and *Sex Superstar*, not an ounce of censorship, but I was like a monk, the only thing that tempted me was a Western with Yul Brynner, it was pretty good, that bald dome of his was so impressive you couldn't take your eyes off it, not even when the bandits were galloping across the plains. I wasn't the only forgotten man in that flick shop, there were neighborhood kids who'd sneaked in free through the toilet, they were bouncing around like bees, from the orchestra to the balcony and back, trying to pick up girls. It's dark and smooth in the balcony, that's where the swooning lovers go, the kind that really mean it, it's no good sitting near them because they never stop pecking and pawing, not even when the lights go on at the end. The bums like me that come to thaw out their feet go to sleep in the front rows. All of a sudden I get to thinking, If this is all you have to do, Ti-Pit, why not go say hello to your curé? So I hike out to the East End, where Vincent does his worker-priest act in his garret. Seven flights of wobbly stairs, and there he is, reading up for his class, he's trying to educate this gang of convicts, not one of them under fifty, and he's deep in a book, *Modern Mathematics*, he says it's called, looked very indigestible to me. "Sit down all the same, Ti-Pit, I'll finish my problem and then we'll make some tea, in the meantime don't disturb me."

There was no heat, I'd forgotten that, and I spat on my hands to warm them. There wasn't any crucifix, Vincent's parishioners, he told me, always got blasphemous when they saw one, all he had was a Bible on a lectern and a cook stove. Then, when I turn around, I

see a kid, a gloomy-looking creep, on Vincent's humble
cot, he's all pinched and green with fear. "Another
pickpocket?" I ask. "Now you've frightened him," says
the curé. "He thought you were a policeman and he'd
have to spend the night in jail. Have you done your
homework, Ti-Pit?"

"What homework?"

"I told you to learn the Sermon on the Mount by
heart. Don't tell me you've forgotten again. Don't stand
there with your mouth open, light the gas and heat the
tea water. You're a man, Ti-Pit, you must learn to
think of others, it's high time."

"I wouldn't want to meet this pickpocket of yours on
a dark stairway," I said. "He looks like a mad dog."

"Don't insult him, he's a child of God. He's not a
car thief like you, only a shoplifter, but the police are
after him all the same. I've told him it's the last time
I'll let him come here. Did you hear that, Luc, it's the
last time . . ."

"Don't sermon me, curé!" Luc yells. I'm thinking
this kid has a dark future ahead of him, because he's
as snotty as they come.

"And that's not all. What do I find in his schoolbag
(he wants us to think he's a man, but he's only a flea-
bitten schoolboy)? Hash is what I find. He not only
smokes it, he peddles it. Do you realize, my son, that
if they catch you, you'll be in for quite a while?"

"Shut up, curé!"

"He's polite, as you see, he's charming . . . He refuses to eat, he thinks I'm going to turn him in this
time; a social worker brings him a bowl of soup every
evening . . . You want to waste away, don't you, Luc,
all right, waste away, you malignant worm! Come on,
Ti-Pit, let's have our tea."

Father Vincent was wearing his same old greasy
sweater. His bicycle was leaning against the wall, just
in case spring came early. His blue eyes were faded
from study and maybe lack of sleep. "Well, Ti-Pit," he
says. "What's up? I'm pretty sure you haven't come to
ask about my health, I suppose you're in trouble again."

"I guess so, but I came for the visit too."

"All right, what's the story?"

"I'm out of work again."

"You're in luck, the snowplows are going on strike tomorrow, you can report with your shovel."

"Christ, no snowplows! It'll be the end of the world!"

"I've told you not to swear at my place."

"Christ, I never swear, so help me."

"You little wretch, there you go again!"

"Holy Mary, I never swear, I tell you!"

"The Lord Jesus forgive you."

I was furious, but I thought, hold it, Ti-Pit, Vincent has lost confidence in you, that's the priesthood for you. But Luc, lying there on his bed, was coming to life, snickering. "You see, Ti-Pit," says Vincent, "you have an accomplice in this young miscreant, after a week of silence, he's laughing . . . You could get up now, Luc, and make yourself useful, sweep my room, for instance, or put my books away. You're not alone on this earth, you know."

"I am too, I'm all alone."

"Anyway, I may be your friend but I'm not your maid."

"You're nothing but a curé, and you're trying to convert me."

"You want me to take you to the precinct tonight? You certainly deserve it. Say, Ti-Pit, why not make him some mulled wine, just heat up a thimbleful of my consecrated wine, maybe that will help Luc smile, I'm sick of his ugly mug!"

"A priest has no business talking to his flock like that," says the little thug.

"You have a nasty temper, my son, and Jesus was a serene man."

"Don't bother me with that guy, I hate him."

"Of course you do, you're a tough guy, you don't love anybody. Just ask Ti-Pit what happens to a thief and burglar like you. The hour of repentance comes only too soon, never fear!"

They were both quick on the trigger, I was enjoying myself. Finally Luc came over to drink his mulled wine and Vincent said, "It's nice to see you up. I was getting sick of sleeping in a chair for a no-good like you."

"Sacrifice is good for priests. And besides, you've got your nerve calling yourself a priest. You haven't even got the outfit yet, where's your soutane?"

"I wonder where I find the patience, the wisdom, to keep a monster like you under my roof. Well, at least you're up, that's a first step on the path to reason. Because you know, Ti-Pit, when he turned up here he could hardly stand on his own two feet, he was raving, you can't imagine the time I've lost this week taking care of this ingrate. Go on, drink your wine, build your strength, because I refuse to keep you here all winter."

"What are you going to do with him?"

"At the moment I don't know. He'll have to help out a little. As everyone knows, it takes two to make a life."

Then seeing Vincent was busy with his studies and had to teach his gang of delinquents that afternoon, I told him I'd pay him another visitation one of these days and started down the spiral staircase. When I got to the bottom the social worker was coming up with a bowl of soup, a Boy Scout girl with a big forehead and an expression halfway between sad and ironic. "Have you come from up there?" she says. "Is Luc feeling better?"

"He's dipping his mug in hot wine," I said.

"We've been worried about him."

"What for? What do you care if he lives or dies? He's just another shit."

"Abbé Vincent and I are very fond of him."

"Why take pity on shits?" I said. "It's no use."

"But it isn't pity, I assure you . . ."

"You're so damn Christian . . . Every bum that turns up you think, My goodness, this is it. It's Christ . . . I've heard all that before!"

The girl blushed, then she disappeared up the spirals.

I shouldn't have spoken so rude to that Boy Scout, I said to myself. She's no Lison, but she treats me respectful, Christ, I don't know how to talk to people.

No two ways, I didn't like myself that day. I thought to myself, As long as you're on vacation, Ti-Pit, why not quench your thirst at the Dancing Cat? I started off again in cadence with the wind, which was growling in the trees. The snowmaker was twisting like a water-spout, still pretty high up in the firmament, but you could see it was fixing to unload before nightfall. I held my hat to keep it from being snatched up to heaven, and pretty soon I'm pushing the door of the Dancing Cat, where you could be sure at any time of day to find the steady customers of the Molson Company drinking their bitter brew. And who do I see, framed in the harsh green glow of the color TV, you guessed it, Papillon in person, but he didn't see me, because he was reading out of his sheaf of papers. The title was "How to Understand Women," and he'd signed himself "A solitary heart"; he sure had that problem on his mind. I holler at him, "Hey, Papillon, don't tell me your blonde hasn't come back yet?"

"Well, Christ, if it isn't my friend Abráham Lemieux! Yes, she's back, my angel, my love, my Jacqueline. I've got her, now the thing is to keep her. She's a rebel, a Female Independentist, and I have to respect her ideas. Let's go eat a bean at the house, at last you'll make the acquaintance of that inestimable pearl."

"We better move out of here, Papillon. There's a Siberian snowstorm cooking up."

"You're nuts, Lemieux. Let us flee through the underground mazes of our magnificent subway, I didn't pay for that subway for nothing. We shall vanish under the skirts of Queen Elizabeth and come up at the other end of town, where my Cadillac will be waiting for us, cool and clean, without so much as a snowflake on its bosom."

"You're dreaming, Papillon, the Bureau of Blizzards says it's going to be the worst since 1914."

"Let's not exaggerate, Lemieux, Holy Mary, it's November, not January. I haven't even taken out my winter underwear yet. Come along, let us pay our respects to the fair, the virtuous Jacqueline.

"Come with me to the close of my heart:
There sits my lady . . ."

So Papillon and me, we squeeze in under the Hotel Queen Elizabeth, it towers over us like an enormous wedding cake. "Ain't it beautiful, ain't it stirring, I ask you, the Great Queen looking down on us like a stone horse, lift your eyes, Lemieux, gaze and swoon, the eighth wonder of the world." While we're twiddling our thumbs on the escalator, Papillon takes a newspaper out of his pocket.

"I've kept this article for you, Lemieux. I thought you might like to hang these beaming faces over your bed, it's straight from the Paris society news, where the intrigues of the princes of this world are sanctified. I thought you might like this family photograph, dear friend and comrade, because you tell me you were born without father or mother, so feast your eyes, poor bastard, this picture was taken at Windsor Castle, on the occasion of the queen's silver wedding, no, that's the honest truth . . . Contemplate it, brother! Here at the bottom is the royal pair, and this is the Earl of St. Andrew, I ask you, Lemieux, why didn't my parents call me that instead of Eloi, Eloi Papillon,

> *"The Earl of St. Andrew, martyr and poet,*
> *Lover of animals, forests and women,*
> *Afflicted heart . . .*

"Kidding aside, Lemieux, isn't that enchanting? And here is the honorable Angelus Ogilvy, the poetry of it, Angelus Ogilvy! And over there you see the divine meadows of Balmoral, a mother's whole family album, they say.

> *"Ah, des prairies amorales . . .*

"Yes, a heaven-blessed mother, who like your Mère Fontaine adores to grill hot dogs in her courtyard."

"Your irony is ferocious this afternoon."

"You want godfathers and godmothers, okay, I'll give you godfathers and godmothers! You're right, Lemieux, it's piling up outside. The deluge is on its way, don't look in that direction, we'll follow the subterranean passages. Which of those bars tempts you, the Irish Pub or the Ace of Clubs, we'll have ourselves an apéritif."

It was a hike to end all hikes, we poked our nose in every door, we'd taken our coats off, a fig for the winter outside the fortress! A lot of folks and folksesses on their way home from the offices were strolling around like us in the hidden city; the cafés, bookstores, and every other place were full of lunatics, there was even a counter where a girl in shorts was selling bathing suits and right near it another where some nut was peddling porno magazines, *Him, Her, We, You,* and *All Together,* you know the kind, and all around us people were chirping like blackbirds in the spring. "There's only one thing lacking in this joyous modern monastery," says Papillon. "Grass, lawns; there ought to be gardens, maybe a few sheep. If the queen has meadows, why shouldn't we, Lemieux?"

"You're asking too much of that woman."

"Consider, Lemieux, that here in the bowels of the earth hundreds of your compatriots, rather than plunge into a snow bath, will find hotels prepared to shelter them for forty dollars a night, a warm bathroom, wall-to-wall carpeting, and, waiting for them on the bedside table, a bottle of Canadian Club . . . Ah, Christ, comfort's not to be sneezed at, let's not carp and cavil, render unto Caesar what is Caesar's and unto Papillon and his peers what should be theirs. Come on, let's plunge into the Irish Pub, that'll provide some consolation, Christ!"

Inside, same deal, it was jam-packed with the common man, all hopping and popping, on the brink of convulsions. "We'll take that table back there," says Papillon, "it's my table, I have an Irish colleague who keeps it for me on days when I come to write my opuses . . . Come on, Lemieux!" But Papillon's table was already taken by two ladies on the fringe of the menopause.

Papillon throws up his arms and hollers, "If it isn't my great friends from the Snow Coast, Thérèse and Eglantine! Come on, Lemieux, magnificent women, I assure you, come to my arms, dear ladies!"

"Papillon, my love," says Eglantine, "sit here beside me, I'll tell your fortune."

So there was Papillon basking in the ladies' perfume.

Thérèse gives my arm a tug and I felt myself blushing under my hair, but nobody knew it, it was dark, there were candles on the tables, intimate lighting they call it. Eglantine's eyes were like glowing coals sparkling in all directions, and her scarlet-painted lips clutched a cigarette; Papillon was wearing his loud hippie tie and right on top of it his separatist flag was waving.

"Four Irish coffees," he orders. "No, make it eight, might as well, to inure us to the snow shovel."

"My friend and I," says Thérèse, "thought we'd spend the night at the Chapelain, they say it's very nice."

"But," says Eglantine of the glowing coals, "what shall we pay with, *ma chère?*"

"I was wondering if, in view of the weather, these gentlemen mightn't be tempted to share the expense with us."

"Alas," says Papillon, "my wife is back, gone are the joys of bachelorhood."

"I understand," says Thérèse of the turned-up nose, "then we'll just dine together, I mean of course if it's agreeable to you, Eglantine, at the Cabaret de Paris; my friend Albert has dinner there every evening, I'm sure he'll have the delicacy to suggest the Chapelain."

"But I don't know your Albert," says Eglantine.

"Oh, that's nothing, Albert has such a good heart."

"You mean the little druggist you broke your engagement with four times?"

"I was shattered, Eglantine, but some things can't be helped. No sex appeal."

"Hmm. Yes, of course," says Eglantine with a thoughtful look. "All right, Eloi, open your hand, here, right next to mine, my dear Eloi, and let me look into your soul with the eye of divination . . . no, my boy, you're not happy, in fact you're two steps away from a nervous breakdown, you worry me, Eloi . . ."

"Nonsense, Eglantine, what are you talking about, I'm so happy it's indecent . . ."

"You're making a big mistake, friend of my heart, you think you've got your faithless little flower, your forget-me-not sealed up in her apartment with her books and paintings, but mark my words, she's going to leave you again!"

"In the first place," says Papillon, "there's one thing you don't realize, I know you have a keen sense of psychology, like all fortune-tellers . . ."

"Yes," Eglantine interrupts, "but that's not all. As sure as I see you here before me, my chubbychub Eloi, my beauty, I've seen the Duke of Guise bathed in his blood . . ."

"Sure," says Thérèse, "but that happened a long time ago."

"That's beside the point, *ma chère,* I saw him, it was a vision, a revelation, don't you see? That's my specialty, my unique gift . . ."

"Never mind about that," says Papillon. "What you fail to realize is that my wife wasn't born unfaithful, her infidelity is an act of purely intellectual revolt. All she wants is autonomy, you see, that's not so very serious. She's not really unfaithful . . . not yet, at least . . ."

"But there lurks danger, Eloi, that's where you're in trouble. Come, give me your hand again, but don't despair, I see a woman with jet-black hair, with eyes like a raven, strong, generous, about forty, no, not quite, let's say at the dawn of her best years, a delicious woman . . ."

"Yes, but, Christ, I love only Jacqueline!"

"Listen to me, young man, that wife of yours with her principles, that famous liberated woman, will destroy you one day, she's proud, she's masterful, but this other woman is all fire and flame, in her past lives she was Iberian Passion incarnate, the Portuguese Nun, ah! if you only knew!"

"It can't be," says Papillon, "you amaze me, Eglantine, where would I ever meet such a madonna?"

"It could be arranged, my love."

"Ah, here come our Irish coffees," says Thérèse, "ah, Ireland, ah, to go away!"

"That's another thing that's lacking here," says Papillon with cream all over his lips. "It would be so simple, so childishly simple, to put in an underground airport over there by the left-hand exit, sure, why not? Let us dream like Jules Verne, let us rejoice our hearts at the thought of powerful 747's. Why, we could meet our friends in the subway station, a few steps would take us to their lovely, sound-proofed lounges, and off we'd go together to fuck the beauty spots of this world . . ."

Papillon was going on like this to the ladies when a character walks into our field of vision, he's thin as a telegraph wire and he tells us he's taking a poll of public opinion. "I, ladies and gentlemen, represent Militant Youth. Would you kindly answer yes or no to my questions? Are you right or left, a contemptible bourgeois or a disciple of Mao?" He had his pencil poised to jot us down, his chart was already bristling with yeses and noes. "Hey," says Papillon, "this is dictatorship. Recreation and politics don't mix, my boy, Christ, can't you see we've come here to relax!"

"All I ask of you, ladies and gentlemen, is a yes or a no."

"Doesn't my face, don't my features tell you," says Papillon, "that Papillon has a social consciousness, nay more, that his naïve heart beats for mankind? In other words, who do you take me for, you jerk?"

"All I ask is a yes or no," says the parrot.

"Go on home to your grandmother!" says Papillon.

Then Thérèse speaks up as prim as you please. "I am proud to inform you, monsieur, that my friend Eglantine and I are daughters of the grande bourgeoisie of Quebec, natives of the eminently respectable Grande-Allée."

"Perfect," says Militant Youth, "I'll take that down."

"But my dear Thérèse," says Papillon, "the Grande-Allée is the petite bourgeoisie of Quebec, meaning no offense, *chère amie.*"

That doesn't go down with Eglantine. "No, my love, it's the grande bourgeoisie of Quebec," she says. "Thérèse and I know our roots."

"I wouldn't have to look far to find a shoemaker in your ancestry," says Papillon. "There is no grande bourgeoisie in our country."

"In olden times we were the lords of Quebec," says Thérèse.

"Lords on the Grande-Allée? Meaning no offense, my dears, you're nothing but beggars on horseback, climbers, upstarts, and snobinettes!"

"Come along, Eglantine, we are being crudely insulted. Come, *ma chère.*"

Stung by Papillon's gibes, they get up to go. Thérèse is looking high and mighty, but Eglantine pats Papillon on the head and says, "I adore you, my chubbychub Eloi, even if you are a bad boy. *Au revoir,* my love!"

"There they go," says Papillon to Militant Youth. "You see what you've done with your poll, you damn parasite!"

"I'll take that down, monsieur," says the parrot.

"You know what you are?" says Papillon. "A pest, a slogan slinger, a labeler, a bureaucrat!"

"I'll take that down, monsieur," says the parrot.

Militant Youth goes on to the next table with his poll. Papillon was pretty well steamed up by that time.

"There, Lemieux, you behold an authentic pain in the ass. He deserves to be taken by the scruff of his neck and chucked into a snowdrift. You might have told him, Lemieux, that when you were a child you were so hungry you ate your fingernails. No, really, brother, they make me good and sick, these quarrelsome louts that try to sound my heart and kidneys, why didn't he ask me while he was at it how many times a week I make love to my wife? I'm reminded of a certain Papineau, a buddy from my Jesuit days, he was as brilliant as the glorious rebel, his namesake. The boys in our class used to say, 'There are two stars in our midst: Papillon and Papineau, Papillon glitters and glows, Papineau shines and outshines!' Christ, it drove me crazy, always this wise guy in my hair. I could talk a blue streak, but Papineau reeled off the applesauce like a talking book of logic, you'd have given him the first prize for eloquence, sight unseen, it was Spinoza here, Thingamabubble there, he'd listen to himself like a phonograph record. I could have skinned him alive, but I've got to admit that Papineau was too many for Papillon. When I'd finally left the unctuous groves of Jesuitry, I thought to myself, Papillon, you can rest confidently on your laurels, you'll never set eyes on Papineau again, he's too brilliant, he'll rise higher and higher, he'll shout louder and louder, but at least you won't have him shooting balloon juice at you every morning in the study hall! So like every well-born man, I get married; without benefit of Papineau I lie down, I stretch out, I write my little books, I paint, I sculpt, in short, I create my inner self, and at the same time I make a modest living teaching the few crumbs of Latin that nurtured my brain in times gone by. For several years Papillon grows in stature and fertility. Then one night I take my wife to a Chinese restaurant because we'd fallen on hard times and at the Ding Dong you could get a meal for fifty-nine cents, tip included, and who do I see all of a sudden? Papineau, Papineau in person, the enemy, the destroyer, and what had he made of himself in ten years? A double, a triple Papineau, as brilliant and hard as steel. Right off the bat, guess what, Lemieux, he asks me if I've read Marx, if I'm 'politicized.' Before I even have time to sit down and eat my egg roll, he lights into me and I start stammering like a feebleminded prince who's lost his kingdom. 'To tell you the truth, Papineau, I haven't read the 1844 manuscripts yet . . . marriage, my wife . . . you know how it is, I'm not as young as I used to be . . .' 'What? You haven't read the 1844 manuscripts, Papillon?' says Papineau, all flushed with triumph, the bastard. 'Why, you're a total ignoramus, and what's more a petit bourgeois, I was too bashful to tell you, but I've been thinking it for fifteen years, you're nothing but a petit bourgeois!' 'Me, Papillon, a petit bourgeois?' I say, trembling from head to foot. 'Is that true? Is that what you've thought of me for twenty years, Papineau?' I could have cried, he'd plunged a dagger into my vanity, Lemieux. Then he flings another question, more shattering than the last. 'And tell me, Papillon, have you read *Religion and Myth in Karl Marx* by Lewis Furthermore?' 'No,' I said, groveling in my stupidity, 'no, Papineau, I even have to admit that the name of Furthermore is unknown to me . . . What with my teaching, you see, and correcting papers at night, not to mention the publication of my books, perhaps you haven't noticed, Papineau, but I've published two more books this year . . .'

" 'I say it again, you're nothing but a petit bourgeois, Papillon.'

" 'Look here,' I say, 'let's not exaggerate, on my mother's side yes, she was always crazy about mink coats, but my daddy, poor daddy, was never able to buy her one. And what about my bicycle, Papineau, surely you remember the three-wheeled bicycle I never had . . . I was a street urchin, with holes in my pants and my face blackened with dust, I swear it, Papineau!'

"But he, the monster, sitting at the Ding Dong with his cadaverous life companion and his two twin boys (Karl and Blaise he'd called them in his devotion, the oddball, real Tiny Twins fed out of a tin can, as pale as alabaster, anemic and green around the gills, I'd never seen such brats, all they ate was rice, all four of them), well, this blasted Papineau keeps hammering at me with his refrain: 'Petit bourgeois Papillon, petit bourgeois,' meaning 'pervert, criminal, anathema,' and my wife and I didn't even dare to pick up our chopsticks and eat our chicken with pineapple. After a while I said humbly, 'Come to think of it, the other day I read in Maritain . . .' But he interrupts me ruthlessly, 'What, still reading Maritain? Your backwardness is inconceivable. For twenty years now you've been talking about Maritain!' 'Yes, but you see, Papineau, I read slowly and attentively . . . in depth, Papineau. I've been reading Kierkegaard too . . .' It was no use. 'What, still reading Kierkegaard? You're decades behind the times, it's appalling!' And then some more of his 'petit bourgeois, Papillon!' That damned Papineau made me feel so humiliated that my head was practically under the table. In the end I said, 'My daddy was a proletarian.'

" 'Did he read Marx?'

" 'No, I can't say he did, but he worked for five dollars a week; he went to work when he was twelve. I'm positive my daddy was a proletarian.'

" 'Not at all, he was nothing but a petit bourgeois!'

" 'How can you say that? You don't know my daddy, you never saw him, I swear by his head he was a proletarian and, Christ, he sweated for his daily bread!'

" 'It was white bread.'

" 'No, Daddy always said it wasn't, that's why I never got my bicycle, and what a trauma that was, like any boy suffering involuntary deprivation at the hands of his father. Daddy always said he'd never known the taste of cake or white bread, there'd never been anything but the black stuff when he was little.'

" 'Petit bourgeois, you're lying!'

" 'No, by the head of my father, whom I admire because he had the courage to refuse Mama her mink coat and me my bicycle; without that iron will to guide my first steps, I might have grown up to be a petit bourgeois, but on my father's side I'm pure proletarian, I swear it by your twins, Papineau.'

" 'Your mother's side won out,' said the viper. 'Now your wife has got the mink coat . . .'

" 'Yes, but we're paying for it in installments,' I said humbly. 'And credit is only the poor man's illusion of wealth.'

" 'Credit is petit bourgeois, America is petit bourgeois, someday, believe you me, America will vanish off the face of the earth.'

" 'Don't frighten me, don't overdo it, Papineau, surely you agree that Platonic moderation is our only hope . . .'

" 'The hope of the petite bourgeoisie, the consumer class. One day you'll be excommunicated!'

" 'Exactly. I was just reading in Marcuse . . .'

" 'Petit bourgeois! Petit bourgeois!'

" 'No, really, Papineau. Think of our friend, the lawyer from Quebec, he too was a proletarian on his father's side, he grew up in Limoilou, you've got to admit that whatever Marx may say in his book Limoilou is proletarian. He, too, used to play in the streets after school, the seat of his britches was worn through and maybe his nose was bleeding from playing powiepalooka with his chums . . . today he boasts of the fortune he's made out of parking tickets, but he started out as a proletarian from Limoilou, just like my daddy! Same as me, Papineau, I swear it by my head!'

" 'Take a look at your paunch, Papillon, you eat too much, you drink too much, you petit bourgeois. You're a pretentious hypocrite, yes, pretentious, and always have been, for twenty years I've been wanting to tell you that, and now at last I am telling you, you're a pretentious petit bourgeois. We, my wife, my children, and myself, are no mere theoreticians, worshippers of abstract ideas, we put our philosophy into practice. We've traveled' (here I broke in and told him in a weak little penitent voice, 'I've traveled too, Papineau, I've been twice around the world,' but he wasn't listening) 'with our knapsacks on our backs we've seen the world, on foot, in boats, in jeeps, we've seen it inside out and outside in; when we got back, we decided to set up our own commune, summer and winter, snow and shine, we live in a tent and eat rice, nothing but rice; our coming here this evening is an exception, it's to warm up our son Blaise, who's come down with pneumonia, call it sick leave.'

" 'How many of you are there in your commune?'

" 'No one has the courage to join us,' says Papineau, 'there's just the four of us, my wife, the twins, and me, but our unity is our strength.'

" 'But what about your grandfather's estate, Papineau? What have you done with your inheritance?'

" 'I divided it among those less fortunate than ourselves. But that, I have to admit, was a failure, because what did the beneficiaries do? They bought Mercedeses and color TV's, which only shows how corrupt our society has become . . . We shall have to destroy this civilization and build another, that's the only solution. And that, Papillon, can only be done by violence, by fire and sword and the searing power of thought.'

" 'Yes, Papineau, that's one way of looking at it . . . But what would you say to dinner at my place next Wednesday with your wife and twins? We'll have rice of course and various other austere dishes, I'm not a gourmand, you know my tummy expands on its own because I'm always sitting at my desk, the fact is I only drink water, Papineau, I'm a sober, frugal man like my daddy, Papineau!'

" 'My wife and I never accept invitations from capitalist society, but just this once let Blaise's pneumonia be our justification, you can count on us for Wednesday evening.'

"Well, Lemieux, that Wednesday all four of them descend on me. If they weren't brandishing their little Red Books, it was all but. My wife and I had laid out a frugal banquet, nothing shocking, I assure you, a pint of red wine, a plate of Kraft cheese. Well, I have to admit (my wife, like myself, has a sprightly palate, you see) there were olives, anchovies, and a dozen little delicacies scattered round about. So in march the revolutionaries, and Papineau says, 'Petit bourgeois, what abundance, what superfluity, it's nauseating!'

" 'The better to receive you with, Papineau.'

" 'It's petit bourgeois, Papillon!'

" 'It's really very simple, Papineau, you can't deny it. A few biscuits to whet the appetite . . .'

"Before we sat down, we wrapped Blaise in blankets and laid him down on the bed, because that twin was wheezing like he was on his last legs.

" 'Aren't you worried about your twin, your little Blaise, Papineau?' I asked him. 'He seems pretty sick to me . . .'

" 'It's only pneumonia, it won't kill him,' says Papineau.

" 'He looks bad. I think . . .'

" 'You petits bourgeois are too soft about sickness; sickness and death don't frighten us. Our aim lies elsewhere.'

" 'All the same, you wouldn't want to lose your little Blaise?'

" 'I don't live for him, I live for my cause. He'll recover. The cause demands it.'

" 'Don't you think we ought to call a doctor, Papineau?'

" 'It's just like you capitalists to call the doctor for every little ache and pain. Death is just another ache and pain, it's not fatal. From the standpoint of history it doesn't count.'

" 'I'm glad to hear you say that, Papineau, but your little Blaise can hardly breathe, I think . . .'

" 'The air of our summits will revive him. He will recover!'

"So Blaise was left gasping on the bed, but my wife and I stayed with him, we fussed over him like a couple of anxious hens, and when we got back to the dining room, what do we see? There's nothing left on the table, Papineau and his bag of bones have eaten it all, they've emptied my wife's fruit bowl with the apples and oranges I wanted for my still life. Well, Lemieux, that was Papineau, the shining light of my Jesuit days, Christ!"

That was the end of his story and it was none too soon for me. "We'd better hit the road, Papillon," I tell him, "or we'll be looking for your Cadillac under fifteen feet of snow."

"Right you are, brother, I can hear the subway blowing its horn beneath my feet."

And off we run, kicking up sparks after all those Irish coffees. In the train there were two kinds of people, the ones who'd been out in the snow and the ones that hadn't. The snow crowd were coughing and sniffling, we were all besieged by winter, with no escape in sight. A bunch of guys from the snowplows were shouting in chorus: "Dig yourselves out, brothers. We're going to sleep!"

"This kind of strike shouldn't be tolerated," says Papillon. "Naturally I'm not thinking of myself, I'm thinking of the widows and old people, look around you, brother, we're the only ones without shovels, even the kids have their rakes, our whole beautiful province is shouldering its shovels, united at last, what an inspiring sight, the polar army of Christ!"

Then Papillon grabs hold of a guy who's stepping on our feet. "I beg your pardon, friend, but tell me, you who've come in from the cold, do you think I'm likely to find my blue Cadillac emerging from the drifts?"

"I doubt it, monsieur, I doubt it very much."

"Christ!" Papillon cries out. "Another goddamned Frenchman in our glorious land! Come, sit down with us, we'll talk this thing over."

"Yes, I am a Frenchman," says the muffled and helmeted man from the snow. "But not from Paris," he adds very sadly. "And I have to admit, I'm not in love with your beautiful country tonight."

"You don't surprise me in the least," says Papillon, "another griping immigrant complaining about the temperature, another Frenchman who wants to lecture us! What's your name anyway?"

"Antoine, monsieur, Antoine Durocher. But I repeat, I'm not from Paris. So you have no reason to hate me."

"I don't hate you, Antoine, I love you. There are all sorts of Frenchmen, just as there are all sorts of mushrooms and Québecquois, but alas, there's only one kind of Parisian."

"I wouldn't know, monsieur, I'm not from Paris."

"What's eating you, Antoine my boy?" asks Papillon. "Does our climate depress you as much as that?"

"Yes, monsieur, the climate, it's too much, monsieur . . . it's so extreme [sneeze], my family and I haven't your resistance, your robust health."

"Of course not, you are the old France, we are the new, the blood in your veins has lost its bounce. Is that it?"

"I'm in no laughing mood, monsieur . . . [sneeze, sneeze]. Besides, you're prejudiced against us, you don't like us, I don't know why, I try to adapt, I assure you, monsieur, but I can't seem to fit in . . . why do you dislike us, monsieur?"

"Not at all, I adore you. Believe me, I have no prejudice against you whatever, aren't we cousins, after all? Especially on a day like this when all nations are one . . ."

"[Sneeze, sneeze.] Ah, what a life! What a life!"

"You don't work for Radio Canada, I hope?"

"No [sneeze], we've opened a branch of the Galeries Lafayette . . . ladies' clothing [sneeze] . . ."

"How's business?"

"Bad."

"Will you be able to pay for your passage home?"

"You see [sneeze] that you don't like me."

"Christ, can't you take a bit of teasing? My word, Antoine, you people have stopped laughing since Voltaire, your smiles have a pinched look . . ."

"I haven't read Voltaire, monsieur, I'm not from Paris."

". . . and you expect us, the last sparks of New World delirium, to vegetate in your dreary Cartesianism!"

"[Sneeze.] *Bon soir,* monsieur, this is my station. I'm sorry to leave you so soon, but it's my station."

"Damn Frenchman, come and warm yourself at my shack, you look like you've come out of the deep freeze."

"I can't . . . monsieur! [sneeze sneeze] *Bon soir,* monsieur."

So Antoine gets out with a lot of other snowbirds. In every station there are advertisements showing guys camping in the summer, fishing for trout and salmon, with the spiel:

Keep the mosquitoes away with Blue Lightning and enjoy a cool summer . . .

"Ah, Christ!" says Papillon, "trout and salmon, if only it were true, but no, we have to go out under the 'pure sky of lofty splendors.' That Frenchman was right, it get depressing after a while. Hey, come on, this is the end of the line . . ."

The exit was plenty crowded, no fear of loneliness, the white cyclone was lashing the street, I couldn't even see how we'd get out of the subway. A lass from the Army of Snow Resisters was stationed there, she plunked two shovels in our hands. "All right, boys, get to work," she says, and along with all the other folks and folksesses we dive into the white bath . . .

"But where's my Cadillac?" moans Papillon. "It was over there next to the lamppost, and now I can't see it."

"Don't cry," I tell him, "we'll find your jalopy, you'll just have to dig Papillon."

"Take it easy, Lemieux, digging is all right for you, you're young and strong, but me with my asthma, you can't expect me to go on shoveling indefinitely. The night will find me dead."

"You damn windbag," I say. "You just dig your hole like everybody else, or I'll poke your eye out."

"Don't be so testy, Lemieux, do I look like I was taking a nap? You're as bad as that blasted Frenchman, so quick to take umbrage."

Papillon wasn't much of a shoveler, he'd move a few ounces of snow and then he'd start declaiming with his coattails flapping in the gale. "Hell, Papillon," I tell him, "I can see you've never shoveled much fluff in your lifetime."

"Fluff, yes," says Papillon, "not anvils."

"Hey, there's your Cadillac, go shovel a bit up front, we'll have to step on the gas to get through."

Night was coming down on top of us, mean winds were crawling up our legs, all around us we saw grimacing faces and eyes glazed with frost. The snowmobiles went flashing by, scooting over the snowbanks like silver fish, you couldn't see the drivers, only the pompons on their caps bobbing up and down against the sky . . . "Hurrah for the snow!" the bastards yelled as they passed . . .

"It's unjust," says Papillon, "all those government blokes have got snowmobiles, why haven't I got one? I haven't even got a sleigh with a dog."

"All you do is bitch, Papillon, just open the door of your Cadillac and let's get in."

"My little Jacqueline will be aghast when she sees me. 'Oh, my precious Eloi,' she'll say, 'you've been out in the cold, come sit beside the electric radiator and rest your poor bruised and bleeding feet in this basin of hot water.' Ah, there's no solace like a wife for a man of morose and mournful thoughts."

"When will you ever shut up, Papillon?"

So we started the Cadillac, we skidded and spun in the sugar, Papillon was feeling better, but that didn't stop his mouth. "My wife is my anchor," he cries out, "my clock, my temple, my harmony, and my symmetry,

you'll see my Jacquelinette, my radiant Jacquelinette!"
And then he starts singing:

> *"My grandma's grandma thought she'd go*
> *Across the great salt pond*
> *To see what flowers grew beyond.*
> *The sun was bright, the wind was low,*
> *She boarded ship at Saint-Malo.*
>
> *She hadn't any finery,*
> *Only a worn-out rosary.*
> *Putting her trust in Providence*
> *She arrived by diligence*
> *From some small town in Normandy."*

"Pull up, Papillon, we're here!"

"Ah, how glad my lady love will be to see her knight of the snows!"

But Lady Love wasn't as gracious as you might have expected, we'd hardly set boot on the carpet when she starts in.

"Well, well, well, if it isn't Papillonnet, and not a minute too soon. The whole neighborhood is out in the street with shovels, it's just come in over the radio, the united front of all citizens. Get down those stairs with your friend, Papillonnet!"

"What!" cries Papillon, completely stunned. "What's the matter, what's wrong, my mamushka, my Jacqueline? Why this wrath, why are you chasing me into the street, what have I done? Can't my friend and I have a cup of bouillon first? We're thirsty, hungry, exhausted, we've been clearing the wilderness for hours, those lovely arms of yours were meant for gathering in, not for throwing out."

"Rave on," she says, "I'm not listening." She's well set up, on the tall side, with a nice round bosom and a ready tongue. "You're right," I tell Papillon, "your better half is quite a dish."

"So she is, Lemieux, but bear in mind, she's out of sorts today, it must be the storm that's upset her." Then he starts billing and cooing again and tries to take his Jacqueline's hand. "My darling, my sugar plum, why are you so stern, speak to your honeybunch, I . . ."

"Not another word! Don't you realize, Papillonnet, that we are experiencing a great historic moment?"

"In what respect, my Christmas pudding?"

"The women are all in the streets. The whole National Front of Womanhood is out there, practically at our door . . ."

"Shoveling, you mean?"

"We have occupied one side of the Boulevard des Epinettes. For the first time in history we refuse to have any men in our midst . . ."

"You mean, my little wild rose, my hollyhock, that they won't let me shovel with you? By your beloved side? In the light of your still somewhat overcast presence? Why, that's impossible. Christ, you're going too far."

"Drink your bouillon and get out there with the patriots."

I could see through the blinds that the shovelers had made a good start on the Boulevard des Epinettes, they were digging tunnels and laughing like mad, and sure enough, the men were on one side and the women on the other. "Hey, Papillon," I tell him. "They're having a snowball fight down there, come take a look, it's the battle of the sexes."

"And you too, Abraham," she says, "you're the same breed as Papillon, my husband and former mate, because from now on we're going to sleep in separate rooms, I've had enough of his conceit, his beastly superiority, and I'm sorry to say, Abraham, I detect the same faults in you. From now on, I'm going to speak my mind to you men, I don't care if it's you or Papillonnet, for my money you're all the same, and I find you intensely distasteful."

"Distasteful?" says Papillon, sweet as honey. "If I've offended you, I beg forgiveness, I fall on my knees, I may have been sightly ambitious, individualistic . . ."

"Watch your terminology, Papillon. Let's be honest for once. The right words are vain and selfish . . ."

"A trifle self-centered, if you will, but selfish, no . . . no, really."

"You're a vain, inconsiderate cad, that's the long and

short of it, Papillonnet, and most men are just like you . . ."

"Me? Your devoted, upright Papillon? No, Jacqueline no, I'm not a cad . . . Ah, Jacqueline, how mistaken you are!"

"Cad! You men are all alike, in love with Woman! It's not me that you love, it's Her . . ."

"Her? Whom are you referring to, my dear?"

"Woman, of course. A myth, a goddess of femininity, a monster."

"Don't forget," says Papillon, "that I'm not the average man, I'm an exotic woodland flower, a poet, a lost soul . . ."

"Bullshit!"

"Don't fly off the handle, my love, calm down, relax as if we were lying side by side in bed, reading and talking, as we sometimes do, you'll have to admit."

"And who's always reading? And who keeps me awake by talking for hours on end? Papillon, always Papillon. He and his poems, his preposterous inspirations. How can I live with such a man! And on Sundays, while you're writing poems to your goddess, who irons your shirts? Me, your slave, your carpet sweeper, your carpet. No, I'm through!"

"Where are you going, my sweet?"

"I've told you: into the street to help my sisters. The children have to go to school tomorrow, you know."

"But what of your brothers, your amiable brothers?"

"They'll have to take care of themselves. Just go give them a hand."

"But you see . . . my asthma . . . my exhaustion . . ."

"Egotist, cad, scoundrel, deserting your comrades when the whole nation is in the streets!"

And *slam*, there goes the door! Papillon collapses into his armchair with a groan. "Open up that bottle, brother, then we'll go toil with our people on the boulevard. But tell me: am I really such a cad?"

"Maybe you've got a few too many Eglantines and Thérèses in your pasture."

"Christ, no, it's not that. It's a psychological gulf between Jacqueline and me, but don't judge by appearances, my boy, because when it comes to the joys of the bed and table, my sugar plum and I get along like two angels."

So we polished off the bottle, and finally Papillon drags himself to his feet. "Okay, Lemieux, back to our shovels. Believe me, this storm, the most ferocious since 1914, will long be remembered . . ."

On both sides of the boulevard it was like a village dance, it made me jump for joy, shovel and all, to see all those guys and girls demolishing walls. It was like a hundred years ago, not a car, not a truck, science spread out all around us, except now and then for the screeching of the joyous shovelers, and on top of it all the wind cutting into the voices and the sound of the shovels. All of a sudden Papillon drops his shovel, he's sighted a chum on top of the snowbank and runs to embrace him. I could hear him yelling. "Hey, Corneille, Louis Corneille, dear publisher, my lone defender, what a joy to meet you here at my very doorstep, do you recognize me? . . . it's me, your son, your friend, Eloi Papillon . . . Eloi!" Corneille can't hear a thing through his earflaps, he pulls them up and yells at Papillon, "Papillon, do you recognize me? It's me, Corneille, I thought I'd do my shoveling in your neighborhood . . ."

"What? What's that?"

"I've got a bone to pick with you, Papillon. About your last trip to Paris . . ."

"What?"

"Your manners, Papillon. I've got to tell you what I think of your bad manners . . ."

"Oh, that was nothing. Nothing at all, Corneille."

"What?"

"What's that place that's still lit up over there?"

"It's the . . . it's the . . . wait, I'll tell you in a minute."

We chucked our shovels and took a breather. Papillon shook the snow out of his eyes and said, "Now I can see, it's the Inferno Club."

"Let's go," said Corneille. "It'll give us the courage to go on."

We held on to each other's coattails to keep our footing, the wind was blowing us every which way. When we finally escaped from the gale, we were all tingling, frosted over like mummies, even our eyebrows were full of ice. There was a big crowd at the Inferno, short-winded citizens, they'd been thawing out quite a while.

Corneille gave our order to the waitress. She had horns on her forehead, only the girls had horns, the waiters had velvet tails, the whole place was full of devils plus the demons of lechery on the walls. The menu was like this:

Whisky sour à la witches' caldron
Martini à la hellfire
Scotch Machiavelli

We were shivering so hard that we thawed out by trying them all. "When we're through here," says Papillon, "we'll be able to shovel in the cadence of the heavenly choir. Ah, now I'm beginning to understand, my dear Corneille, why the Montreal-Miami planes are so crowded at Christmas time."

This Corneille had a good mug, a waving mane falling down over his shoulders, and graying sideburns. He tosses off a quick one and says, "Yes, Papillon, I wanted a word with you about serious matters. Will you finally listen to me?"

"I always listen to you, my dear publisher, my friend. Who would publish me if you didn't out of the kindness of your heart? Now what have I done to make you deign to reproach me?"

"As I was saying, Papillon, your manners are execrable."

"What do you mean, *cher ami?*"

"Your Paris publisher, famed far and wide for his 'Albums of Rejected Verse,' after all you owe him a modicum of gratitude. True, it was I who begged him to publish you when he had no faith in your talent, he always said you were nothing but a vulgar windbag, but all the same his tolerance and condescension did bring you the consolation prize for your contribution to his Imperiled Poets of the French Tongue series. Then you, in your usual insolence, your ungodly arrogance, accept my generous gift of a trip to Paris but you don't even have the courtesy to show up for your prize and meager crown . . ."

"Yes, but, Corneille, it was the first prize I wanted."

"Once again, Papillon, you shamed me before my friends. Your Paris publisher, who is not a calculating man and has only your literary future at heart even if he did tell everybody in sight that you were nothing but a crude peasant . . ."

"Me, a peasant!"

"Don't interrupt. You write, I'll talk. Your publisher arranged a glorious reception for you at the home of his revered friend the Duchess of Mimosa, there was orange juice, tomato juice, a spread for the gods, we were all there waiting for you in our Sunday best, the intellectual and diplomatic cream of Quebec, not to mention the Paris 'Let's-cultivate-Quebec-it-ought-to-bring-in-something-someday Society' . . . we were all there, proudly waiting for you, and you, vile knave, you never showed up!"

"Listen to me, Corneille, my only friend, it's the first prize I wanted. Not even a French Canadian pessimist wants a consolation prize."

"It's a beginning. You lack perseverance, Papillon."

"It was the first prize or nothing," says Papillon. "I assure you, friend Corneille, even an Angora cat, an eminence of the animal kingdom, would turn up his nose at a Parisian consolation prize."

"The truth, the abject truth, Papillon, is that, unbelievable as it may seem, you, the shining light of my Rise and Shine Press, detest the French. That's why you didn't turn up for your consolation prize. Come to think of it, you snubbed the Governor's prize as well, because you detest the English. Is there anyone you like, you blinkered bigot?"

"I like you, friend of my heart."

"Then listen to me, you'll have to turn over a new leaf, Papillon, your provincialism, your Joual particularism, is making you narrower and narrower when you ought to be unfolding your petals in universalism, an artist who doesn't have an open, adaptable mind is no artist. Take Gogol, there was an open-minded man, or your friend Flaubert . . . Why do you hem yourself in like this? If you eliminate all oppressors, real or imaginary, there won't be anybody left on earth, don't you see, and it's childish to imagine that the Joualonese are better than anybody else, not at all, they're jealous of each other, jealousy is their crowning vice and it takes every conceivable form, oh yes, they're just as capable of cruelty as anyone else, they may be less tyrannical because they haven't anyone to tyrannize, but man is man or worse; fire, as we all know, is always worthy to be called fire, but man is a different kettle of fish . . ."

"Have you ever had a French mistress for a week, or even for a night or an hour? Now there's an experience you'll never forget . . ."

"Let's not mix sentiment with publishing, I'm speaking of your boorish behavior in Paris, not your amours. I nearly expired with humiliation when I heard that Madame Lucette Potauvin carried off the prize that should have been yours for her *Reminiscences of a Former Nun* and spent the money on a cruise to Venice. Glory be, to think that I pay you royalties you haven't even earned! When I opened my publishing house seven years ago, I went into debt to encourage you, because I believed in your slightly paralyzed afflatus."

"You're my only friend, Corneille, I've admired you since I was a child, you're the only crusader we have left. And today no one appreciates you as you deserve. I shall write poems in your honor, yes, when you're dead, I'll speak of you, I'll glorify you in phrase and fable . . ."

"Let's get back to the present, Papillon. We were speaking of the present. Madame Potauvin wasn't the only one to outstrip you, you thinking tortoise, even the author of *The Maple Leaf in the Wind* has overtaken you, not to mention Jojo Cafard, the precocious fifteen-year-old, published by New Celebrities in Longueuil and acclaimed by all France because, as the critics over there say, he writes 'pure Joual.' And do you know what makes that barnyard adolescent's Joual so pure? It's because instead of saying '*merde*' as they do in Paris, he says '*marde*,' which, according to the Joualologists exiled in Paris and the Parisians who set themselves up as Joualologists, has a deeper resonance. You see, the last clarinet is always the sweetest and you, Papillon, are dragging your crutches in the rear-guard of the avant-garde . . . Oh well, as you know, I've always accepted you as you are, you're not the only Joual freak I publish, and even if you're not a Federalist, a universalist like me, even if you are a bigoted party man, envenomed against the French on the left, the English on the right, and the Americans in the middle, because, knowing you as I do, Papillon, I'll bet you don't like the Americans either, don't try to tell me different, you liar, you don't like anybody, but even if you exasperate me with your party politics, Papillon, what can I do, I have to put up with you . . ."

"That's your weakness, Corneille, your only weakness, you're too much of a universalist, too magnanimous. Watch your step, my dear Don Quixote, someday that nothing-human-is-alien-to-me windmill will turn around and bite your head off."

"Like all party men, you understand nothing."

"I don't want to fight a duel with you in the snow, Corneille, let's shut our traps and stop talking politics. Why, only the other day I read in *Burgeoning Thought,* which you yourself publish incidentally, that one of your chums, like yourself a universalist and spawner of utopias, has just started a party for people who hate parties, the Giraffe Party he calls it, anybody can join who wants to, anybody who wants to can make motions, the floor is open to worker and aristocrat alike. Now there you've got something. There I'm behind you, Corneille."

"I have another friend," says Corneille, swallowing the cherry out of his whisky sour à la witches' caldron, "who's just founded something even more daring."

"Yes, yes, I know. I suppose you mean the Socrates Party."

"That's what he called it at first, but nobody came to the meetings."

"That's right. Now he calls it Sodom Power, I hear all Quebec is joining up. Splendid, just the rocket our sky needed! But I repeat, Corneille, I've always admired you. Why, I remember the articles you wrote for *I, You, We Accuse,* when I was still with the Jesuits . . . And after that, remember? . . . you flung yourself into the defense of the unemployed. Ah, what a dauntless spirit you were then, crusade followed crusade. I said to myself, Papillon, that's the man you must resemble when you grow up. But I don't even come up to your ankle. Luckily all kinds are needed in the Valley of Joualonie! And who was more corrosive than you in repudiating, in words of course, first, foremost, and forever in words, the ignoble lords of the manor, the tyrants who crushed our poor defenseless people in their barbed fists. Long live Corneille! Down with tyranny, down with lies! You were our conscience and our witness, ah yes, someday I'll frame you in verses."

"Yes, but for the moment, Papillon, let's discuss your affairs. How is your *Irreversible Moon,* your little book of poems, getting along? Have you worked on it this fall?"

"Sometimes I spend a whole night on a single rhyme, so you see, my friend, it advances slowly, very slowly . . ."

"Through the leaves of your verbiage I seem to perceive that you need money."

"Yes, my dear publisher, friend of my heart, alas yes."

"I'll advance you this check for your *Irreversible Moon,* but as I know you, you'll circumvent me again by spending twenty dollars an hour on your psychoanalyst. Am I right?"

"What can I do, my friend, my dear Corneille, it's my wife's affectivity that's on the blink."

"I'm not paying you a three-year advance to encourage psychoanalysis, it's just another party, you know. There are limits to my patience . . ."

"No, Corneille, my bread, my honey, it's limitless, you are my divine mercy on earth."

"But why do you still waste time on those liturgists, those shrinks? What have they got that you haven't got? Just tell me . . ."

"They've got Freud, and I only have my feeble and sometimes slightly beclouded lights."

"You exasperate me, Papillon, but I suppose it's none of my business if you want them to caress you with words like neurosis and metempsychosis. It's never too late to learn a new catechism."

Then Corneille looks at me and says, "But you, Abraham, why don't you say anything, my boy?"

"Because you two keep shouting to high heaven," I told him.

"That's a fact," says Corneille, suddenly conscience-stricken, "I haven't been listening to you, I'm always listening to this Papillon whom I nourish with sugar and salt, and who's always handing me the same line."

"You ought to publish Lemieux," says Papillon. "He's got what it takes, he's Joualonese to the gills, he's an orphan, hence no Oedipus complex, he's poor, hence no political party, he doesn't even need one, he sniffs in the air of the times, he's a home-grown product, pure wool, the bastard doesn't talk, so he must be thinking, ergo, he's writing dozens of novels in that muttonhead of his."

"Talking about novels," says Corneille. "What's become of that dubious erotic novel of yours?"

"Ah, my dear friend, a tragedy! The lawyer from Quebec has stolen it from me, now he's writing it— *The Story of Y*. Ah, little Y, what will become of you in the company of that abject cynic? He'll deflower and delouse you! And you know what? He's planning to publish it at the Drooping Priapus Press, and you can bank on it, Corneille, it will do even better than those bathtub novelettes *Snow and Sex* and *Sex and Snow*.

At this point Papillon goes pale and green, he's just recognized a phantom coming from the depths of the Inferno. "Christ," he says, "who do I see coming toward me again? Christ, it's Papineau, it's Papineau again . . ."

Sure enough. There's Papineau standing across the table from Papillon, giving him a big handshake. "Papillon, comrade," he says, solemn like. "What a great night to be alive, all of us side by side, building our Great Wall of China in brotherhood."

"But, Papineau, we're not building the wall, we're shoveling it away."

"No," says Papineau, "tonight we are raising the

bulwark of our solidarity. Oh, Papillon, my heart is overflowing! But what are you doing here, Papillon, drinking and belching when your comrades are at work, shoulder to shoulder, shovel to shovel?"

"Me?" says Papillon with his tail between his legs. "Me? Well, I'm resting from my labors in the company of Corneille, my publisher and friend, and Lemieux, a comrade and scion of our noble proletariat, yes, Papineau, I swear by my head, he's a proletarian to the hilt, though alas he's never read Marx. As for Corneille, his name speaks for him. Who in his youth has not read the powerful, the courageous articles of our beloved Corneille?"

"I know you, Monsieur Corneille," says Papineau, all in a fever in spite of his running nose and the snow cascading down his chasuble. "Like all naïve school-boys I used to read your articles, I was flabby-minded enough to admire you, yes, flabby-minded, Monsieur Corneille, for today I despise you . . ."

"Really? Why?"

"Petit bourgeois!"

At that Papillon rose as one man, his eyes were on fire. "No! No!" he cries out. "You can't talk to my friend and publisher like that, Papineau, you bloody Virgil who invariably crosses my path just as I'm fearlessly settling down for a chat in the bottommost pit of hell. Tar me with your 'petit bourgeois' brush if you must, but spare my friend Corneille!"

"But I am a petit bourgeois," says Corneille meekly. "Why should that bother him?"

"It's not true," says Papillon. "Christ, the hero of my childhood a petit bourgeois? Never!"

"I recognized you, Monsieur Corneille," says Papineau, still in full swagger. "Your picture is in all the papers, wherever I look I see this militant who's stopped militating, who publishes books by the hundreds and never defends anybody but his authors, in other words himself, this petit bourgeois opportunist."

"A man defends those he believes in," says Corneille.

"Listen to me, Monsieur Corneille. We militants hate all artists and writers, we hate the whole lot of you. You stand in the way of our march to freedom through violence, you're all alike with your consumer needs, you need a table to write on, a canvas to paint on, you need this, you need that, abject petits bourgeois one and all, from Emile Nelligan and his lyrical flowers to your protégé Papillon and his cracked lyre, not to mention yourself, whom I once had the weakness to admire, you're all the same, parasites, dreamers, products and tools of imperialism! Murderers! Assassins."

Papillon saw that the conversation was going sour. "How's your wife doing?" he asks. "And your little Blaise? And your little Karl? Are they well? Blaise hasn't died, I hope . . ."

"Not at all, he's resuscitated. One night we all thought he was dying, the night after that scandalous dinner at your apartment, you abominable capitalist, but I picked him up in my arms and recited Marx to him, and next day he was cured, not only cured but converted to the sovereign doctrine of my master. That boy will grow up to be a revolutionary someday, I shouldn't wonder if he slipped a bomb under your door, you petit bourgeois."

"And how's your wife, Papineau?" asks Papillon, quaking at the thought of his TV set blown to kingdom come. "How's your wife, comrade?"

"She's outside with her sisters."

"I see. But permit me to tell you, Papineau, comrade, we are comrades, aren't we, maybe not in Marx but at least in Jesus Christ, remember how we used to play football together in the old days? . . . The gulf between us can't really be so great . . ."

"Petit bourgeois!"

". . . permit me to tell you that my wife is out there too, on her snowbank, shoveling with her sisters, as you put it. You see, Papineau, we have the same language and almost the same wife. Yes, the world is changing and, believe it or not, so am I . . . possibly for the better, who knows? . . . I'm learning to cast off the dross, to live simply, like you and my daddy . . ."

"Someday my little Blaise will blow you up . . ."

"Why me?"

"You and the rest of them, Papillon."

"I haven't done anything. Yes, I own a Cadillac, a

bad mark against me, you'll say, but the friend of my childhood ought to be able to forgive a little thing like that. Remember, we were choir boys together, for fifteen cents a Mass . . . remember?"

"I have a heart like everyone else and an excellent memory," says Papineau. "And I'll prove it. Out of pity for you, out of sympathy for my childhood friend, I intend to surmount my profound revulsion and name my future son, now in his eighth month and nearing completion, Maritain, in memory of our dead friendship, dead, I say, you lousy petit bourgeois. Yes, I'm going to call him Maritain."

"No!?"

"Yes, Maritain Papineau. Luckily the Papineau retrieves the Maritain."

"Thank you, comrade, thank you! It's plain that you have a . . . how shall I say? . . . a humble soul, yes, that's it. How humble of you to think of my humble and so unpopular Maritain. But your wife, comrade, eight months gone and hard at work you say? Isn't shoveling counterindicated in her condition? . . . Doesn't it worry you a little?"

"It's just like you capitalists to attach such importance to childbirth and prenatal care. What do those things matter from the standpoint of history? A woman's suffering—or a man's for that matter—is mere dust on the marble of our eternal foreheads."

BUT PAPINEAU had hardly finished his sentence when a gang of shovel girls, with Papillon's Jacqueline in the lead, invaded the Inferno, shouting and yelling. The chief devil, holding his velvet tail in one hand to keep it out of the beer foam on his tray, tries to stop them. "What's going on, mesdames? Keep your voices down, if you please, we are in hell!" Jacqueline and some girl that's right next to her pipe up, "Our sister is going to have a baby any minute, look how pale she is, where can we put her, monsieur?"

"Go upstairs and make yourselves at home," says Satan. "This is all we needed!"

"We shall bring the child into the world by ourselves," say the sisters, and up they go to the Eat in

Purgatory Restaurant, to make their sister comfortable "far from the eyes of importunate men."

"It's my wife," says Papineau. "Can I go up?"

"No, monsieur, no men are admitted."

"But it's my beloved wife, my future child, my embryonic thinker who is about to be born," says Papineau. He's as excited as everyone else, the windbag. "My wife . . . my child . . ."

"That's just too bad. The sisters have no need of you. You will be informed in a few moments whether it's a boy or a girl."

"Christ," says Papillon to the friend of his childhood, "why not sit down with us, comrade, and drink to my future royalties? Drink a Highland Supreme Scotch, that would pick up a steam roller!"

"Oh no, I couldn't drink," says Papineau. "I'm too shaken . . ."

"Shaken, comrade? Come along, that's not like you."

"We shouldn't call him Maritain, that's enough to make him miss the exit. And to think that I'm not there, I, his father. Really, those women are going too far. Our sisters, I mean. Our female comrades are too emotional. The revolution isn't for them, it's for us, for us men. Don't you agree?"

Just then Papillon's Jacqueline comes running down as if she'd carried off a trophy . . .

"Our sister's brother has just been born," she says.

"What do you mean, my sister's brother?" says Papineau.

"Your son, comrade, your son, can't you hear him mewling his first song of revolt? Ah, comrade, we're so glad for you, we your sisters!"

"Can I go up now?" asks Papineau, trembling all over like a leaf in the wind.

"Sure, comrade, come on up, we'll celebrate!"

So Papineau goes up to his sister and Corneille says, "It's been an agitated evening, Papillon, but now let's get back to our shoveling. Rome wasn't cleared in a day."

We went out through the whited portal of the Inferno and looked around. It was all white and quiet, the wind had stopped whistling, our brothers and sisters

were bent over their shovels and we could see boys
and girls who seemed to be rowing down the boulevard
on their snowshoes . . . We listened to the storm dying
away and pretty soon our feet were nice and warm.
That's the way it happened that night.

3.

TWO DAYS after the storm we were still floundering
in powder. Even the unemployment mill closed down,
they knew nobody was very keen on working. The
waitress at the Spaghetti at All Hours was sitting behind her counter with her arms folded, drooping and
sighing. "The spaghetti is still on the Ile Sainte-Hélène,"
she says, "the trucks are stuck in the snow at the other
end of the bridge, I can only give you some of last
week's pancakes, Monsieur Ti-Pit, we're even out of
hot dogs." There weren't any newspapers, etc., and
the students, instead of doing nothing as usual, were
sliding down the Boulevard Saint-Laurent on skis.

Then one morning the snow men climbed up on
their plows and pretty soon we could see where the
streets were. At the Jeanne Mance, Mère Fontaine was
weeping and wailing because our neighborhood bum,
the old geezer who'd been singing serenades under my
window, had been so full of joy when he left the tavern
the night before that even with Mère Fountaine yelling
at him to come inside and sleep it off, he hadn't
noticed the snow piling up under his nose, and an hour
later our flea-bitten troubadour was froze to death,
nothing left but a corpse. Mère Fontaine took out her
handkerchief and said, "Ah, Monsieur Ti-Pit, another
of nature's victims, gives you food for thought, remember those newlyweds who took a flying leap into the
river because they'd forgotten how to steer their
Peugeot, think of their surprise, Ti-Pit, the wedding
banquet, their warm bed with kisses, and then dropping

into eternity all of a sudden . . . I only hope, Monsieur
Ti-Pit, they had plenty of enjoyment first, because they
don't get much of that in heaven, I'm told." Mademoiselle Mimi and her precious Jean-François had no such
problem. Mimi hadn't left his bed except at night to
flit over to the Dear Boy for a while, with his blond
curls peeking out of his hood "and his slender person
swathed in mangy fur," as Jean-François said. He was
always running Mimi down; for his money Mimi was
nothing but "a tart, a crispy-crunchy piece of ass to
buck and bugger"; that's the kind of thing this Jean-
François said to Mère Fontaine. There was style in his
lingo, but you can't deny it was coarse. Mère Fontaine
would say, "Poor Mademoiselle Mimi, it was an unlucky day for her when she met you, Monsieur Jean-
François. You fuck her but you don't love her."

"I have my reasons for not loving him," said Jean-
François. "You don't understand. If I were to become
attached to anything but his ass—pardon the word, but
I suppose you've heard it before, you weren't born
yesterday, as the saying goes—well, it would be fatal,
it would devour me."

"I know my Mimi," says Mère Fontaine, "even if
he waltzes at the Dear Boy to earn his living, it doesn't
mean a thing, it's only because he's so talented at
transvestying and his willowy thighs attract the gentlemen."

"Bah! Your Mimi's a tart. I have my reputation to
protect, I act in high-class plays, do you think I'm mad
enough to throw everything away for a delinquent kid
who gets the wriggles for everybody that comes along?
You've never seen him at the Dear Boy, Mère Fontaine, he's a scandal. Besides, I don't care for fags and
queens, they nauseate me!"

"It's un-Christian of you," says Mère Fontaine.
"You're a queen yourself, Monsieur Jean-François."

So then Mère Fontaine settles down in my pad with
suggestions for Mademoiselle Mimi. "You're fond of
Michel, Monsieur Ti-Pit. Why wouldn't you go to the
Dear Boy and give him a little encouragement? I'd do
it myself, but they don't admit the feminine sex, I'm
speaking of my own, which is only too visible, my

opulent charms, I mean, but you, so virile, so broad-shouldered, Monsieur Ti-Pit, they'll welcome you like the hockey king at Town Hall. It's Mimi's seventeenth birthday and my maternal instinct vibrates for the poor thing, especially now that his family has disowned him."

"I can't say that the Dear Boy tempts me," I tell her.

"Do it for my sake, Monsieur Ti-Pit."

So I head for the Dear Boy. It was kind of a holiday night just about everywhere. The taverns kept their lights on until dawn waiting for the delivery trucks, and the folks poured in. There wasn't anything to eat, but the cafés on rue Saint-Denis were full of people talking and bouncing around. The wine was flowing free, and even in the bars they were serving liquor on the q.t. So I slip into Mimi's grotto at the Dear Boy. Mimi was sitting on the lap of an athletic-looking type, all muscle. He jumps up when he sees me.

"Oh, thank you for coming, Ti-Pit! In a few minutes I'll be on with those aged nymphets you see behind the curtain with their legs in the air . . . they don't like me but I can't help it . . . I thought my darling Jean-François would come, but maybe he's forgotten, he's such an important person, maybe he had to be at his theater . . . I still love him madly, you know, even if he keeps telling me I'm a vicious little drab, but you, Ti-Pit, you know it's not true and he only says those things to make me spoil my makeup with my tears."

"Why don't you knock his block off?"

"Love. You don't know, Ti-Pit, you just don't understand . . ."

Mimi was all warmed up for a chat when a guy comes in, he's about twenty, his jacket is open at the chest, he's wearing boots that come up to his knees, he looks like a Cossack. "Hey, there, Mimi," he says, "your chum isn't one of us, what's he doing here?" "I invited him," says Mimi, "it's Lemieux, my pal from the Jeanne Mance boardinghouse. "Women and normals like him have no business here," he says. "I'm telling him for his own good. One of those rutting queens might mess him up at the exit."

"How goes it?" says Mimi to the Cossack. "We haven't seen you at the Dear Boy in a long time, Danny darling. Still got your old man in tow?"

"I've got him all right. It's getting sticky because he's not so young any more. But I'll never walk out on him, he picked me out of the gutter when I was only thirteen, it's pretty near time for our silver wedding."

The customers were waltzing around the tables. The old man was sitting in a corner, reading a book and sulking. "Daniel," he says, "Daniel, my boy, come sit down and have a drink."

"Nope," says Danny. "This is my night off."

"Why are you being so disagreeable?" says the old man.

"You're pissed because I'm conversing with Mimi, is that it?"

"You're a promiscuous catamite," says the old man, flipping the pages of his book. "This is the last time I take you anywhere."

"You mean you're supposed to be faithful?" Mimi asks.

"Lots of queens go for my uniform, but mostly I keep them at arms' length, it makes the old man so sad when I don't . . . And you know, Mimi, it's nice to have a home, don't worry about me, I go out with girls when I get too sick of him."

"Daniel, did you hear me?" says the old man. "Come here and sit down or we're leaving."

"Shut up, you old nance," says Danny. "You know what you can do with your money, you whited sepulcher, you old hollow-balls!"

"My goodness," says Mimi, "you sure don't use kid gloves with your old man."

"Why should I? I let him make love to me, I knock myself out to please him. I dress the way he wants, I do what he wants. Do I have to sing his praises too?"

"All the same," says Mimi, "there are some things one doesn't say."

"He's deaf, he doesn't hear a thing, and anyway it's true, he is a whited sepulcher."

"Why do you say that, Danny darling? The more I

look at you the handsomer you seem. Why wouldn't you be unfaithful to the old boy now and then, eh, Danny?"

"I've told you the truth," says Danny. Mimi's cherubic little hand was toying with the braid on Danny's lapels and the old man, with his profile in his book, was purple with jealousy. "You'd have to dig into my past to understand, Mimi, but right now like this, just before your show, there isn't time . . . In his outside life, you see, he plays respectable, he fools everybody, hell, even here this evening, look at him hiding his nose in a book, the hypocrite!"

"My act's about to begin," says Mimi. "I've got to slip into my girdle and folderols. Come see me afterward, Danny darling, I'll have a kiss ready for you . . ."

But the old man grabs Danny by the jacket and pushes him into a chair.

"That's quite enough, Daniel. Understand?"

"What's enough? What have I done?"

"I don't care for your licentious behavior. You seem to forget all I've done for you. Your conduct is inexcusable."

"Damn nance!"

"Be still!"

"I've had enough of your daddy act. Sometimes you give me the shits."

"Usually you're more reasonable. What's going on tonight? You're handsome, Daniel, you're intelligent. Why do you behave like a juvenile delinquent? Why are you always trying to destroy everything I'm trying to do for you?"

"Save your sermons for the choir boys, you old sodomite. You can't kid me."

"I've always been your friend, Daniel. I've always tried to help you, but suddenly you seem to detest me, I have to admit I'm surprised at you. Is there anything you need? Just tell me, I'll get it for you tomorrow."

"Keep your presents, you scum. Tomorrow I'm going to take this uniform and cut it up in little pieces . . . hear?"

But then Mimi's act began, she came out with a bevy of semi-middle-aged Angelinas covered with ostrich feathers. When it came to the French cancan and high-legging it, Mademoiselle Mimi was the Queen of the May. She slithered like a sexy snake. The customers were all in heat, clapping and shouting: "Hey, Mimi, treasure of the boards, do it again! Encore!" And that fiendish acrobat, sometimes disguised like Little Red Riding Hood and sometimes like a brazen bathing beauty, went on with the quadrille. The only one that didn't applaud was Danny's old man. He turned to his open-collar Cossack and said, "Is it him you want? Is that it?" "Button up!" says Danny. "It's perfectly simple, Danny, you only have to tell me, all I ask is that you come back to me by noon. The key will be in the mailbox as usual. But come back, understand?" The old man gets up and leaves the grotto, hanging his head.

I said to Danny, "You've got to admit, your old man has dignity."

"Sure. But it's easy to see you're not one of us, Lemieux, you haven't worked at this trade all your life. He gives me the shits, it's not his fault, but that's the way it is. Come on, I'll buy you a drink even if you're not a member of the club . . ."

"Looks like you've got plenty of money."

"Sure, and everything else, all the suits and hats I want. But it's a funny thing, sometimes it comes over me like this, I have to chew him out, it doesn't mean I don't love him."

Mademoiselle Mimi pirouettes over to Danny and says, "What did you think of me, Danny darling?" "Not bad, not bad, but it's not the kind of thing that pops my fly buttons . . ." "Is it because you've suffered so much?" Mimi asks. "Could be," says Danny. "The old man's gone home to bed. I only hope some naughty queen doesn't try to rob him in the street . . . it can happen."

"Don't worry about your old man, Danny. He'll get over it."

"What about that actor that was such a puritan?" Danny asks. "You still got him?"

"Yes, but he didn't come tonight. I thought he'd come

after midnight . . . 'cause, you know, he's no tramp, she doesn't come out in broad daylight . . ."

"Another whited sepulcher," says Danny, spitting on the floor. "They make me sick, all these guys that bugger themselves, a lot of Narcissuses, like my old man, always worried about what people will think. What I'd like to do is expose the lot of them."

"Yes," says Mimi, "because you're a real man. But now I've got to hurry. It's almost time for my second dance."

Just then a big, tall vamp comes up to Mimi and says, "No you don't, young man, you've done your number, you've shown your legs enough for tonight, just put on your jeans and split. It's Yvonne's turn . . ."

"Go on," says Mimi. "How are you going to dance with that stuffed corset and those plush tits? You've been an old maid too long to attract the gentlemen, my dear."

"Clear out, I said," says Yvonne in a high falsetto rumbling with virile undertones. Bristles peered out from under her pink make-up and there were tufts of black moss where her bodice had slipped down. Her bosom stuck out like the prow of a ship, she practically put it in Mimi's face. The rabbit fur on her neck was trembling with fury.

"You're young today, Mimi baby," she screamed. "But one of these days you'll be old yourself, and with the life you lead, you little tramp, it won't be long. I'm not giving you more than four years before your tripping toes are crippled with rheumatism."

"That's no rabbit fur you've got over your winsome lips, dearie," says Mimi, always the bitchy tease, "it looks to me like skunk."

"You won't always be the rising sun of the Dear Boy, you little cricket of the garbage dump. I know how depraved hussies like you end up, I've been to bed with the schoolgirl type, meaning no offense . . ."

"I don't believe it," says Mimi. "Who'd want a big male like you with hands like sides of beef? Who'd go to bed with you at your age, my sweet?"

"What do you know about he-men, you marvel of

the dance floor? I can see you've never had a stallion.
You don't judge a male by his hands, but by his phallus,
you shameless Naiad!"

"I wouldn't want yours for anything in the world,"
says Mimi.

"Do you know how you'll end up, my little darling?"
says Yvonne. "With T.B.! You look undernourished
already. You've got T.B. if it isn't the syph. That's
right, sweetheart!"

"Shut your trap, you old fag," says Danny. "Beat it
behind the curtain or I'll puncture your rubber bust for
you."

"Put that knife away, Danny darling," says Mimi.
"It's not worth it for an old queen."

"Just try it, you sucker of old men's cocks, he only
does old men, that's his weakness, what a waste, my
beauty, plenty of handsome studs would be glad to
oblige you, my pretty, what do you see in old men, old
age is crabby, it has one foot in the grave . . ."

The battle was on, Yvonne had muscle, one two
three, he'd pushed the Cossack against the wall, and
the customers were cheering: "That's the stuff Yvonne,
give him a good spanking, the snotnose!"

"I'm just wondering whether to kill you," says
Yvonne in the flush of victory. "Look, here's your
knife glittering in my fist, what do you think of that?
You look mighty green, Danny boy, want me to cut
you up a little?" Danny was no coward, he thought
he'd risk a kick. "Danny, Danny," Mimi pleaded.
"Don't! That queen's not worth it, Danny darling!"
But Danny was a scrapper, he ended up with a bloody
lip.

"That does it," says Yvonne. "Bleed awhile, sonny,
and get out of this club quick before I cut you somewhere else!"

So it was Yvonne and not Mademoiselle Mimi that
got the applause that night. "Come on, Danny," says
Mimi. "We'll be better off in the street without all these
envious cunts . . ."

"Yeah," says Danny, "all these cunts in heat, they
give me the shits."

Out on the street Danny's lip was bleeding so bad he

pretty near passed out under the lamppost. Mimi
stopped the blood with snow, then put his arm around
the Cossack and we took him back to his old man, who
said to Mimi and me, "Thank you, my friends. It's not
the first time this has happened. Sleep well, my children."

So that was the party at the Dear Boy.

WHILE I was unemployed Père Baptiste turns up at
the Jeanne Mance. "Well, Baptiste," I tell him, "it looks
like we're both out of a job!" "It's hard times for me
and the old woman, Ti-Pit, since the Rubber laid me
off. Come on down to Peel Street with me. Ti-Guy,
my eldest, the son-of-a-bitch, is living there in sin and
lechery. Mère Baptiste says to give him a kick in the
ass and make him come home." "Take it easy, Baptiste,"
I tell him. "Maybe your eldest has only slipped a
bit . . ."

"I'll break the bastard's back," says Baptiste. "It's
easy to see he didn't go hungry during the Depression.
He's not dumb, he could have worked up a better career
than me at the Rubber, didn't I stick it out for twenty
years?"

"You sure did, but look where it's got you."

"It's not like the old days, Ti-Pit. You can't say like
father like son; how did he get this way, that's what
I'd like to know? This damn generation, they're all
lunatics, and my Ti-Guy is the looniest of the lot! He
started on liquor, then he stole pills from the drugstore,
now it's the dreamy needle, one time he grabbed the
boss's typewriter and chucked it out the window, that's
how screwy he is. He would have jumped after it if they
hadn't put him in a strait jacket and sent him to the
nuthouse to cool off. He was out of that strait jacket
as quick as a bedbug but just as wild as ever, he hadn't
calmed down at all, I don't know where he gets it,
there's nothing dreamy about Mère Baptiste, she's all
rolling pin and good horse sense. But right now he's
got to come home and work for a living or, Christ, his
folks won't be able to pay for their plot in the cemetery."

It was Ti-Guy himself, in an ankle-length robe like
a priest and greasy hair hanging down over his shoul-

ders, that opened the door of his garret. "Welcome to
my home, P'pa," he says like he was glad to see him,
but his look was far away and his eyes were popping
out of his head. He flaps his wings in the direction of
some guys and girls that are busy painting the place
in fancy colors. The kitchenette was orange and they'd
even painted the coffee pot sea-green, and one guy
with JESUS on his T-shirt was doing the crapper in
lavender. "Every color in the rainbow," says Pére Baptiste. "Some rat's nest you've got here, you little bastard!" "Take it easy, chum," I tell Baptiste, but it's no
use. There he is, slapping Ti-Guy around and growling,
"What have I done to deserve a no-good son like you!"
Ti-Guy was off in the clouds. "What's that you say,
P'pa? You say you love me? Thank you, P'pa. Thank
you for coming and telling me. 'Cause you see, P'pa,
I never go out. My pals come here every day to bring
me my sugar. Is it true there's a blizzard outside,
P'pa?"

"Listen to me, you crummy little snotnose," says
Baptiste. "You got to come home, you're the oldest, you
got to take my place at the Rubber, no kidding. Ti-
Guy, you want your parents to die in the ditch?"

"I love you, P'pa, and God loves you too, you and
M'ma are like the lilies of the field, you'll want for
nothing. God will look after you, P'pa, for you the gate
of death won't be as narrow as the gate of life."

"Is this what your trips do to you? You're completely
nuts!"

"Oh, P'pa! It wasn't a bad trip . . ." Ti-Guy was
standing on a chair, he'd lost the thread completely. "I
remember . . . I'd just escaped from Saint-Jean-de-
Dieu with a girl, she had plenty of money, her name
was Anne, she committed suicide a month ago and it's
all for the best, everything's for the best, a razor slash
on the wrist and it's all over, that's the secret of life
slipping away, you see, P'pa? Anne and me, we went
into the desert . . . it was so beautiful . . . you'll never
know, 'cause you'll never take a trip. I'll be going back
to the desert pretty soon . . . I wasn't afraid of anything
. . . we had Arab friends, they loved us, Anne and me,
and never asked any questions . . . and then we were

alone . . . our friends disappeared . . . dots on the horizon . . . we called them, but they didn't answer . . . we were thirsty, our tongues were scorching hot . . . we were terribly afraid when dawn came, our heads were throbbing with cries, the big red sun walked into our tent, it got nearer and nearer, it wanted to destroy us, it was thirsty too . . . same as us . . ."

"You'd better get back to Saint-Jean, a bit of shock treatment will do you good, you little stinker, you make me sick with that gown and your bleary eyes, you had a future at the Rubber, but no, you didn't want it."

"I love you, P'pa, and God loves you too . . . don't be afraid . . . I'll be going to the desert soon and there won't be anybody, just Anne and me . . . not a soul . . . silence . . ."

"You're living in lechery and sin, you'll go straight to hell!" says Baptiste.

"Lechery? Oh no, P'pa. All desire has left me . . . the one thing I desire is the desert . . ."

"That's the truth," says a girl in a T-shirt, with a paint pot in her hand. "He's lost interest in sex, and that's from the horse's mouth . . ."

"What have I done to deserve such a son!" asks Baptiste, practically in tears. "Come on, Ti-Pit, I can't stand it any more."

"I know a priest in the East End," I told him. "Father Vincent. He's the real stuff. He could bring a gallowsbird back to the straight and narrow. Why don't we drop your screwball Ti-Guy on his doorstep?"

"Too late," says Baptiste. "Too late. He's doomed and shot to hell. Christ, I wash my hands of him, even if he did use to be my dear little boy. The devil take him!"

That's the kind of father Baptiste was, no guts. With murder in his heart he went back home to his old woman.

I counted my money, five dollars, only five, when I owed Mère Fontaine sixteen. I didn't even dare to show myself in the doorway. Then at the Cat I run into Papillon, and he says, "Why not share your misery with a philanthropic bourgeois? Come on, take this and shut up!" "Look here, Papillon" I say. "Don't strap yourself for me." "Christ, nobody asked for your opinion, take it, little brother, and button up."

"Still scribbling?" I ask him.

"This time it's something serious. I'm writing a true story."

"And how's your wife doing, Papillon? And your Latin class?"

"My wife is at home, my students are conferring with the strikers, that's why I've abandoned my lair, Lemieux. You see, my house has been invaded by the National Front of Womanhood, but in the meantime Jacqueline is home at least. The dear little thing, she needs to express herself, she's only a woman, a sensitive soul, a frail and fragrant violet . . ."

"It's lucky you're married to your writing, Papillon."

"You've hit the nail on the head, Lemieux, in your superb Joual, mingled, interlaced, amalgamated, married, that's the word all right. You see all these papers, Lemieux? What superabundance. And all to show Corneille that I've rubbed shoulders with Lady Paris, whose charms he is always praising. This, brother, is the story of a woman whom I once identified with George Sand, with Madame Bovary, and who wasn't worthy to be your cleaning woman . . . but let it pass . . . I see you're yawning, you illiterate son-of-a-bitch . . . but all the same I'll give it to you in a nutshell. So one day this lady, Justine by name (Christ, to think I once punctuated that name with sighs worthy of Lamartine!), writes me from the depths of her Sixteenth Arrondissement, to tell me what, I ask you, brother? To tell me she's read dibs and dabs of my poetry. A feminine hand holds a censer under my mustache and instantly Papillon, the jerk, reels with emotion. '*Chère Madame,* How can it be that you deign to read me, whom no one reads . . .' By return mail she sends me, written in an aristocratic hand, these delightful words: 'Modest poet, dear friend, I sense, I divine your austere solitude . . .' So Papillon catches fire, he cranks out poem after poem for his unknown lady of the Sixteenth Arrondissement; he carries on like a two-legged jackass, and this loquacious ninny says to himself, I love Jacqueline, but Jacqueline is Womanhood, I know her well, we sleep together every night. But Justine is something else, she is the Muse that haunted Musset's heart ... the passion, the torment! ... ah! You get the picture? After a year of this dubious correspondence between two nitwits, Justine writes me a letter, still in the most exquisite good taste of course, asking if I mightn't in my idle moments (as if I had nothing else to do) find her 'a humble position as lecturer at one of your universities ... Oh, nothing presumptuous ... perhaps a course or two on French civilization? I remain your disciple, dear poet . . .' You know my kind heart, for three months I run myself ragged for Justine to find her a job, she sends me her pedigree, a sheaf of diplomas, and a list of lectures she'd given from Montmartre to Louisiana. What could I do? I write her by air mail, special delivery, inviting her to come and kiss our soil. So I'm decking myself out in my Sunday best when Jacqueline says to me, 'Hey, Papillon, what's going on? Have we a date in high society?' 'Who me, Jacqueline, my sugar plum? Not at all, just a brief excursion into nature's beauties. It's autumn, my love, the leaves are searing and dying . . .' 'Shit!' she says, as scintillating as ever. 'Liar, you've already deceived me in thoughts, tomorrow it will be in deeds, I can hear the cock crowing your betrayal, Papillon.' Well, brother, the following will show you what to think of the human race, even if you're not listening ... I leave my humble dwelling, I chase out to Dorval to welcome my Justine, my foreign bloom. Because she was European, hence exotic, I thought she must be woven from the rosy substance of ecstasy, I was floating on azure. At Dorval, I drink one gin and tonic after another, followed by gin and orange pop, at the Bar des Esquimaux, my heart was going loop the loop, like a jerk. Just as Justine's flight is announced, an irrepressible hiccup erupts from my stomach, Christ, I take a Bromo Seltzer, I take another, it's no use. I line up at the gate. I recognize my Justine by the little passport photo she'd had the delicacy to send me, but she, the bitch, seeing me hiccuping like a machine gun, passes me by without a word, carrying her little 'fuck-in-town' bag in her hand and holding herself inflexibly

aloof, even though I trotted along behind her saying,
'But, Justine . . . it's me . . . it's Papillon.' It was only
at the exit, before getting into an eight-bucks-a-throw
taxi, that she suddenly says, 'Forgive me, my friend,
my eyesight is poor . . . I didn't recognize you . . . maybe the picture you sent me was rather too flatt—it's a
matter of light and shade . . . How delighted I am to see
you! . . . Come, the taxi is waiting . . .' 'But give me
your bag, *chère amie* . . .' 'No, don't bother, it's not
very héavy . . . why, you're charming, adorable, just
as I imagined you, what a joy to meet you, my friend,
I had a little trouble with the language, but otherwise
it has been a marvelous trip, I'm so happy . . . But
come and sit beside me, *chéri* . . .' Jolted in my vanity,
I say to Justine, 'What's that, my dear? Difficulty with
our language you say?' 'Yes, your accent, it's not as
pure as ours . . .' That was only the beginning,
Lemieux, of the amorous Papillon's humiliation. I soon
found out that Justine had flattered me and my poor
little rhymes with a view to obtaining certain of my
deplorable North American privileges: not love but
money, kid. Why, the very first night, set up in a
sumptuous hotel room at thirty dollars a day, she made
no bones about criticizing the bashful Papillon's manner of making love. She kept flinging the windows wide
open, when he, always discreet though seething with
passion, kept closing them. That very first night she
started calling him her 'noble savage,' any minute I
was expecting her to say something about our wretched
'few acres of snow' or the 'Quebecan's tragic solitude'—
the mystery of the Canadian soul that every Parisian
tourist thinks he has penetrated. It's a fine phrase, my
boy, as haughty as sovereign reason. Its special advantage is that it shuts us up for good. Once we've
been told about our tragic solitude, we're helpless, clas-
sified, and filed away. And under her veneer of charm
and elegance I failed to see the despot who held me in
her clutches . . . Hey, Lemieux, look over there, isn't
that my Jacqueline and her sistren? . . . I thought she
was home . . . What's she cooking up now? Another
feminist rally?"

Papillon wasn't seeing things. Jacqueline was barging into the Cat with a gang of girls in tow, all singing, ready to mount the barricades. Papillon was flabbergasted. He clears his throat to make a speech. "Ladies," he says, "you are familiar, I trust, with the inscription over the door of our taverns: MEN ONLY. Has it ever occurred to you that there may be a reason for preserving this old English custom? Because sometimes, my dear ladies, things go on here that would offend your sensibilities." "Shut up, Papillonnet," says Jacqueline. "We've rubbed out your MEN ONLY and written, in our language, WOMEN TOO. We will not be moved from this tavern. It's a sit-in, if you don't like it, you can fuck off."

"Come, come, Jacqueline, look here, ladies, let's not exaggerate. Why shouldn't we have our own place of recreation? Don't you find this spectacle degrading? Admit it. These old men, these moldy derelicts—surely their stench must offend your refined nostrils . . . Observe those decadent urinals . . ."

"Shut up, Papillonnet!"

All over the room the old soaks were grumbling, half in their sleep. "Hey, no dames in here, no, no, we ain't come here to see our wives and mothers!" Even the owner jumped up in his fat and called out, "Ladies, we can't have this at the Dancing Cat. Kindly leave or we'll call the police . . ."

"Let him!" says one of the girls. "It'll give us publicity."

"Christ!" says Papillon. "What is the world coming to?" But then he puts on his silkiest tones, maybe that would go down better with the ladies.

"Ladies," he says. "You all know that I stand for conciliation. I respect free speech, to which, I am well aware, both sexes are entitled. I therefore ask the gentlemen to allow you to state your demands . . . and even, should there be any, your grievances against us . . ."

"No, no, no dames in here," the old soaks repeated.

"Come on, gentlemen, let's not be disagreeable. Haven't these delicious creatures, these objects of our adoration, as much right to express themselves as we have?"

"*Objects,* Papillon, you've put your foot in it again!
That's why we've come here for a sit-in or a sit-on, to
bury the floor-mop-woman, the dishwasher-woman,
and, whether the men like it or not, usher in the I-lead-
my-own-life-woman. Understand?"

"Hurray," shouts the girl at the head of another gang
who'd just shown up for the demonstration. They're
wearing big heavy boots and they march in with a banner saying SAPPHIC POWER . . . "And you, ladies," says
Papillon, mopping his forehead. "What can we do to
help you? The floor is yours . . ."

"Fuck you!"

"Now, now," says Papillon. "That's no answer.
We're all nice people here, couldn't we just have a
peaceful talk? What is the cause of your dissatisfac-
tion? Tell us your desires, my dear friends, your aspira-
tions, your . . ."

"Fuck you, man!"

"The police are outside," says the owner. But the
girls didn't turn a hair, there were almost fifty of them,
plus Eglantine and Thérèse and some others with a sign
saying BE PROUD YOU'RE A WOMAN, A WIFE, MOTHER.
Papillon, all wiggling and beaming, goes over to them.
"Ah, my friends, what a pleasure to see you here, my
dear friends of the excellent and honorable petite bourgeoisie of Quebec . . ." "No, the grande bourgeoisie
of Quebec," says Thérèse. "Yes, yes of course, the
grande bourgeoisie, why not? Embrace me, my sisters!"

"We disagree, Eglantine and I are opposed to all
this. We too wish to express ourselves."

"What is more moving, more inspiring for a woman
than motherhood?" says Eglantine. "What is your opinion, Papillon, my love?"

"It's pure transcendence," says Papillon.

"We are proud," says Thérèse, "to declare that we
are first and foremost women."

"Bullshit!" yells Sapphic Power.

"Shit!" says Papillon's Jacqueline.

"Yes," says Thérèse. "We are proud to be women.
Born and raised in the high society of Quebec, we wish
to assert the nobility of our womanhood."

Meanwhile the cops were doing their job. One by one the girls, stiff as boards, doing the dead-woman-carried-away-by-the-bandits-of-the-law act, were piled into the paddy wagon that was waiting outside. "Christ," says Papillon, "my Jacqueline, my sugar plum, is going to spend the night in jail." All the starch had gone out of him. The only ones that hadn't been taken in were Thérèse and Eglantine and their lady friends from Quebec.

Eglantine of the eyes like glowing coals comes over to Papillon and says, "Papillon, my dear Eloi, didn't I tell you when I was reading your palm the other night that your wife would bring you nothing but trouble? Have you thought about the Other Woman, the woman who is all passion, submissiveness, voluptuous docility? Do you sometimes think of her, my dear Eloi?"

Outside the Cat I left Papillon simpering with Thérèse and Eglantine and beat it back to the Jeanne Mance to see if maybe some news of a job had crept in. But there was only a letter from Ti-Cul, mailed at least a week ago, the paper was still wet with the storm. Here's what that crud had to tell me:

Dear Ti-Pit, You won't be surprised, you've known me since our time in the Orphanage of the Dearly Beloved, where the whores that bore us dropped their bad eggs, so you won't be surprised to hear that I'm writing you again from behind bars in the fortress of law and order. If words are missing here and there, it's because these damn   cut holes in our vocabulary. It didn't take the damn   long to arrest me; I had a nice racket going before they turned the double lock on me. Me and some pals were specializing in high finance, we were riding high until we were caught stealing checks, you know the system . . . out of mailboxes, postoffice trucks, etc., it takes quick fingers like you used to have, Ti-Pit. We were going strong until those damn   holes trapped me in their meshes. I was even thinking of marriage, no kidding, to a kid

that was my assistant, a real signature artist. They
only gave me two years but   me if I don't
out of this   dungeon! You can expect my ap-
parition, maybe before Easter, being that Cri-Cri
(that's my blonde, she sparkles like a movie star, you'll
see) and me have a job in the works. It'll make a big
noise too! We got plenty of inspiration. We don't do
things by halves, you'll see, chum. I seen out of my
window that it's been snowing buckets, curses, a lot of
people are sliding around outside while I'm cramped
up in this damn   but how are you getting along,
Ti-Pit? I got your address from Father Vincent, your
chum, but me, you know, I say   all sky pilots,
even the ones that jazz up the Mass, and if you lick
their   you're nothing but a damn Christing
traitor. You got to get hard not soft, Ti-Pit, that's the
only commandment for me. Remember when you
and me took that bus to the States, thought we'd go
to Old Orchard, we hadn't stolen anything, we hadn't
done anything, I'd only looted Jos Langlois's pocket
a bit to pay for our tickets, we were taking it easy in
the Greyhound bus, batting the breeze with some
other beggars who'd saved up for three years to see
the   U.S.A., them and their snotnosed kids, we
were having fun, all hopped up with hope, even the
driver was full of beans, gallivanting his bus all over
the road, we hadn't been drinking, we were just folks
enjoying a trip, remember, and then at the border this
gang of Nazis start looking us over, in a couple of
minutes all the joy was gone, everybody was scared
shitless, even the kids were afraid to move off their
seats, me and you were afraid to move off their seats,
me and you were way in the back of the bus, those
damn   come up to us yelling, 'Go home! Get
out of here!' We bumbled a little in English, but those
          knew how to tangle us up in guilty silence,

you said we were going to visit Old Orchard, Old Orchard had always been your dream, you said, you damn jerk, sometimes you give me the shits, you and your dreams, they just laughed, you could see all the way into their man-eating mouths, they had teeth like machine guns ready to grind us up, they threw us off the bus, we had to fill out papers and sign forms like criminals, and I wasn't a murderer then, not even a bad bum, I was young and tender, but you wait, I'll show them I can play the same game. They had nothing against us, they just didn't like the cut of our jibs, they thought they'd practice on us, but we got even. that night we slept in a field on our side of the border, then about 3 a.m. we took a path I knew through the woods and brambles, a chum that escaped had told me about it. "That way," he'd said, "you can get to the States on your own feet, you'll have time for a drink out of the brook, you can even cook a hamburger to drive away the mosquitoes . . ." And remember, Ti-Pit, after we'd crossed the border, it wasn't just the guards that didn't like us, everybody gave us dirty looks, they could tell by our rags, they thought we were bums, beggars escaped from the poorhouse, they didn't like our smell, but we saw their damn Old Orchard anyway, remember? We'd put one over on them, but hell, we'd sweated for it, the gulls over the sea, that water that looked so warm it turned your stomach, I'm telling you, Ti-Pit, nature's a lot of shit when you can't touch it, when you can't swim in it like other people. I'm telling you this, Ti-Pit, because I know you've been getting ideas from that priest of yours, that Vincent, you think you'll have an easier life if you don't kill, if you don't rebel, it's not true, Ti-Pit, your Vincent has sold you a bill of goods, don't go soft, dammit, get hard. So long for now, chum, Yours, Ti-Cul.

Christ, I thought, my Ti-Cul has certainly changed, he's not the same guy any more. In the days when the two of us were on Jos Langlois's farm, he wasn't so tough. And those days unrolled in front of me on Mère Fontaine's cracked wallpaper. I saw Jos Langlois and his wife and his three sons, three more brutes, they were trying to catch the ox and chain him by the muzzle, you never saw a sweeter-looking ox, with thick curls all over his white muzzle. Ti-Cul had guts, he says to Jos, "I'd like to see somebody chain up your jaws and plant an iron hook between your teeth, make you piss blood through the nose like your ox!" Jos Langlois and his gang, they all jump Ti-Cul, Jos Langlois yells, "I'll teach you how to talk to me, you bastard, we took you out of the kindness of our hearts, when the brothers were good and sick of you, orphan-asylum trash, that's all you are, expect us to use kid gloves on the likes of you?" They beat the hell out of him, but that didn't stop Ti-Cul from saying, "Don't worry, Jos Langlois, I'll make you pay for this someday, you damn skinflint, you won't be piling up shekels forever, what you do to your ox I'll do to you someday . . ."

Then Jos Langlois's wife spoke up. "Let him go, if you kill him you'll answer for it in court . . . He'll croak soon enough without your help. The hangman knows how to handle his kind."

So Jos Langlois and his three brutes worked off their rage whipping their animals.

I was still floating in images of my days with Ti-Cul when I see Mère Fontaine hovering on the edge of the lamplight.

"It's only me, Monsieur Ti-Pit, I've brought you a fresh-ironed sheet in case you get company soon. We haven't seen much of you these days, Monsieur Ti-Pit, have you been out on one of your expeditions?"

"No, just shoveling snow with my fellow citizens."

"So many things have happened while you were gone, Monsieur Ti-Pit, Pierrot has just signed up for a lumberjack in Newfoundland and his Nicole has been weeping night and day. Is that a way to treat a woman, I ask you, Ti-Pit, they were so fond of each other. And then Mademoiselle Ti-Pit, or Madame if you prefer, has been sleeping in your bed with a strange young man . . ."

"Christ, Madame Fontaine, I told you not to let Lison bring men into my pad!"

"I took pity on them, it was such a cold night."

"My pad's not a cathouse, I repeat."

"And only this morning," Mère Fontaine goes on, "I rented Pierrot's room to two young girls, night workers they call themselves, no saints of course, they don't come that way any more, ah, here they are. Very well, I'll leave you young people to yourselves . . ."

Josée and Monique were their names, they tell me they're living together "like man and wife, see, we ain't no convent chicks, we wouldn' kid you, because you know the score. Mimi says you're okay, a good chum, even if you're not a queer like him." These two are bedded down in room 9. Josée pulls a knife out of her jacket to show me, and then she shows me a supply of chewing gum and cigarettes, kid stuff. "How old are you two?" I ask them. "Fifteen, why? We take care of ourselves, we work, we can even drive motorcycles, the knife is only to keep guys from attacking us, say we're nineteen if anybody asks you, our folks are looking for us." "I bet you go with men at night." "That's the quickest way when you've got to eat," says Monique. "We're not particular, as long as we keep together, we've got the life we want, we don't ever walk the streets like pros on account of we're minors, we hang around the railroad stations, and we've got our rules, we've always got to be together, it's safer. But sometimes you run into gangs of thugs and there ain't much you can do, not even two strong girls like us, some of them are dirty and give you diseases. One time some guys dragged us into a cellar, big bruisers as tough as Hell's Angels, we thought we could break out, I'm the muscular type, I can swim a mile and once I won a motorcycle race, but there it was no soap, we had these twelve frigging bastards on our hands, they jump us all at once, talk about fucking marathons, brother, I wouldn't wish it on you, you'd have been in purgatory even if you're not a Christian, there was one big sadist that tries to ram Josée with a milk bottle.

Since then we've had knives to defend ourselves with, that's a help, just so our parents don't drag us back to the ant heap, there are ten kids at Josée's, we've got eight . . . you get mighty sick of all that bawling and blubbering, and besides, M'ma has a weakness for the bottle."

THE GIRLS from room 9 and me were soliloquizing like this when we hear Mademoiselle Mimi and Jean-François talking pretty loud on the stairs, it certainly wasn't the turtledove season that day. Jean-François says to Mimi, "Yes, I know you've been unfaithful to me again, I can see it by that simpering puss of yours, you little drab!"

"Why would I do such a thing, sweetheart? You know you're the only one I love."

"You stink of vice and depravity, Mimi, even if you are the queen of the queens. I have ample proof that you've let that little fag, your Danny darling, as you call him, turn your head and unbutton your fly."

"What proof, Jean-François, my angel? All I did was kiss his lip because it was bleeding, it was only to comfort him one night on the street . . ."

"Liar!"

"Anyway, to hell with it," says Mademoiselle Mimi. "You don't own me yet. It's not written in the Bible that we're married for all time. You just refuse to live, Jean-François dearest, you're always sulking, always talking about the theater and the books you read, can I help it, sometimes it's no fun . . ."

"Go fuck your Danny darling, I'm leaving . . ."

"No, no. Don't leave me, I beg you . . ."

Just then Mère Fontaine's telephone rings in the kitchen. "It's for you, Monsieur Ti-Pit, the Unemployment Bureau might have a job for you on an ambulance . . ."

"But I wanted to be at the infirmary."

"Never mind, take the ambulance in the meantime," says Mère Fontaine. "You see, the ambulance men are on strike, they need volunteers."

"What about the pay?"

"They say they'll give you twenty dollars a week. Will that do?"

"Yeah, that'll do."

So I grab the phone. "Very well, Monsieur Lemieux," they tell me. "There's been a smashup on the North Expressway, five cars reduced to jelly. You can run right down and pick up the survivors."

On the stairs Mademoniselle Mimi was holding Jean-François by the arm to keep him from leaving. "So now you're the undertaker of the highways, eh, chum?" he says. "Hell, Mimi," I tell him, "you take what you get." So that was the end of my furlough, I was working again.

4.

MY AMBULANCE driver was an old guy in a cap, he told me he'd been on the job thirty years, it didn't exactly galvanize him any more, meaning it was up to me, practically all by myself, to take care of the populace in transit to paradise. He was no more interested in his passengers, dead or alive, than if he'd been driving a gang of society folks in a cab. He didn't even hear the wailing of the siren.

"You're awful nervous," he said to me. "What's wrong with you?"

"This thing is no joke. Five cars all in a jelly, I don't even know where to look for the charred bones."

"Take it easy, son, it's only death."

"Yeah, but it's nothing to laugh about."

"Nor neither to cry about, son."

That's what he was always saying. During our lunch break he'd read the comics. Before we had time to swallow our cheeseburgers, the bell was after us to go somewhere else. "Eat first, son," he'd say. "There's no hurry. I haven't finished my comics."

"No hurry, you say? You're a funny guy, for sure," I tell him.

We'd cross the whole East End, so our male nurse, who sat in back with his life-saving equipment, could do his stuff in some tenement, and then we'd have a carload of kids on our hands, burned, poisoned, and what have you. I'd ask the driver, "What about this kid? You think he'll live?"

"It's been a long time since I cared whether they live or die."

"That's his mother over there weeping and wailing."

"What good is her weeping to us? They say the Blessed Virgin wept at the foot of the cross, it didn't help much. All I know, son, is that you've got shaky nerves. Blood is always the same, it doesn't change, I've known that smell for a long time. People are always the same too, the same old puppet show. Monsieur in his tailcoat, madame so sure of herself, still holding her little evening bag in her gloved hand when we pick her carcass up off the roadway; could be monsieur hasn't even got a scratch, maybe he's just whiter than usual, with his eyes open like he was counting the stars romantic-like. The kids? Maybe they were asleep in the back seat, and the one that's still alive is out in a field somewhere whimpering, 'Papa! Mama!' For once we get a mixture of all the social classes, all the same hash."

"You damn coffin driver! So it just makes you laugh?"

"No, son, I've told you before, it don't make me laugh and it don't make me cry. Only one time I had a good laugh. I was carting this old bitch, her heart was conking out on her, but that didn't stop her from bossing people around. She was dressed fit to kill. 'Monsieur,' she says, 'don't you dare let any of those priests give me extreme unction, it would bring me bad luck in the other world.' When we get to the hospital, there's at least three roly-poly priests waiting for her, not so much to give her the last rites as to get her to make out a will in their favor. The old lady's mind was on the way out, but she was stubborn. 'I don't want any priests closing my eyes. It would bring me bad luck.'

Christ, son, even you would have laughed. So her gold went with her to the other world, just the way she wanted."

The sound of our damn siren got me down, but I managed to get through the day with dry eyes. I'd hardly hit the sack at the Jeanne Mance when Ti-Guy, Baptiste's kid, starts thumping through my head. So I climbed back into my winter togs, the icy wind is good for black thoughts, I said to myself. I walked a long way, I wanted to see if they were putting up the Christmas garlands on rue Sainte-Catherine and if those guys on ladders were decorating the big pine trees with angel's hair and colored lights. I ended up on Vincent's spiral stairway.

"You've come at a bad time, Ti-Pit," he says. "I'm boning up for my chemistry class. But come in. Luc has left us, taking the bit of money my social worker and I had in the till."

"Hey, that kid's a natural-born crook!"

"So he is. But he'll be back, I think. But what about you? How are you getting along?"

"I haven't come to preach my cause this time, it's on account of Baptiste's kid. I dreamed last night that he'd jumped in the river, he had a stone around his neck. What do you think of that?"

"That was only a dream, Ti-Pit."

"I know. But wouldn't you come to Peel Street, just to see if . . . ?"

"Listen, my boy. I haven't time to associate with all your friends. You can see I have work to do. Why these wild ideas?"

"You're just like Baptiste. Always thinking of yourself. What kind of a Christing bad Christian are you, anyway?"

"Stop cursing!"

"I'm not cursing, I'm blaspheming. There!"

"But even supposing your friend is desperate, what do you want me to say to him? You seem to think I'm some kind of healer. If your pal doesn't come here of his own accord, why should I go and bother him? Tell me that."

"He can't go out, he's always waiting for his fix, he's

helpless. He hasn't been out for a'month. He lives in a dream, all he talks about is the desert. But I'm going to see him, not that it's any of my business, only that Baptiste has dropped him and, Christ, I don't think it's right . . ."

"To think I thought I was finally going to have a quiet evening. Hand me my coat, we'll walk, I can't afford the bus right now. And whatever you do, don't tell him I'm a priest, that would humiliate him."

"Or wouldn't it by any chance humiliate *you?*"

"My feelings are no concern of yours."

WE WALKED along in silence, Vincent was sulking because I'd busted in on his evening. He was sighing, "I'm only an old egotist, that's the way it is." And then with a sly look at me, "And so are you, my friend, so are you." Looking at the Christmas mangers they were putting up along the street, he said, "Bah! look at that poor Joseph with his silly smile, he looks like a shop-keeper, and that Virgin devoid of spirituality, the only one that feels any pity is the ass . . . And you, Ti-Pit, feasting your eyes on the windows of Eaton and Company, you covetous child, what has caught your imagination now?"

"Christ, it's all a lot of trinkets for the stinking rich, the Faber families of the world!"

"You're always insulting the rich."

"I'll hate them to my dying day, the Fabers and the Rubber Company inclusive."

"You've told me that a thousand times, my boy . . ."

"I'm telling you again."

"Envy is a sin, you know . . . It seems to me there's envy in your anger . . . It's not healthy anger."

"Healthy or not, it's my business."

On Peel Street Ti-Guy's girl opens the door. "It's funny you've come," she says. "Ti-Guy tried to hang himself this morning. He's all right now. We've given him something to calm him down. I'd been trying to break his habit for a few days . . . as you see, it didn't work. He was always talking about Anne and the desert, it was giving me the shits . . . I beg your pardon . . . ecstasy is a bore, it's been going on for months."

Ti-Guy was stretched out on his bed next to the wall sprinkled with red stars. He was as white as snow and he had a mark on his neck.

"Ah, Gyslaine," he murmured, "I told you they'd come, the people who love me, the people who love me. Is it still so cold outside?"

"I like that wall," says Vincent. "It's cheerful, a lot more cheerful than my gloomy walls. What do you think Ti-Pit?"

"I think it looks like hell."

"You say that because no one has taught you to love warm colors. But believe me, they help a man to live more serenely with himself . . ."

Vincent didn't dare to tell me in front of the others what he really thought, but I was tuned in on his meditations, and this is what he meant:

"It's not your fault, Ti-Pit, you don't appreciate warm colors because you've always been surrounded by the gray walls of prisons and orphan asylums."

Gyslaine says to Vincent, "If you like, we'll paint your walls." "Fine," says Vincent. "I'll expect you and Ti-Guy tomorrow morning. Here's my address . . ." "No, don't expect me," Ti-Guy sighs. "Don't let anybody expect me. Oh, it's so nice . . . out there . . . with her . . . far away . . ."

"First," says Vincent, "let's heat up some soup. We're all kind of hungry. What about you, Ti-Guy, aren't you hungry?"

"I'll never be hungry again, never thirsty again," says Ti-Guy, still wandering, waving his arms and weeping without knowing why. But Vincent and Gyslaine heated up the vegetable soup in the kitchenette and I heard Vincent whistling a song. "You sing when you hadn't ought to," I told him. "It's better to sing than to let yourself die like Ti-Guy," says the girl. "He's making everybody sick with his tears, maybe your friend is right, it's better to sing, hell, there's nothing interesting about misery, it's the crappiest thing on earth . . . I wonder why I love him so much, a guy that's spaced out from morning to night . . . love is crazy, I guess . . ."

"Give me a hand," says Vincent, coming in with the soup, "this boy has to eat."

"No, never again," says Ti-Guy in tears. "Never again. My friends abandoned in the desert . . . do they eat? No . . . hardly anything . . . and remember, Anne? . . . the tourists were greedy . . . We were greedy too, and they, the slaves, brought us water . . . and bread . . . remember? You said, 'It's a sin, the only sin, to accept things as they are.' I have to go away . . . we're rotten . . . I'm rotten . . . and there's something else I never confessed, the camel, remember, Anne? . . . the tourists threw him roses . . . nobody noticed his bleeding jaws . . . he chewed the roses . . . the thorns . . . and nobody saw . . . but you . . . No, no food, never again . . ."

We held the dish of soup in front of him and managed to spoon it in, Ti-Guy had to swallow it, like it or not. Then he fell asleep. "Fine," says Vincent. "Now let's close the door and leave him in peace."

"Hey, you," Gyslaine asks, "are you a doctor or what? We've had doctors here before, but they gave up in a hurry, there's no cure, you're wasting your time, he'll come to a bad end. It's too bad, we really loved each other."

"We must be vigilant," says Vincent. "All is not lost."

"Oh, so you're a new-style priest? You're not like the rest of them, but I can smell it a mile off."

"A priest? . . . Is that what you think? I should say, on the contrary . . . Priest . . . no . . . not yet . . . far from it . . . not if the priesthood is a worldly calling . . . All right, I must go now. Coming with me, Ti-Pit?"

"Never mind, we'll be at your place tomorrow morning, Mr. Priest."

"Coddle him a little, he doesn't tell you so, but he needs it."

"You're wrong, Mr. Priest. It's easy to see you don't know anything about it."

"I meant, coddle him like a child," says Vincent. "See you tomorrow."

In the street I shook Vincent and said, "Why did you

sing like that? You see a guy in torture and you start singing . . . why?"

"Because I felt like it, that's all. Sometimes you're small-minded, Ti-Pit. Don't you understand that for your friend Ti-Guy it's too late . . . there's nothing to do but . . . sing . . ."

"Too late? Then what does your religion amount to? Nothing but false promises to the wretched."

"I don't think I ever said I had the power to console anybody. Anyway, that's enough, I have nothing more to say to you."

"Christ, you can't always shut me up like this! You've helped me, I'd have been strung up by now if it wasn't for you, why can't you help him?"

"With him it's different. He can't face the misery of the world and he's letting it destroy him. I'm afraid he hasn't got the courage to fight it . . . To love life, you need a kind of courageous cowardice . . . yes . . ."

"You're not a real Christian, that's for sure."

"You exasperate me with your smug pity. You think you're sympathizing with others, but you're only reassuring yourself. It's no use talking about it any more. Don't be angry, but I'm going home . . . alone. You wear me out."

So that crazy savage that calls himself a priest just walks off, leaves me standing there all by myself wondering why he's racing down the boulevard like that. I yelled after him, "Hey, Vincent, maybe you're a Christian, but I don't like your character." All the answer I got was wind and silence . . .

AFTER LEAVING Vincent I was as blue as a month of Mondays, I couldn't think of anything else but hightailing it over to the Cat. There at his table, under the spots and stripes of the TV, was Papillon, talking to his chum Corneille. He seemed to be applauding himself—so brilliant!—and his tie was jiggling in the breeze. "Yes," he says, "by his befuddled consciousness Papillon swears to you tonight that someday Joualonie will belong to the Joualonese."

"I was referring to your grossness," says Corneille,

"your rudeness . . . your atrocious manners. Will you finally listen to me?"

"But, my revered publisher, what have I done now? Have I tripped and danced too much, have I twittered too much, have I gone too far in murmuring and burbling the indignation of my people?"

"You don't murmur and burble, *mon cher,* you roar with nationalistic fever wherever you go. The whole city is deafened by your blasphemous psalms. In the subway, under the bridges, in the wind, in the rain and snow, there's Papillon raising his banner."

"Hurray for Papillon!" says the scribbleroo, giving me his hand. "How about a drink, Lemieux, my Christing chum? Whatever you may think, Corneille, you have here in Lemieux an inspired proletarian, one more primitive Joualonese to publish. His thus-far-unwritten confession is entitled *A Joualonese Speaks Out.* What do you think of it? Never despise a book just because it hasn't been written! What do you say, Lemieux. No, he won't say a thing, the stinker, that's his way: silent creation. Are you always going to keep your jaws closed as tight as a nun's twat, Abraham? Here's my notebook, here's my pen, brother, I'm all ready to take you down, to get stoned on the treasures of your tongue, and you say nothing, you miser."

Then Papillon starts telling us how people were writing him "from every corner of Joualonie, yes, *mon cher,* same as to Margot, the Big Sister of the Lovelorn." And he unfolds his letters under Corneille's nose. "Listen to this plaint and weep, divine Corneille, it's from one of our red-tape workers.

" 'Dear Monsieur, Dear Poet,

" 'I have seen you on television and for the first time in forty years my heart leaped. I recognize myself in you, monsieur, I am you, your words flow from my lips. When I read your novels I encounter myself in each of your characters, and in your poems, what shall I say . . . I am your breath! I feel that you are speaking to me and me alone. How have you been able to understand me so well, you who do not know me? I bow to the mystery. Yes, my heart leaped three times when I saw you, you so noble in stature, when I saw you, who were already standing, stand up and declare without shame: *Here I stand in the words of my people.*' "

"You really said that?" cries Corneille. "It's idiotic . . ."

"Okay, let me continue, *cher ami*. 'Yes, Monsieur and dear Poet, you have raised me up when I was crushed to the ground. For almost twenty-five years I have been working at the courthouse of our city. Born a scribe, monsieur, a scribe I shall always be. In all these years my salary has been the same and I have always led a stable life. The one good thing about a life like mine is that nothing changes, that destiny in a manner of speaking has forgotten me. But I too have a secret, monsieur. My secret is that I too, like you, WRITE! Since you have always known how to describe my innermost thoughts, you will understand me when I say that to write is to die a little. And so, dear Poet, bright and early tomorrow morning I shall send you (for now I dare to, to see you was to believe) directly from the courthouse, where under the cover of my faded documents I write perpetually . . . yes, with joy in my heart I shall send you . . . my ten children, that is, a dozen manuscripts, surely you who understand me better than anyone will have the patience to read them. Perhaps you will even help me to get your friend Monsieur Corneille to publish them. Ah, dear Poet, in speaking to you I am speaking to myself, I beg you in advance to forgive my illegible handwriting, like all scribblers I have learned to contract my letters almost as it were to the vanishing point (but that has already been said, has it not?) in order to save paper, and permit me to tell you why: You see my room costs me $13 a week, and my ink 50 cents . . .' "

"Papillon, that will do!"

"You don't understand humankind, Corneille, I read my pen-pusher's manuscripts through to the end, it was a kind of journal entitled *Twelve Variations on Myself* by Richard Petitfour, bureaucrat. Each one begins like this, you might call it a Te Deum of resignation:

"This morning it was very gray, almost black. I got up. I put on my socks and looked open-mouthed at the ceiling. I thought, This morning, yes, this morning something will happen to me at last. I waited for two minutes. Nothing. At nine o'clock I was at my office as usual.

"And each of the manuscripts ends like this:

"This evening when I got home, it was black, almost gray. There was nothing to do but undress and go to bed. Once again I opened my mouth and looked at the ceiling . . . Might this at last be hope? Where is God? I exist, but why? Was there anything new, anything overwhelming on the ceiling? Nothing, still nothing. I exist, undeniably I exist, but still nothing happens."

"Why, what prodigious inspiration!" says Corneille. "But that's not all, Corneille, listen to this charming lullaby, this archaic perfume from the hand of a sexagenarian stenographer:

"Dear Poet,

The person who is writing you is a humble stenographer, a secretary in the twilight of her spinsterhood, whose only close ties in this world have been with blotters and the boss, in short, monsieur. What am I but a sponge writing out balance sheets for a monstrously rich firm, the victim at rare and none too happy moments of the boss's mustachioed paternalism? One day, while I was reading your short story 'In the Paradise of Tender Flesh' (I am told you wrote this masterpiece at the age of fifteen, in the burgeoning copse of puberty. Are you by chance a libertine, monsieur, I have real Monsieur de Sade, you know . . .), a whole world of delicious, unknown sensations was revealed to me . . . It is true that with you one does

not read, one perceives, one does not see, one lives
through the eyes. Who but you, beloved master, would
think of praising us, old maids of the offices, ants of
the mechanical tickety-tick, who but you would think
of courting, as you write so well,

> *Our flickering virginities*
> *Extinguished by the robe of Duty . . .*

You alone, dear Poet. I press my bosom against you
and the bower of your tender Paradise.

> Sophie Desrosiers, aged 58
> Servant of the government

"Ah, Corneille, my friend, how I love to bask in the
sweet caresses of my readers."

"Get that goofy look off your face," says Corneille,
"and listen to this . . .

"Dear Monsieur Corneille,

You are a worthy, respectable man, a man of great
talent. [Hear that, Papillon, you're not the only one.]
We the rhetoric class at the Free School [You know,
Papillon, that new school, all the teachers were driven
out with rulers and inkwells and now the pupils insist
on being addressed as professors, a simple experiment
. . .] have signed a petition against you, monsieur,
because for almost fifteen years now you have been
publishing that insipid poet Eloi Papillon . . ."

"Hey," says Papillon, puffing like a locomotive,
"those kids . . . they're going too far . . . me insipid?"

"Shut up and listen!

"The midget Papillon is a blemish on our Literature.
Do you know why, monsieur, because he CONTRIBUTES
NOTHING, NOTHING TO HIS COUNTRY, monsieur . . .
and nothing to us . . ."

"Those kids are drunk on words. Now look, Corneille, what could I give them that they don't possess already in their arrogance? No, nobody understands me . . ."

"I continue," says Corneille . . .

"First of all, Monsieur Corneille, has this puny author even a glimmer of talent? You alone have the naïveté to publish and republish him, some thirty of his worklets are ruining the reputation of your otherwise estimable house. We happen to know that the Paris publishing world, to which we students look when we want to know whether one of our own authors is worth reading, yes, we happen to know that the publishers of Paris make no bones about despising the works of this common usurper! Like St. Thomas we insist on touching Paris before loving one of our writers; if Paris says no, we despise him. This Papillon whom you so fanatically champion is unworthy of the slightest interest. We are therefore, dear publisher, signing a manifesto against him, which will be distributed on our campus.

Louis-Marie Cochonaille, Free School, senior year
Chrétien Lambert, Free School, junior year
Hector L. T. P. P. (anonymous)

P.S. For us, of course, our academic status is pure allegory. We are Knowledge and Enlightenment.

Louis-Marie Cochonaille, president of the F.A.G. (Free Association of Geniuses)"

"The damn snobs!" says Papillon.

"And now listen to this one, it's from one of those steely-eyed madmen who take care of your mind for you, a psychoparasite by trade:

"Dear Monsieur Corneille,

I hardly need express all the admiration I feel for you . . . [never mind, I'll skip a few lines, why vex

you with the compliments people pay me?] . . . a few
of my patients and myself have studied the works of
your unfortunate (and deranged) Eloi Papillon in
depth and concluded, thanks to the light of our
science, that this writer's entire production inclines to
dementia. We have here a hopelessly deformed libido,
whose principal obsessions I list here: double phallic
presence, undoubtedly a symptom of impotence, his
image of himself as father of the nation . . ."

"Corneille! Stop!"
"What, you're not interested in the diagnosis of Professor Ernest Cool of the University of Montreal? It's
worth forty bucks an hour."
"Let's drink to the health of my friends, Corneille,
and of my enemies as well, may their numbers decrease
in perpetuity, amen! But what's eating you, Lemieux,
your lips are shrouded in silent gloom. Is it on account
of the ambulance tomorrow morning?"
"I guess so. All that blood! It's no joke."
"Sufficient unto the day, chum. Take your beaker
and rejoice!"
Papillon and Corneille were sluicing down their
beers with the swiftness of thought, they were old hands
at it. Their faces were flushed with argument, but without a wrinkle of drunkenness. Finally Corneille says
it's time to wind up the festivities, he was due to meet
his proofreader at 3 a.m. But he wasn't really in
any hurry. "All right," he says to Papillon, "for friendship's sake I'll give you another few minutes." And
Papillon comes back with "For friendship's sake, I have
something more to ask of you. I want you to start taking care of yourself. Look at the life you lead, you're
hell-bent for the graveyard, proofs in the middle of the
night, in the morning your humanitarian appointments,
in the afternoon the cocktail circuit in honor of your
authors, not to mention your gastronomico-Bacchic
trips to Europe, you worry me, *mon cher,* even you are
getting old. Bear in mind, eternal oak, that when you're
gone this frail reed is likely to bend beneath . . ."
"You may bend but you won't break," says Corneille.

In answer to which Papillon, hand on paunch, clouding himself in smoke from one of Corneille's cigars, expressed the opinion that "a light pen isn't always a tender-waisted handmaiden" and that "women often mistake weight for depth." The fogs of memory carried him away to the Thérèses and Eglantines of his life. "Yes, Corneille, let's face it. When my Jacqueline, my sugar plum, was in jail for the night, singing,

> "Freed at last from man,
> Our aggressor,
> The husband of our chains,

"what did I do? I consoled myself with the perfume of those two voracious flowers, ah, Thérèse! . . . ah, Eglantine! I lulled them to sleep by singing:

> "I am handsome, I am faithful, I am durable,
> But you, my sweet, will you endure me?

"In the morning Thérèse and Eglantine went home to their respective bourgeoisies, but who do you think turns up at my place? Papineau's wife, in tears. 'My poor pussycat,' I say. 'What's wrong?' And that sensitive soul informs me that Papineau, my abominable one-time classmate, has been unfaithful to her, the poor darling."

"When?" Corneille asks. "Before or after the birth of little Maritain Papineau?"

"Before, after, and during, mon cher. First thing, I say to Papineau's wife, 'Have some of my tarte aux oignons, you can talk later.' Weak from hunger, the poor thing staggers to the table, and I rejoice in the unabashed sensuality of her appetite. 'Ah, have you any idea what it's like to eat rice for ten years? And to think that while I was toeing Papineau's ascetic line, my husband was secretly eating pork chops and coq au vin with his mistress! You don't mind if I take a little more of the tarte, Papillon? And a bit of cheese and some more wine? May I, comrade?' 'Fill your belly, ma chère, fill your belly—as you say, it's between comrades . . .' 'You wouldn't have some ham and a few slices of bread, would you, comrade? You don't mind if I help myself?' 'Shovel it in, comrade, shovel it in!' 'Ah yes, to get back to Papineau, my husband,' she says with her mouth full, invigorated by her succulent repast (what would Jacqueline say, her whole week's marketing at Stringbird's was vanishing into the maw of this youthful Marxist). 'I know he's right when he says you're nothing but a petit bourgeois, Papillon, but you're his only friend, so naturally he has to put up with you, you wouldn't happen to have some butter and jam to put on the bread? Thank you, comrade, thank you, you can open another bottle of wine if you like, I'm thirsty, comrade, I can't remember when I last had anything to drink. But getting back to Papineau, my husband and comrade: he always had his head shaved like a monk, his body looked as if he'd been fasting for years. How could I guess he was indulging his materialistic appetites elsewhere? Even when he was making babies he seemed to be doing it with his brain . . . his touch was like metal . . . brrr . . . it makes me shiver to think of it! But who's got Karl and Blaise and the whole gang of little Papineaus on her hands? Me! And this Papineau, who managed to make me think he was chaste even when he was making love, what does he tell me now? That he's discovered "the ecstasy of a perfect sexual bond with his mistress in Westmount." Oh, comrade, I'm hungry, I'm thirsty! But why aren't you eating?' 'I'm eating in you, my charming comrade, I mean, it's pure bliss just to watch you . . .' 'A few cream tarts would hit . . . what, you have some? And maple syrup? You people want for nothing, you really are a despicable petit bourgeois, this has got to change, Papillon, my husband is perfectly right. Ah, Eloi, you don't mind if I call you Eloi? It's the wine, it's the joy. Do you remember when that shriveled prune of a Papineau came back from India? Right away he told everybody that he'd spent a whole year in piety and meditation at the feet of a chief guru and that he himself had become a guru. Everybody had to call him Guru Papineau Oudidida, all very corny . . . And who was his most devoted disciple? Me again, his wife! I was his guinea pig and proving ground. Day and night we meditated, he did breathing exercises before climbing into bed and before getting up. He'd go into a trance and ask his faraway guru for advice, and sometimes he'd say to me, "No, not tonight, he doesn't want it. He says the atmosphere is not propitious." "It's none of your guru's goddamn business," I'd tell him, but he went right on consulting with his forehead on the floor, it was no fun, I'm telling you. Even when the atmosphere was propitious, the shadow of his guru would fall on us at the critical moment, you're a man, comrade, I guess you know what I mean, and there was the guru's grunt mingling with our moans. Ah, comrade, I know you're only a mediocre, half-witted petit bourgeois, as my husband is always saying, it's true you're useless to society and come the revolution we'll have to cut your throat and chuck you into the raging fires of our Ideal with all the rest of the dead wood, but I bet you at least, comrade, don't quote Marx while you're in bed with your wife. I'm hungry, I'm thirsty, why don't you still my hunger and quench my thirst? Comrade, come to my bosom . . .' 'Me? I couldn't do that,' I say, 'I'm married . . .' 'Petit bourgeois concepts! Marriage . . . pooh! You ought to be ashamed, it's a comrade's duty to feed his comrades when they're hungry . . .' 'No, no!' I protested. 'I adore Papineau, I'm his only friend, comrade, I can't deceive him with his beloved wife . . . no . . . no . . .' Then the poor thing put her breast away, buttoned her blouse in rage and vexation, and left me on this fanatical and familiar melody, 'You're nothing but a filthy capitalist, Papillon!' "

Those little stories poured out of Papillon like a babbling brook, not a chance of his running dry before morning, but I thought I'd better hoist anchor all the same, there'd be a whole raft of smashup victims waiting for an ambulance bright and early, we had to be on time to pick the bitter fruit. "So long, chums," I said, and put my lid on. Papillon followed me out into the street and grabbed me by the coattails. "Christ, Lemieux," he says, "you're the death of the party, you haven't opened your mouth once and now you're slinking home to your attic, that's no way to treat your friends, you Joualonese traitor!" "I can't drink too much," I tell him. "It makes my heart pound." "Let it pound a bit, friend, you're all tied up in knots, let me set you free." He was puffing with his asthma, but that didn't stop him from declaiming (in another second he'd have shinnied up the lamppost). "Ah, my friends, my Joualonese brothers," he rants, "you who love happiness and freedom, let us, you and me, become the masters of Joualonie!" He was all fire and flame, I guess it was the cold wind and the sound of his own voice caressing the air. Looking back, I saw Corneille leading Papillon back to the tavern and heard him say, "Will you never shut up!"

Dead on my feet, I crawled home to my boarding-house. The entrance was black as pitch and in the hall-way I stumbled over two shapes intertwined till death do us part. "Christ," I say, "what's this tangle?" "No," comes Mimi's voice, "don't put on the light, wait till we get our pants on!" "Who's that with you, Mimi, what's the big idea? You've got your room for your love life." "Yeah, but we were in a hurry; hey, Danny darling, where's my belt?" "Here it is," says Danny, "and here's your comb, it fell out of your pocket." "You're lucky it wasn't the postman," I say. "How can anybody be in such a hurry? It's hard to believe." "I know," says Mimi, "it's all Danny's fault. The mere touch of his hand turns me into an electric shock." "Shut up," says Danny. "That's no way to talk." "It's God's truth," says Mimi. "You send me to the bottom of the sea, Danny, and while we're basking in paradise, my Jean-François is wasting away all by himself in the clink." Danny turns on the light, his cheeks are as red as a fire engine and he's squirming with embarrassment. While he's hooking up his braces, Mimi, making the usual big noise, tells me all about it. It seems Jean-François was picked up at the Faerie Queene Club by a cop in drag, so Mimi and Danny and a few friends were taking up a collection to spring him. "You mean there are cops that go cruising just to chuck you boys in the freezer?" "It's true all right," says Mimi, "those pigs are real swine. You're off your guard in those clubs. When somebody new comes around, you don't look him in the eye, you start from the bottom up, it's easier to make up your mind that way, but how are you going to tell what kind of a creep you're making a pass at? The guy comes over and whispers, 'Let's go outside a minute.' The minute you're out the door, he pokes his gun in your back and after that the whole thing is organized like a gangster movie." "We've got almost fifty bucks, we need a hundred to spring him," says Danny. Danny was smoking, probably to hide his embarrassment. "When you caught us in the act just now," says Mimi, "we were just taking a little break between collecting. We're going around to Liberated Sex, maybe those guys'll help us." "They're drips," says Danny, "they just talk a good lay." "That's the truth," says Mimi, taking sulky Danny by the neck. "There's nobody like you, Danny, you go to my head like champagne. You're the best lay I ever had!" "That'll do," says Danny. "And don't breathe a word to my old man, see, he'd have a stroke."

"The silence of the tomb, Danny darling," says Mimi.

"You going to see Jean-François at his free hotel?" I ask them.

"It's been a lovely time for Danny and me," says Mimi, "but we think we'll have enough in the kitty tomorrow to get him out. That's why we're always in a hurry, because when Jean-François gets back, we'll have to listen to his moaning. 'Ah, Mimi, ah, Danny! my career . . . my career is over! I've lost my reputation . . . woe is me!' Like a lady that's lost her virtue. Ah, sweet Jesus, he folds up easy, not like you, Danny darling (here Mimi runs his hands through Danny's hair and Danny doesn't like it), don't get mad, you're as virile as those handsome French sailors you see parading in the summer on the Terrasse de Québec, in their tight white pants and their blue berets with the red pompons . . . oh, it's so lovely! . . ." "You just leave those sailors alone," says Danny. "And how's your old man getting along?" I ask Danny. "Not bad," he says, "he's just started a new business with religious books, it's shitty, but the bread rolls in and it takes a lot of bread to keep an old nance with a taste for pretty boys . . . that's the way it is . . . Sometimes I try to help

him out with a bit of casual fagging, but old guys like
that are always proud, you've got to watch your step."
So then Mimi and Danny beat it to the gay jungle to
round out their collection . . .

For once Mère Fontaine was asleep on her sofa,
buried in her magazines, Grisly Murders, The Seamy
Side of Montreal, and all the rest of her night companions. Back in my pad, Lison was sleeping on my
bed, so I spread out my coat on the floor and lay
down, griping, "Christ, once they get their claws into
you, they never let go!" Then the dreams started up.
My damn ambulance driver was frolicking on the
edge of a meadow, toting his latest victim of the freeways over his shoulder like a sack of potatoes. The
blood was pouring out of his nose and I'm dragging
along behind him. "Can't you see you've got him head
down?" I said. "Don't you know they croak quicker
that way?" "It's all one to me, son," he says, laughing.
"Hell, it's no skin off my ass.

> "There were three students on vacation.
> They'd just taken their examination,
>   tra la la
> Happy this morning, dead tonight!"

The victim's parents and sisters and fiancée were all
around us, the driver lays him down in the grass and
starts to roll a cigarette. "Good God, save him!" says
the mother. "Do something. Can't you see he's in pain?
He's my only son, he's just passed his examinations,
first in his class . . ." But the driver had his sly little
smile and didn't budge. "I need to smoke first," he
says. "I've been on this job for thirty years, see?" A
sound was coming out of the ground, out of the blood-
stained grass, out of the blue and gray sky . . . It was
this medical bozo's breathing. His black eyes were half
glazed already. "Observe," says the driver, "it always
starts with the eyes. That's the way Death comes down,
the stinker . . ." That breathing was still behind me,
and the voice of the student's mother, she was kneeling
beside him. "Between us a veil . . . dark on one side,
transparent on the other . . ." Then I wake up. Mère

Fontaine was holding a plate of toast under my chin.
"It's almost seven, Monsieur Ti-Pit, they'll be waiting
for you on the job . . ." Lison was still asleep with her
face to the wall, so I followed Mère Fontaine into the
kitchen to shave. "You've been having bad dreams
again, Monsieur Ti-Pit," says Mère Fontaine. "I don't
think that ambulance is the right thing for you . . ."

While I'm standing there with my brush full of
lather, other memories from the days of Jos Langlois
and Ti-Cul tugged at me (Mère Fontaine was turning
the pages of the St. Joseph calendar she kept on top of
the cupboard, she always skipped pages in the winter
so's to make the warm weather come faster). One day
Jos Langlois's wife had said Ti-Cul and me were just
animals, we might as well sleep in the barn, which
suited us fine, we were all alone with the pigs and
horses and the smell of straw. We'd steal a case of beer
and bring it in for the night, but sometimes that bastard
Jos Langlois came in to spy, we could smell him in the
dark, he had a spade in his hand and his shadow
moved from left to right, and we couldn't shut an eye
for fear he'd decide to kill us. One time Ti-Cul whis-
pered in my ear, "You'll remember, chum, you'll remember that when you were thirteen you had masters
like this and you were their slave, and someday you'll
come back and cut their balls off, swear it, Ti-Pit,
swear it on my head." And when I wasn't too crazy
about swearing, Ti-Cul swats me and says, "In that
case, Ti-Pit, you're nothing but a coward."

"As you see," says Mère Fontaine, "Monique and
Josée are still out. What a life for those poor little
things, luckily they have each other to love in the daytime. Another winter's day to live through, Monsieur
Ti-Pit, another day of mourning . . ."

"Why, Mère Fontaine," I say, "you've got the blues
today."

"Oh, I almost forgot, I bought you some body lotion,
Monsieur Ti-Pit, it kills all B.O. smells, as they call
them, shall I slip some under your shirt?"

"You mean I stink?"

"No, but you smell strong," she says. She rolls me in

lotion and finally I push her away. "My job is waiting, Mère Fontaine," I tell her.

Then who do I see on Sherbrooke Street, which the snowplows had pretty well cleared? Ti-Guy, looking like a scarecrow on his bicycle. He pulls up at the curb beside me and says, "As you see, I've taken out my bicycle, it's such a lovely morning!" "Are you crazy? I bet you're the only bicycle at large in the whole town and your head is bare, you want to catch the flu?" "No," says Ti-Guy, "I don't feel the cold, and I'm very happy, you know, we painted your friend Vincent's attic, he's a priest, but I forgive him, I love everybody and I can feel that everybody loves me . . ." He still had his long robe on, every known color, and his hair hanging loose, he looked like he was taking a vacation under the sun of Mexico. "You got to pull yourself together, chum," I tell him. "Old Baptiste is having a rough time, he doesn't understand people that take shit, he thinks you're a hell of a son . . ." "Poor Papa," says Ti-Guy, "poor Mama, they've suffered a lot, but someday, you know, they will be first . . . how about you . . . would you like some sugar? I've got more than I need this morning, that's why I'm feeling so good." "Listen to me, Ti-Guy, what did Vincent say to you?" "Oh, Vincent said such beautiful things," says Ti-Guy. His eyes were veiled and it was only morning. "He told me that if he were the priest that had to give the last rites to somebody about to be hanged, he'd take the host and break it in two . . . He said a prison chaplain that's willing to do that is as bad as the hangman, guilty of the same crime . . . that's what he said . . . say, did you ever see a hanging? I did."

That's the way it was with Ti-Guy. One word could change his whole horizon. All he saw was the end, always the end.

5.

HEARING THAT wavering siren, that clarion of
death chasing us down the roads on a chilly morning,
and fighting my way through the mobs of wage slaves
on their way to work was enough to make me envy
Pierrot, who'd written his Nicolette at the boardinghouse that the tundra, the far north, was the life, the
miles on miles of timber, the silent plains, the glittering
snow, that was the life that put rhythm into a man's
heartbeat. Ti-Cul and me, we used to talk about building an igloo in the woods, we were out in the bushes
smoking Jos Langlois's pipe, but there was always some
cop roaming around, looking for tramps, so we'd have
to beat it back to the cow barn, and Ti-Cul would say,
"We only get to breathe cow shit, the mountain air ain't for
earthworms like us." Right then the guy beside me
wasn't Ti-Cul but my ambulance driver in his EMER-
GENCY cap. He was a degenerate. "You know what
we got in our buggy this morning?" he says. "The big
sister and the little brother. That kid don't weigh no
more than a feather, the spiders of cancer are eating
him away. The Bigshot up there has got His nerve with
Him, eating His little children. Nothing's too crummy
for the Great Tormentor, this kid is only twelve, four
months he's been wasting away in his mother's big
bed; his sister thinks it's gone on long enough, she
wants them to inject him with galloping death at the
hospital, she's right, because the Big Boss that lives up
there in the clouds don't give a damn."

"Shut up, you make me sick!"

"You'd better listen to me, son. No use getting
worked up, it's nothing."

He goes on talking; once you hear the tortured cries
of an innocent babe just starting out in life, he says,
you lose your respect for everything in this world, we're

all of us lumps of shit under the blue summer sky. That's the way he'd talk. And then he'd think about his comics and laugh himself sick. Meanwhile, I'm thinking about the time when I'd just got out of jail and Vincent was putting me up. One afternoon—Vincent was giving me a dose of the Gospels and I didn't understand a thing—the boss priest comes in, a skinny, dignified guy in glasses, a chum of Vincent's. I guess he thought Vincent needed a sermon. "Yes, my child," he says. Vincent was already looking glum, he didn't go for the "my child" routine. "Yes, my child, how can you live in this wretched place when we can provide you with excellent living quarters. It doesn't befit a man of your calling . . . of your cloth . . . to live so humbly." Seeing that the patriarch looked tired after climbing the stairs, Vincent made him sit down and suggested tea as usual . . . "Yes, thank you, my friend . . ." said the old priest, raising his hand as though in blessing, but stopping just in time because that wouldn't have gone down so good with Vincent . . . "I see you're squandering your salary giving shelter to these unfortunates" (here his eyes grazed my person). "It's unnecessary, my friend, we have our rehabilitation centers . . ." All along, Vincent was grunting inside, but then he explodes. "I thought you'd come to see me as a friend, but it's just to find fault with my mode of life . . ."

"But, my dear child, I see nothing to find fault with except perhaps your tendency to irritability, your violence, which indeed are grave defects . . . We all know how much you have helped these disillusioned souls . . ."

"Helped? And what makes you think these souls are disillusioned? And why souls? I'm interested in people, not in souls . . ."

"Don't get excited, I speak to you as a friend, as a father . . . you know what affection I feel for you, I have been your only defender. The others disapprove of you because of your rages, I am more tolerant on that point, in my opinion it's a matter of health. Nobody's nerves would stand up under the life you lead . . . I know that . . . I understand . . ."

"I'm violent, extremely violent," says Vincent. "Why deny it?"

"Let's not exaggerate," says the patriarch wearily, "you always exaggerate, my friend."

Vincent was fuming, and stamping inside, but his priest looked so frail he didn't want to throw any thunderbolts; he even calmed down enough to mutter, "I thank you for coming to see me, you're a faithful friend . . ." Then he turns to me, grumbling, "You could put on a clean tablecloth when His Reverence comes to see us. Go on, get a move on!" Then the patriarch says he understands "the great bitterness that sometimes comes over you." Years ago, he says, stooped under the weight of his memories, he had tried to pass on his "fruitful mission in Gaspé" to Vincent, but the priests in the other villages had protested that Vincent "went too far, yes, too far in the Lord's teachings. You see, my friend, you were threatening the social edifice, many of your fellow priests are not equal to such penitence, such a state of poverty, you had no right to demand it of them . . ."

"I know," says Vincent. "Sometimes my rebellious spirit led me astray, and it's true that I can't stomach rich priests, but whether it's here or in Gaspé, I'm all right, I always find my place in the world, you mustn't worry about me."

"Nevertheless, my son, you are subject to the orders of your superiors. You must obey, you are a priest, hence a servant of God, you must not put man before God in your egoism. In Gaspé you were at home, we uprooted you, but perhaps it was necessary for your own good, there perhaps you were beguiled by the image of a worthy, grandiose poverty . . ."

"There's no such thing as worthy, grandiose poverty," says Vincent, who was getting hot under the collar. "Besides, as you know, I am not a man given to sentiment and emotion. Even at the seminary I had a reputation for coldness . . . indifference."

"Who is asking you to be more just than God? Of course there is greatness in the fire that consumes you, but what the Church demands of you is first and foremost obedience, and forgive me for saying it again: a little Christian meekness . . ."

"I am incapable of acquiring that quality."

"And yet it's a simple matter if one has faith. You yourself know that violence is reprehensible, and in your case perhaps a sign of unchecked pride. Why then should you knowingly turn your back on sentiment, on tenderness? We are all weak sinners, God doesn't ask us to struggle perpetually against ourselves . . ."

"I have always struggled to live," says Vincent. "It's an old habit with me. And unfortunately the struggle for life is rarely gentle . . . Anyway, I don't like to talk about myself."

"Just one more thing," says the priest with a sigh. "Your tormented childhood doesn't justify you in doing violence to others . . ." Then he picks up his cane and rises. "I must admit," he says, "that I don't understand you. You don't love God enough to accept being more or less defeated by life . . . With you it's always this wild struggle. Very well, I say no more, I shall leave now . . . Don't forget me, old age is a lonely thing for a priest . . ."

Vincent took the old man out to the landing, then he sat down at his table. He was pale and lost in his thoughts. "What do you expect me to do with meekness?" he grumbles.

Then there was this abbé fresh out of the seminary, a black-haired, hot-blooded scrapper, he'd bust in without warning and before Vincent could get his breath he'd start hollering, "No . . . I can't go on like this . . . the Church asks too much of us . . . absolute chastity is impossible, it's madness . . ."

"Another fit of lust, eh?" says Vincent impatiently. "Why do you tell me these things? If your desire is too much for you, give in to it, that's all."

This fresh-baked abbé would complain that Vincent was a cynic and took no interest in people and their problems. One time Vincent grabbed him by the arm and said, "Maybe what you say is true, but I say you were misguided, this isn't the place for you, you'll never be a priest." The young priest starts to tremble and says to Vincent, "If something terrible happens to me, you'll be responsible!" He beats it downstairs and right under Vincent's window this battler in petticoats throws himself under a milk truck. They pick him up all contusioned but not dead, and while they were patching up his leg at the hospital, Vincent and me would go see him now and then with chocolates for the ward. The abbé said to Vincent, "I hate you because you understand people too well . . ."

When his leg was mended and he was all well, this abbé had worse ants in his pants than ever. Come spring he was living with a woman, and when he came back to Vincent's hovel he wasn't on the warpath any more, he only said, "There are men like you, Vincent, but there are also men like me, mere pawns of desire."

After he'd finished resting me up, Vincent found me a job on a building, and then another as a mechanic's helper, and a third in an ice-skate factory. He'd always say, "This time, Ti-Pit, you'd better keep your job, because I'm going to throw you out pretty soon . . ." "Do I bother you so much?" I'd ask him. "Yes, because an old bear like me has to live alone and I'm never alone . . . Sometimes it seems to me that all I've ever wanted of God was just that, a little solitude in which to think of myself . . ." "Selfish, hardhearted bastard," I'd think. "All priests are the same." Couldn't he see that for me the outside was just one big empty space full of nothingness?

"Actually, Ti-Pit, you'll be happier yourself without me. You won't have to go to Mass any more, you won't pray, don't try to kid me, son, I know you."

"You don't know me at all! Christ, what's the good of fishing bums out of the sewer if you're going to throw them to the wolves? Just tell me that."

"We're all of us thrown to the wolves, as you put it."

That heretic just couldn't see what it meant, dropping me like that, no lamp burning behind the curtain when you come home from the factory, no disagreeable son-of-a-bitch at the head of the stairs to cheer you up, summer and winter dragging your ass in the desert like an old rag. I hadn't any friends but the beggars on Boulevard Saint-Laurent, we'd go out looking for bargains together, a coat, a pair of boots, there'd be a whole mountain of filth to choose from, sometimes for a buck you'd get a treasure crawling with lice, maybe a leather jacket or a lumberman's coat, and then for fifteen cents we'd get a club sandwich and a drink of 7-UP, that's what life was like without that hardened sinner of a Vincent.

Then one day while I'm hanging around a pinball machine rigged up with a lot of naked women, their nipples light up like candles when you hit the jackpot, I make the acquaintance of Mimi over a bottle of Pepsi. He's wearing his tight black jeans and there's still a bit of powder on his eyebrows, left over from the Dear Boy the night before, he tells me. He says he's going to a wedding in Quebec, seems he had this chum, a priest on rue Saint-Jean near the Ramparts, who gave his blessing to "marriages between the same sex." "So you see," says Mimi, beaming, "I'm inviting all the bums I know to come and drink champagne. That's the way Georges and Jocelyn want it, a Catholic wedding with promises to be faithful and the whole shooting match. Me, I'd rather have a ball every night, I'm a wandering minstrel, as they say, but they want to settle down, they've just bought a farm on the Île d'Orléans, they take their marriage seriously."

"I've never seen Quebec in all my natural life," I tell him. "What's it like?"

"It's a riot, you'll see, come on, some society dame that's soft on me is giving us a lift . . ."

Naturally, being winter, the party was indoors, Mimi's Georges and Jocelyn had plenty of cabbage, they came of good families with gilded high-finance daddies. They'd loved each other ever since they'd played with hoops, so everybody approved of the marriage, except Jocelyn's mother, who said she'd had "higher aims for my son." But his father said, "They'll make a good thing of commercial art, they've got business sense, don't worry . . ." The dancing and festivity cheered Jocelyn's mother up, and then when it was all over the wedding crowd went out on the Château Frontenac bobsled run and drank up great mouthfuls of wind from the river. That's where Mimi picked up Jean-François, he was miming at the Chez Lulu Café, seems he was all dreamy-sad that day, as languid as a frozen snake. After the ceremony Georges and Jocelyn took off for their nuptial island. "Ah, Jocelyn, my sweet, we'll never have any grand-children," says the mother, kissing her son goodbye. "We're thinking of adopting a few later on . . ." says Jocelyn, and away he goes to his happiness.

On this same trip I also met Lucie and François, a very cantankerous pair, they couldn't look at each other without starting a fight. Lucie was toting their six-month-old chick-a-biddy on her back. They were down and out, but that didn't stop them from saying, "Come and have dinner with us on rue Sainte-Ursule." The grub didn't amount to much, cats might have liked it, and their moods swung around like a weathervane. Some days François would smash a chair or two against the wall, the prick of hunger, I suppose, and his Lucie, wiping the baby's ass philosophical-like, would say to me, "Ah, you wouldn't believe it with all this ruckus, but it started out like a great love story, the baby changed it all, Romeo and Juliet had no kids as far as I can remember, that's why their love never went sour on them." After fighting hammer and tongs, as often as not they'd swing to the other extreme and do a Bacchanalia standing up just like that, or in the bathtub, while the bitsy-witsy in his diapers would be doing his exercises on the cold floor.

The more alone you are, the more family ecstasy you run in to, people were pairing up all over the place, you threw a blanket over your sorrow, what else could you do? When there was no more gravy to put on the bread, François would work off his temper crawling through the dirty snow in his back yard, looking up at the motionless sky that didn't give a damn whether he fed his baby that day or not. Then, encouraged by the cold and his morning sport, he'd tell his wife, "I've got an idea, Lucie, I'm going to the Beaux-Arts shindig and swipe some clothes." Away he flew on the wings of his idea and came back home with a big pile of coats, hats, and galoshes. "The boys were all stinko under their beards, it was easy . . . They're friends of mine, they'd understand. Look, this is my prof's trenchcoat, it'll keep you warm, Lucie."

Christmas is a bad time for a jerk that's all alone, the evening comes down sweet and calm on all these family folks, and you say to yourself, Where are you going to stow your carcass tonight, in jail or at the Home for Pathetic Souls? Or maybe you'll line up outside that convent and the Little Sisters will give you a slice of rotten meat while waiting for their novices to come back from Communion. You don't know, you walk, you pass apartments so close to the street that one step would take you onto the carpet. Some school kid is stuttering his lessons before going to bed, Grandpa is opening his newspaper, it's like a show with voices and sound effects that say, "This is my happy home. This is my happy home," but the closed door says to the bum that's scratching his nose under the street lamp, "No, not here, go somewhere else, no admittance." Hell, after a while you learn to get along without other people.

"What are you dreaming about?" says my driver. "Your mind isn't on your work, son, you're off in the clouds, what's eating you anyway?"

"You damn undertaker, don't talk to me."

"You got the blues, eh, son? The job is getting you down, that's what it is. I know. In a couple of days death won't mean a thing to you . . . then you'll be a man, son."

AT THE hospital, just as we're taking the little cancer patient, flat as a pancake on the stretcher, to his eternal destination and his sister's walking along behind him with a courage that was too good for this world, my spooky driver says to me, "Hey, son, you seen *Montréal-Matin?* There's been a grand murder out in the sticks, no kidding, an orgy, they don't know who did it, maybe a gang, anyway, they did it right. The rich farmer shot square through the head, his wife bound and butchered, his big strapping sons mowed down by gunfire. Ah, son, a bloodbath like that warms my heart."

"You monster! The only thing you like is blood!"

"Sure I like it. That's justice, *our* justice. We don't talk, we know it doesn't do any good, we kill. With corpses you can talk, they listen."

"Christ, but it's sinful to stink up the earth with blood like that."

All the same, while going through my routine, I kept thinking about that damn massacre, it seems the killers made off with the old man's cash. All around the farm there were trails of blood, they'd even caught one of the sons in a ditch and trampled him after the massacre, Christ, what a sauce, what tasty seasoning, for Christmas dinner! It took a fiend like my driver to roll himself a cigarette and curl up his lips with delight. "Yeah," he said. "It had to happen, it was high time, you don't understand, son, but if some colonel told me to go burn half of Montreal, I'd do it tonight. We've suffered enough, it's time to act. You know why they did it? In the papers they talk about 'cold-blooded murder.' That don't mean a thing, that's a journalist trying to squelch his conscience. I know the reason why. There's always revenge in a massacre like that. They think the serfs will never grab the whip, but they're mistaken, son, and those criminals that stepped so graceful into that sleeping house with their guns in their fists, believe you me, they're free men now, that makes two fewer slaves in the world."

During our break I opened up the paper and one look told me it was Jos Langlois and his brood that those barbarians had gunned down out there in the country, at a time of night when only the foxes and hares are stirring. Christ, it was plain as day, Ti-Cul and his Cri-Cri were the killers, because I see on page 2 that some convicts had escaped. I hadn't believed Ti-Cul when he prophesied his apocalypse in his letter. I sneak out to the toilet quick and vomit up my guts. The driver stops me on the way out. "Been puking, son? If you'd done it, I could see why, this way you've got no right." I wanted to run back to the boardinghouse and tear up Ti-Cul's letter in case Mère Fontaine went poking through my stuff, but the driver says, "Tell me the truth, son, what are you so quivery about? You're all green. You can tell me if you've heard anything about that revolution out there, maybe you're in the know. I can see you've done a spell in the kid house .... You've never said anything, but I've got a nose for dregs."

"They put me in for stealing cars, see, nothing crummy, just shut your trap or I'll clout you!"

"Don't talk to me like that, son, I could be your uncle or your godfather."

I was thinking maybe this dumb Ti-Cul would write me, maybe the damn butcher would try to mix me up in his crime, sure, that was it, the bastard thought I'd two-timed him because I'd forgotten the old days at the orphanage and decided to go straight and live without him. Ti-Cul would try to trap me, because he was a mad dog, an animal hungry for blood and torn flesh, he had his reasons, as the driver said, he'd eaten mud and shit, sure he had to vomit them up, but why did he have to do it this way? You won't catch me, brother, I says to myself, you won't catch me. You won't pull me into your crime. I know what Ti-Cul is thinking: I need an accomplice in blood, somebody to share the blood with. Otherwise it's no fun. So let's go find Ti-Pit, he's only an empty bottle anyway, and fill him up with poison. "You see, Ti-Pit, when you got no love in you, you got to fill yourself up with hate, you feel better that way." That was Ti-Cul's proverb, and now he was after me, wanting us to hang together.

That same day the newsstands were full of something to gladden every idiot in town: in no time at all, a week maybe, the lawyer from Quebec had brought out his bestseller, *The Story of Y,* in installments. In all the stations there were posters showing Y in knee socks, eating Eve's apple. Everybody was rushing to buy, but I had no heart for it. At six in the morning the stations were full of white-collar stiffs snapping up Y for their sandwich breaks. They hardly had their eyes open yet, but that didn't prevent them from grabbing their ration of porno, and the funny part of it was that, for their money, blood and sex were the same thing . . .

Okay, but Ti-Cul's letter! I run back to the boarding-house to put my lighter to it, and there's Mère Fontaine dishing out pea soup that didn't attract me at all. I thought I'd never be hungry again, but Mère Fontaine insisted, so I ate like everybody else. "What's on your mind, Monsieur Ti-Pit? Is it Mademoiselle Lison? Oh, everything's fine, you know, she's getting a curettage that will flush her baby down the drain with the other waste products of this earth, it can't be helped, that's the way it is. And Mademoiselle Mimi is in seventh heaven, Jean-François was let out this morning, he's more mournful than ever and he keeps saying to Mimi, 'Oh, my future is clouded forever on account of you, you little drab.' But all the same it's Mimi and Danny and the ladies of the Common Pederastic Front that got him out of the coop."

Sitting beside me, Ti-Paul the butcher says, "Have you read about the crime at St. Whozis, Ti-Pit? Isn't it sublimely revolting? It's the talk of the town. Don't you think it's vile?" "I don't think anything at all, it's the police's business, not mine!" "It's not like you to say that, Ti-Pit," says Ti-Paul. Then this colossus stretches and stands up in his bloody-grimy undershirt. He turned my stomach, but he wasn't a bad guy, he'd even reached into his own pocket to help get Jean-François out of stir.

I'D JUST flopped down for a nap when Mère Fontaine comes in. "Monsieur Ti-Pit," she says. "There's a school friend of yours downstairs. Should I tell him to come up?" "I've never been to that school," I tell her. "Who for the love of God can it be?" "A nice-looking young man, in a tie and a slightly tired felt hat, I'll bring him up." It was Ti-Cul in person, he hadn't grown any, he still came up to my shoulder, and he was swimming in Jos Langlois's clothes. I said to him, "Christ, you think I don't recognize that hat?" Then I saw he'd changed the color of his hair, he'd practically changed his skin, the tricky bastard. "Shut up, Ti-Pit. Come on, we're going to the Bar Latino Americano, it's dark and quiet, I want a few words with you . . ." "No dice, you gallowsbird," I tell him, but he holds his knife blade under my nose. "Careful," he says. "Ti-Cul has his fan all ready." But I could see the knife trembling in his hand. Down in the street I say, "I'll listen to you okay, if you've got something to say, but don't expect anything from me, no, Ti-Cul, find yourself somebody else, you're nuts to move around like this, everybody knows that you and Cri-Cri are on the lam." "Don't worry about us," he says. "We didn't fly the coop by ourselves. There's four more touring the country . . ."

AT THE Latino he sank into his fur collar and spoke in a whisper, though there wasn't so much as a mouse in the bluish smoke of last night's cigarettes. "So you think I'm the big butcher?" he says. "You really think Ti-Cul could do a thing like that?" "Yes," I tell him, "stop kidding around, I know all about it, it's you and you make me sick, Christ, do you make me sick!" "But supposing I only masterminded the job," he says. "Think it over, Ti-Pit. Maybe I tipped those guys off for laughs . . ." "No," I said, "don't lie. You're the killer!" "Hey, not so loud, we're not in the confessional yet, or in court. Christ, you're my chum, you're Ti-Pit, that means something, doesn't it? Cri-Cri is holed up with the whores, but I've got to travel, I thought you'd come with me, you're practically my brother, we'd share the bread, old man Langlois had a pile tucked away in the straw and I knew where, I knew my Jos, I'd seen him poking around with his lantern. This chum is lending me his Pontiac, we could evaporate down to Old Orchard, I'll give you all the clothes you'll need, the border will be a breeze if we dress up nice. Well, how about it?" "No, Ti-Cul, no soap. You can see Old Orchard by yourself. Get this, Ti-Cul: it's finished, I'm not your chum any more and it'll be goodbye any minute now . . ." "No, you don't! I'll rip your guts out first, you can't chuck your brother so easy." I watched him, he was trying to nail me down with his eyes. So he'd had it in him, I'm thinking. Even at the orphanage he'd had it tucked away in some dark corner, the devil had used Ti-Cul's pale face for a mask, nobody'd known it, but maybe that bloodbath was in the making even before Ti-Cul had foundered on our shores, and far, far away from Ti-Cul, the victims were eating, drinking, and playing their cruel tricks without a suspicion that one fine day they'd be torn to pieces. Maybe that massacre had been spawned at the orphanage when the candidates for parenthood picked pissy blonds in preference to dark kids like Ti-Cul and me, when they went for babies with dimples and cunning little hands, anyway, one thing for sure, the ladies had no use for black hair. Right now I could see that Ti-Cul still had his yen to be blond, there were yellowish glints sticking out from under his hat, but his eyes glittered black and there was no way of painting them blue . . . "So now you've got the hair you dreamed of," I tell him, "but you'll never be a real blond, so what's the percentage? Christ, what did you do it for? Thrills? The pleasure of being strung up one of these days?"

"The monks used to say I was a savage, descended from savages; it handed Langlois a big laugh. Well, it's true and I've proved it. They expected me to make a career of scalping and that's just what I've done. I don't regret a thing. I only need to remember the song they sang for the orphans they rented out for fifteen cents a week:

> *"Ti-Cul, the little nigger,*
> *Ti-Cul, the little nigger,*
> *Ti-Cul, you got no teeth,*
> *Ti-Cul, you're black all over."*

"Don't laugh too much," I tell him. "You haven't got time. Where are you going from here?"

"To see the world with you, Ti-Pit. Get me?"

"Forget it. I'm not your brother and I'm not your shadow."

"We'll sneak away as soon as it's dark. You can't desert me, Ti-Pit, we're in this together . . ."

"No," I said. "You deaf?"

"If you don't come, you'll regret it."

"I can tell you a hiding place, but you won't want it, it's too risky . . ."

"You mean Vincent the priest? Oh no! If the Pope invited me to lunch, I wouldn't go. Christ, you don't know me, Ti-Pit, priests give me the shits. But all the time in my cage, Ti-Pit, I thought about you, I thought we'd team up like when we had our little shack in the woods and shot hares and drank beer, remember? And now you chicken out on me, you're yellow!"

That barbarian couldn't see I didn't like him any more. For his money, swiping Jos Langlois's hat and shooting his head off were all one, he saw no difference between our trip to Percé, when we'd had ourselves a swim while the cops were warming their asses in the sand, and rubbing people out in their sleep. As far as he was concerned, blood and water were the same article. "Maybe," I said, "you're just nuts. Maybe you don't even know you've done anything wrong . . ."

"Shut up!"

Even after he'd disappeared in the darkness, I could hear his damn wheedling in my ears . . . "You'll go to hell with me," he says, "because you'll never be able to rest easy again. Never again, because of me, Ti-Pit, your shadow and brother in suffering . . ." He said he'd come back and carve me up good, he thought he could break me down with threats. "One of these days, or maybe nights, I'll cut your gizzard out," he says. He even followed me into the street. We came to that stinking corner where practically all the garbage cans in town were piled up because the garbage collectors were on strike, and I'm thinking that there, in among the piles of old snow, in among the stink and slop of last week's meals, under the blinking neon eyelids of the Chinese food sign, Ti-Cul would burden his soul with another crime for my benefit. But Ti-Cul held back his dagger. "Christ, Ti-Cul," I tell him. "You're like a salesman selling bottled death . . ." In the end he was scared and ran off into the night, but I was sweating like a pig. So that damn spook would be coming back. Christ, why had I ever been pals with that thug, who was always chucking fire into my quiet copse. "Ti-Cul and Ti-Pit are made of the same stuff, you can't turn shit into honey."

Wherever I went, people were talking about that depressing massacre. Even Vincent asked me about it. "Hey, Ti-Pit, haven't you read about that shocking business? The newspapers are full of it." "I don't have to read about blood and guts," I tell him. "I've got enough with the ambulance." Vincent's room was all painted by then, Ti-Guy went for colors all right, the more the merrier was his idea. "My room is like a garden now," says Vincent. "And Luc is back, still sick of course. Life goes on, that nice social worker is bringing him soup again . . . But you, Ti-Pit, you seem far away. What's on your mind?" "None of your business," I say. "But watch out for that pickpocket of yours, he'll make off with your purse again . . ." "I can't change his nature," says Vincent, "or yours either. And as I see it, what's mine is his. But tell me, have you any news of Ti-Guy?" "I saw him on his bicycle, pretending to be a bird. It wasn't a very promising sight, I assure you." "Why don't you see a little more of him these days?" says Vincent. "Maybe you are a bit too wrapped up in yourself."

Being that he was always up in the sky with his drugs, Ti-Guy was the only one who didn't know that we all have our hands covered with blood. He'd be lying there, flying through the firmament in his sheet. "It's true," he'd murmur. "I've thought about it a lot, if Jesus loves me, why should I worry? Everything is so beautiful . . . if you only knew how beautiful the world has been . . . for the last few days . . ."

"You got religion now? You're not in the desert any more?"

"It's a desert of snow . . . can't you see it? Oh, I'm so happy . . . delivered forever . . . I used to be anxious . . . nobody understood me . . . but that's all over now . . ."

He told me how anxiety had plagued him since the dawn of his existence when he'd seen Père Baptiste leaving for the Rubber Company every morning. The factory was poison, he said, it withered the human spirit. Père Baptiste had spent his whole life licking the dust under other people's boots. "Poor Papa," Ti-Guy sighed. "Poor Papa . . . but what can I do? . . . I don't want to be like him . . ." So he'd escaped from under the parental heel to live all alone as a pilgrim . . . "Blessed are they which do hunger and thirst," he sighed. The wings of famine hadn't caressed him very long, soon he had started feeding on "impalpable, invisible air . . . ah! you see, I lost my appetite for everything else . . ." The habit held him in its clutches, from then on he had seldom left the ethereal mansions. "The earth receded day by day," he said, "and I heard the soft music of heaven . . ." It wasn't just the charlatans' pills that had hollowed him out, it was love, too. From daisy chain to daisy chain, his body was wrapped in cotton. "Ah yes, a balmy pleasure that never ended. Toward morning a whole gang of us went out into the streets. It was snowing. In a lonely church an old priest was saying Mass. Fresh from our orgy, my friends and I took Communion . . ." Another time he said, "No, you can't understand, these states can't be explained . . . You fly away to the arms of Beauty . . . you give yourself to everyone, at every moment, all wickedness is behind you because you love without restraint . . . in the peace of absolute freedom . . . in visionary anarchy . . ." "I see. But this anxiety you were talking about? Why did it come back like a wood-worm?" "I loved . . . I loved too much . . . I had to break away from my body . . . And now I've done it . . . Now I'm free . . ."

I could see this Ti-Guy was off his rocker. I grabbed him by his anemic shoulders and said, "Get up, Christ, get up, don't you see that your dreams are a tomb? Come on home with me, I'll feed you, your bones are sticking out." But he only held me by the hand and said, "Nothing . . . nothing to worry about any more . . . not a wrinkle on the snow . . . nobody will come and wake me saying, 'Help me!' There won't be any-body far away saying, 'I need help!' No . . . nothing . . . silence . . ." It was like holding a handful of ashes. Gyslaine, his girl friend, comes over and says to me, "It's been worse since he saw your friend. Up till then he talked about Anne, now it's Jesus, I think I'd rather have Anne back. Between women there's no harm in a little jealousy, between Jesus and me it's a different problem . . . But don't worry about him, it's no use . . ."

Then Gyslaine read poetry to Ti-Guy, that seemed to quiet him, he'd repeat the lines after her:

"What has become of my heart, that abandoned ship?
What remains of it after the brief storm?
Alas, it has sunk into the seas of Dream."

But misery wasn't my only companion that Christmas season. I went to see Laurence, an old pal that worked for the Spotless Cleaners on rue Saint-Denis. This Laurence had been like a mother to us apprentice gallowsbirds, she sweetened our captivity with towels and handkerchiefs that still smelled of soap. "You'll be out soon," she'd say when she saw us grazing in our pasture. Some of the chums said Laurence had ideas of bedding down with us when we got back to the land of the living. They didn't see that fucking was the least of it and Laurence was something else again. For my money that woman was kindness in person, the salt of my earth.

"Ah, it's you," she says when I take my cap off in her doorway. "Come in, come in, I was beginning to think you'd forgotten me this year . . ." There were three kids. One little boy is doing his homework next to the stove; the other boy is bigger, in the sulky mists of adolescence, "a rude, insulting lout," according to his mother. The girl has torrents of hair front and back. "You sure are a mother, Laurence. Doesn't it get you down, all these puppies underfoot?"

"No, I have no regrets, but it's a hard life sometimes. Come on into the living room, we'll have a little talk."

The two teenagers giggled and peeked at us through the curtain. "Christ," says Laurence, "how many times do I have to tell you that when I have adult company we want to be left alone?" The coals were humming on the grate, the carpet was littered with schoolbooks, still open.

"You sure got family ties," I said. "You know, Laurence, sometimes when I see you with your kids, I get envious, no kidding."

"Children are problems," says Laurence with a sigh, and opens a bottle of whiskey. "This calls for a celebration," she says. "Get about your business, you kids."

"Don't drink too much, M'ma," says the insolent son.

"You're fat enough already," says the daughter.

"What do you think, Ti-Pit? It's true that a woman of forty-five can't hope to be the rose of yesteryear. It shows in the hips. Not that I really go for liquor, it goes for me. Here's to your health and your happiness, Ti-Pit. What do you think, don't I need a husband to keep my chicks out of the vegetable patch? Look at these adolescents, they're too much for me, they pimple, they break out. That's right, kids, what you need is a father, the belt is a great educator."

Here's how that pimply teenager spoke to his mother: "You're nothing but a tramp, M'ma, you sleep with everybody that comes around, my whole school knows it, they're all talking about it, M'ma." "Let 'em talk, son," says Laurence. "Now you've got a chance to prove you're a man, tell 'em your mother's private life is nobody's business, not even God's . . ." The girl was more affectionate, she kissed her mother's tangled hair just where I used to kiss it in the old days, her forehead was shining with sweat and her cheeks were flushed. "You are fat," says the girl, "but I love you all the same. Is it all right if I go to the dance tonight with my chums?" "What dance? Where?" says Laurence. "Oh, you needn't worry. It's at the parish school, the abbé will be there to chaperone us." "Are you sure of that?" "Oh yes, M'ma, and I promise not to let any man take me home in his car like last time . . ." "I hope not," says Laurence. "I don't like to see you all alone in a car with a man pulling up your skirt, I don't like it at all . . . it's not right . . ." "Yes, but you've taught me how to keep from having babies, M'ma, there's nothing to be afraid of, you know . . ." "That's no excuse," says Laurence, "I don't want you doing that again . . . I try to bring you kids up right, I live only for you but I expect a little respect in return . . ." "You're right, M'ma, I honor and obey you, okay, but can I go to the dance?"

"On condition that you come home before midnight."

"Oh yes, M'ma, I swear I will."

"Last time you swore by all the saints and I heard you slipping your shoes off at 3 a.m."

"This time I promise, M'ma. Because I know you love us and I don't want to make you feel bad."

"Don't try to wheedle me, little girl, I know you!"

Laurence told me that children nowadays talk too free and easy to their parents, they don't sit and dream in the sunset the way they used to, "there's no such thing as childhood any more. This young adolescent, for instance, takes his girl to his room, and he thinks I don't know it. To think that they know all about orgasms, etc., at their age, why, I was at least twenty-five before I unveiled the statue of my first man." "Yes," I said, "but you weren't bashful after that!" "So what, I was only making up for lost time. All the same, I think these kids overdo it, they're in too much of a hurry, it worries me, as a mother, I mean. At the age of twelve, for instance, they decide they're atheists, really, I ask you, and at thirteen they think it's time to lose their virginity. They do it because it's on the program, that's what worries me. Fortunately, my youngest is still learning his catechism. It's not that I'm in love with Catholicism and all that, but it gives them certain principles, after all I don't want them to turn into delinquents. I've seen too many and they're too unhappy. But you, Ti-Pit, how are you getting along? Still at the Rubber Company?" "No, I was fed up." "So you're just bumming around. Don't you ever think of getting married? Oh well, you're still young. At your age I didn't think of it either, but now with these hungry bunnies on my hands . . ." "Isn't there some star satelliting around you? Some steadfast knight?" "No, steadfast he's not, but he's nice-looking, an Italian waiter. He has a gift for romance and acrobatics in bed, but the idea of marriage depresses him, especially with this gang of mine. Try and find a lover bold enough to foist this crew on himself, especially Roger, that's the eldest, he's so persnickety . . . he's first in his football league, if only his tongue weren't so sharp . . . It's his precocious sex life, that's what I think, Ti-Pit, all that juice they lose, it knocks them out. To think that last winter I'd been saving up to buy him an electric train and then, right under my window in the dark, I catch him at it with a girl . . . It's food for thought, you know. We mothers don't have the same place in life as we used to, because we haven't the same children, actually we haven't got children at all . . ." "You mean," I said, "that you're all alone with middle age coming on?" "No, it's not that. The children put life into the shack, they bring home friends to eat and sleep and all that, they make music, you know how it is, but they don't seem to be my kind even if I did spawn them, there's no one to talk to, the women in the neighborhood don't fuck right and left the way I did in my springtime, they're all respectable ladies with big fat husbands who kiss them goodbye every morning outside the garage door, but nowadays, I suppose you've noticed, the bottle means more to me than bed, it's better company. When you get to be my age, you begin to think that life is pressing in on you from all sides, that's why you go conventional and start thinking about somebody to protect you, he wouldn't even need to be very attractive, ever since I was born I've been protecting other people, now I'm tired . . ." "That's the truth," I said. "In prison you laundered and fondled us . . ." "But what's become of your friend Ti-Cul? You remember the way they used to stick him in solitary now and then? Ah! That was some more of the world's injustice. Tell me, why were they always punishing him?" "Because he went on hunger strikes," I told her. "He was always ready to mutiny, the wardens didn't like that." "And now he's in jail again?" "Yes, I guess so." Laurence poked the coals. I had the shivers for fear she'd suspect about Ti-Cul, but she didn't read the papers any more, she told me. "I haven't got time with my little scamps. Who'd have thought I'd get to be a big fat mother like all the rest of them? Take you, Ti-Pit, you remember the days of my passions and frolics, you can see that I've lost my glamour for you young guys, I've lost interest in sleeping around, all I want is a friend . . . somebody as solid as marble. See what I mean?" "Yes," I said. "Maybe a friend'll turn up someday, but they're harder to come by than money." "I haven't given up," she says. So we parted as usual on a note of comfort, telling each other that the downgrade would be easier going.

I was escalating into the subway when I see Papillon, more agitated than ever, tagging after his pal, the lawyer from Quebec. "Lordship of Quebec," he cackles, "would you look at that? In all our underground thoroughfares, nothing but *Y, The Story of Y.* It's a scandal. Robbing poor Papillon of the only triumph of his career . . . You'd better repent, *mon cher,* or I'll sue you . . ." "Calm down," says the lawyer from Quebec, "my intentions toward our little Y are strictly honorable, and after all you were only the seed-planting ram, not her father . . ." "No, you don't!" says Papillon, "I'm the father, I had the bump of genius, all you had was the businessman's concavity, the pit where the dollars fall . . . Ah, villain of Quebec, is it true you've squeezed ten thousand dollars out of her in these few days?" "Definitely," says the lawyer from Quebec, as smug as you please. "But don't worry about your future, Papillon, you'll help me to administer my New Era Home for Derelicts, that's where I'm investing the money, you see, it will be the pride of all future generations . . ." "What are you talking about, Lordship of Quebec, what kind of a home? A welfare hotel? Christ, you're crazy!" "Not at all," says the lawyer from Quebec. "Like most men I am impure, though I don't look it, but sometimes I get these philanthropic impulses and I'm determined to establish a haven for derelicts in distress, I've already discussed my plans with an architect friend, like my derelicts a lover of pubs, we're thinking of a hostelry with inclined, undulating forms, something like the Tower of Pisa, regular proportions might upset our guests, they lean to the blurred and confused . . . The sheets on the beds will be of all colors, as flamboyant as flags, the better to dream in, there will be enormous refrigerators replete with beer, a perpetual banquet for my derelicts. Ah, Papillon, if you weren't so perverted, so gone on motorcars, you'd understand my noble sentiments; what am I after all but a millionaire cenobite, is it my fault if I have to guarantee the future of my wife and children for the next twenty years at least? But in spite of all that, the impulse comes over me, I dream of wearing a monk's robe . . ."

"But what about me, you goddamned monk? What becomes of my dreams in all this? I've been dreaming of a new Cadillac." "You'll have it soon, Papillon. Say, did you know that the authorship of *Y* is still unknown? They think it was written by a schoolboy in short pants. I'll read you the reviews while drinking your health, Papillon."

"I am her father and her lover," says Papillon to his lawyer from Quebec. "I have held Y in my arms and enshrined her in my heart." Then the inspired old, punching bag finally recognizes my mug and says, "Join our cavalcade, brother Lemieux, we're going to pop a champagne cork to celebrate the approach of Christmas . . ." Already the subway like an enormous lung was exhaling "Christian Midnight" and "Angels in Our Villages," a ragout of pagan hymns that would have sent Vincent up the wall, but I liked it all right, even if the lawyer from Quebec proclaimed in his pomposity, "There you can see how sad people have become. Ah, sinister epoch that wallows in syrup and soap opera!" What he didn't realize, it seemed to me, was that the light on the horizon and the sound of crystal in paper trees makes people dream, especially when they're not very bright.

We went to the Queen of Clubs bar. Papillon was still wailing about his Cadillac. "I want it for New Year's in my manger, between the ox and the ass, understand? With our hard winters, my once Herculean car is on its last legs, it groans in every joint, the starter wheezes, the lights go out, the brakes fail me." In addition, Papillon accuses his chum of "deflowering my little Y while I was struggling through the brambles of my *Irreversible Moon,* that was a treacherous thing to do, considering we've known each other since our Jesuit days. Yes, I have to admit, I feel mortified . . ."

"Let me read you this, Papillon. As Y's parents, we're entitled to these testimonials of admiration. This is what you might have read yesterday morning in *Free Choice* magazine:

" '*The Story of Y,* signed "An Anonymous Moralist" (we have as yet been unable to identify the author with certainty), possesses unquestionable literary merit

. . . It is a novel of heady freshness, a daring fairy tale for all!' And here's what the *Mystical Review* has to say:

" 'In this sensitively written book we cannot fail to see that the sphere of the soul takes precedence over the lower sphere of the flesh. Though the subject matter is occasionally repugnant (the love affair of a child with an elderly priest; how revolting! we know that such a thing could never happen in our country), the author never succumbs to vulgarity. On the contrary, he employs a profoundly religious terminology, and the martyrdom of Y, struggling against the embraces of her tormentor, evokes the sufferings of each one of us on the cross of desire.' "

"Well," says Papillon, "if the style is so 'profoundly religious' that a rape becomes a fable and a lecherous priest comes off looking like an honest man, where's the sense in your little sexual fairy tale? If you ask me, the whole thing is a lot of wasted sperm."

"But that's life in a nutshell," says the lawyer from Quebec.

THEN WITH the champagne bubbling in our beakers, Papillon goes mournful, lamenting that his Jacqueline was wandering again.

"The poor little love bird," he says, "I understand her less and less. And now I'm jealous. Do you know why, Lordship of Quebec? Because she's taken to stealing my political causes. It used to be me that poured out his heart to the Joualonese people, but now she's taken over . . . She shines in their midst like a new emblem of victory. 'Sisters, brothers, friends,' she cries out, 'let us unite . . .' A tremor passes over the multitude. A woman's wingbeat and blessing has touched them, they listen with bated breath, they hug and kiss each other, even the *profanum vulgus* is awake to her feminine charisma . . . Oh, I'm so unhappy!"

"Write, Papillon, that's your trade."

"Yes, but listen. I wrote a little masterpiece in Joualonese; it was so pure it almost stank. I thought, My compatriots will recognize themselves in this. I'd spoken like the man in the street, the woman of the sidewalks, the child on his scooter, dispelling the symbolic and rural shadow of Maria Chapdelaine. What happens? Once again I was bitterly attacked, *mon cher,* the critics said I didn't understand the Joualonese soul, can you imagine, me not understanding my Joualonese brothers! . . . that was in *Babble and Destroy* magazine; my muse has been suffering torments ever since . . ."

"They think you're not Joualonese enough?"

"They say the perfection of this subtle tongue escapes me."

"Don't be discouraged, Papillon. You've got to be more Joualonese than the Joualonese. That's the secret.

We're blithely sipping our nectar when who comes along but that skinny Militant Youth bastard, that pilgrim of the subway corridors. He shoves a leaflet under our nose, hisses "Stinking bourgeois cruds!" and splits. Papillon and his shadow from Quebec throw themselves on the leaflet, it bowls them over. Papillon starts to yell, "Look at that, Lordship of Quebec, the wretched of the earth, the assholes, are throwing a Christmas demonstration, say, maybe this derelicts' paradise of yours wasn't such a bad idea . . . We've got to be there, we, the intellectuals and burblers of the thinking class. What do you say? What an opportunity to speak to my people . . ."

"I'm sorry, Papillon. I shall be spending Christmas with my family, with my wife, my dogs, my children. I stand for law and order, I love my wife and children."

"Christ, you're nothing but a Pharisee with clean socks and smelly feet. I'm ashamed of you, look at Lemieux here, a true asshole if there ever was one, he'll be there. Why, this will be the apotheosis of my mute people so long condemned to silence, the vagabond in search of his roots will find his voice, you think I'd walk out on Lemieux and his comrades for the sake of three Christmas Masses and a turkey leg?"

"A poet needs experience," says the lawyer from Quebec dryly. "There's sure to be trouble, Papillon, I prefer not to be there. When the tempest subsides, I shall be present to defend the humble."

"Christ," says Papillon. "You don't deserve to be a Joualonese!"

I read the leaflet too, the assholes were rumbling with anger, sounded almost like Ti-Cul, hand in hand they'd march "through the long night of injustice," that's what they wrote. It looked like red-hot rebellion and the national constabulary threatened to reeducate the sons of the people if they went too far, a platoon for every asshole, they suggested—why not, who ever heard of agitating down the boulevards when the good folk were getting ready for the virgin delivery of Christ? But never mind. The assholes, the little people who'd always lived like moles in their hovels and kept their mouths shut, would be marching by the thousands and Papillon was fixing to join them. "What a grandiose tempest for Christmas!" he cries out. "Our Joualonie is waking at last, what about you, Lemieux?"

"It's none of your business if I'm waking or not!"

"Say, aren't you edgy! I bet it's that horrible massacre that's got you stirred up . . . escaped convicts it seems, they haven't been caught yet . . . a hideous crime . . . we all know that, but sometimes it's that touch of infamy that rouses the consciousness of the poor and downtrodden . . . You see, Lemieux, sometimes good springs from evil."

"No good ever came of a crime like that," says the lawyer from Quebec.

"Right," I said with my eye on the lawyer from Quebec. "It was just plain stinking murder."

"There are thousands of Langloises in our midst," says the lawyer. "Probably each one of them is thinking, Those thugs could have knocked at my door, my own family could have been exterminated just as gratuitously and irrationally. That's the kind of thoughts such a disaster should inspire, Papillon."

But Papillon was still up in arms.

"You make me sick, Lordship of Quebec, you're only a damn paterfamilias that wants to protect his home. The law of your heart is: Everything for my little darlings. My idea is that maybe this crime was necessary in its way, those rebels are our own people, impetuous Lemieux's, how do I know? Has it never occurred to you, Lordship, that if someone had spoken to them, if someone had treated them like human beings, this disaster might have been avoided?"

"I doubt it," says the lawyer from Quebec. "It's not so simple."

"Ah, if they'd had a spark of pride in their Joualonie, in you, in me, in themselves, their rebellion would have taken another form. They'd have marched in the van of all men of good will, holding high the banner . . ."

"You're dreaming," says the lawyer from Quebec. "If you were awake, you'd pity the victims of violence."

WHITE CHRISTMAS! Long ago, when Ti-Cul and me were at the bottom of the pit, we'd hear the sleigh bells tinkling around our prison. Ti-Cul had feelings in those days, he wallowed in visions, in dreams of sleighs and snow, but for us it was dungeon time, the princes had sent us a box of goodies, the guys in death row were smoking Players cigarettes by the mouthful, we didn't get many visits, there was always this weeping mother that came to tongue-lash her son. "You goddamn thieving adventurer, sweet Jesus, why should this happen to me, what have I done, I dedicated you to St. Theresa when you were born and this is how you repay the blessings of your religion!" But Laurence would come in smiling with her turned-up tits, taking a package and a kiss and a kind word from barred door to barred door. "You'll be out this year, don't forget . . ." And now Ti-Cul was out in the fresh air but laden with malediction, he'd have gall and wormwood for Christmas. Maybe he'd set sail for the States the way he'd told me, maybe he'd hole up in some godforsaken corner of the woods, same difference, he was through. Meanwhile, the lawyer from Quebec would be brandishing his electric carving knife at the head of a table overflowing with a fifteen-dollar ham, a crispy turkey, and wine. "Let us eat and be happy," he'd say to his brats, "but let us not forget that many people on this earth are less fortunate, you are priv-ileged children and don't forget it . . ." Mrs. Lawyer from Quebec would cling tenderly to her husband's arm, her delighted chickabiddies would cling to her skirts, oh how lovely it would be! Under the gold-spangled tree, her heart and nose told her, there would be new and unheard-of vegetable peelers, a no-wind Eternity watch, runproof panty hose, etc. . . .

"What are you thinking about, Lordship of Quebec? The shadow of gloom has descended on your brow."

"I was thinking of my happiness," says the lawyer from Quebec.

Ah, he tells us, wouldn't his gadget-happy wife and little snotnoses be surprised if only he had the nerve to bring a crowd of his derelicts home for midnight punch. Ah, he could see it all, those hairy, grimy hands on the pink-flowered tablecloth, the ham snatched away by cannibals, the effluvia of those beggars sprawled in the armchairs, his brats standing around making faces. But in the end he changed his mind. "No, to take them to my home would be to insult them."

At that point Papillon told us he'd be going next morning to Utopia House, that was his name for the loony bin, where a chum and fellow poet was vacationing. "He went off his nut, *mon cher*, and you know why, Lordship of Quebec, no, you're too materialistic and thick. My friend Oscar used to be a poet, the adventure of words laid him low. Poor Oscar Joyeux, he was so brillaint, it's very sad."

"I know," says the lawyer from Quebec. "Words, like money, are a peril to weak minds."

"Stop right there! A little respect for my friend! Oscar Joyeux was a thinker, a scientist of the word, hasn't a man a right to invent his own language? Wherever he went, he sanctified the Word, glorified his incomprehensible language, his alarming dialect. At the age of eighteen he recited:

> *"Edora branch of aloes boom boom*
> *Maiden claws dogmeal doo doo*
> *White masturbated zither yoo yooey!*
> *Apple of memory . . ."*

"How did he make out at twenty-five?"

"None of your mockery, Lordship of Quebec, let us not mock a solitary seeker who lost his way . . .

Heaven bless you, Oscar Joyeux, you who wrote and spontaneously declaimed these verses one night from a seventh-floor window of the Hotel Windsor:

> *"My echo my birthday dusho dish mia,*
> *Lr . . . Loor . . . outside your retina is watching me*
> *Monster crawling' in the barley cricri noowa*
> *Haunting Humb oopt decomposed brain*
> *Silken indoumgrieffiellel.*

"Of course you'd have to hear him do it," says Papillon, "it's a sigh rising from the entrails of a cave, it's the singing grass . . ."

"Yes," says the lawyer from Quebec. "I understand . . ." And he took another swig of champagne to wash it down.

"So you see," says Papillon, still in high gear, "tomorrow he's going to read me his works and I'll read him mine. We'll smoke a cigar together, and then poor Oscar Joyeux will return to his solitude . . ."

He went on to tell us that his chum Oscar Joyeux spent his time at the Transcendental Meditation hostel getting up a scrapbook on the deceased of the year 1925, that was his obsession, he'd cut out old newspapers and scribble epitaphs:

> *I mourn for Paul-Marie Gagné,*
> *Baptized and deceased on July 5, 1925*
> *At the age of two days.*
> *Smallpox strikes where it will*
> *And God reaps His harvest. Amen.*

And further down the page:

> *I sigh for the soul of Onézime Miton,*
> *Deceased in the dawn of his eighty-eighth year—*
> *He died on his feet one night while shoveling snow—*
> *And for his Lucie Miton, eighty-eight,*
> *Who died of sorrow in the same night.*
> *God taketh away but God forgiveth. Amen.*

"Yes, indeed," says Papillon, "my charming Oscar is really haunted by death, he's even asked me to cut all the death notices out of the papers for him . . ."

Listening to Papillon, I said to myself, What a lunatic won't think of next. It seems this feverish idea man,
this Oscar, had built a miniature city out of cardboard
in his bats-in-the-belfry cell. "There were streets and
stores, a church and a hospital," says Papillon. "Every
comfort for the deceased of 1925. Besides, he had a
map marked with red dots to show where each of his
protégés lived."

When Papillon asked him why he'd chosen to build
for the dead, Oscar answered, "They're better off with
me than in the ground with the worms. Anything could
happen to them down there, all those contagious diseases, maybe even the Spanish flu. But think of all
those other years that are still waiting for me. It's
enough to drive me mad. Luckily, Papillon, I've kept
my sanity, I can say to my friends of 1925:

> *"You are in purgatory, my friends, my reeds*
> *Zoom . . . zoom . . . dilated pupils . . . tr . . . yes true.*
> *The fire is going out*
> *Children beneath the heel of the Ogre God*
> *Duk . . . duk . . . dub little doggies . . .*

" 'You see,' said Oscar as I nodded in approval, 'I
speak to them like human beings and it does them
good. They fall asleep like water lilies in the gentle
summer breeze . . .' "

I said to myself, They're better off than us guys that
stay awake, all we've got to plunge into is a pool of
beer at the tavern, we can't flirt with the water lilies
or sound off oracles like Oscar Joyeux, it wouldn't go
down. And then I remembered a young hayseed my
age, we called him Ti-Foin because the hay stuck out of
his ears. He had feet like an ape, if he'd climbed on
the table to eat nobody'd have been surprised. His
shoulders were so big you could see him a mile away,
but he was fragile underneath, the move from the
sticks to Montreal turned him inside out and he took
to drink, not wine or whisky, only beer, he sloshed
down Molson's till it came back up at him, he couldn't
stop the flow in either direction. One time he lay down

to sleep in the middle of Sherbrooke Avenue, that's when Vincent gathered him in. We took him up the spiral staircase, Vincent on one side, me on the other.

"You ought to be ashamed," says Vincent.

"Why?" says Ti-Foin. "I'm lost. The city ain't for me. But I gotta make money for my ma. And, holy tabernacle, making money is corruption!"

"Is your mother very old?"

"Sixty, but a woman's through at that age on the farm. Had too many kids, beginning with me . . ."

"Go to bed and sleep," says Vincent, "we'll talk in the morning." But our hayseed wouldn't buy that. "No! No! No!" he said. "I wanna talk to you tonight, 'cause you're a man. I've never talked to anybody except the trees and my father's dog. Gimme a beer, drink with me, then you can go to bed, not before." Vincent said he couldn't "encourage a drunkard in his vice by drinking with him," but Ti-Foin was adamant. "No, damn it no, I won't sleep till you drink with me."

Vincent looks my way and says, "Bring us three beers, Ti-Pit." He's in a wicked humor.

"What about your principles?" I ask him.

"Never mind. My principles are my business."

We drank our beer. Ti-Foin was so stewed he was wobbling on his chair. "Well?" says Vincent. "You wanted to talk. Talk, my friend . . ."

"Thass right, wanna talk to you . . . I sure wanna talk!"

"About what?" Vincent asks.

"Gotta drink some more, I ain't got no words, see?"

"You won't get them by drinking . . . you must have some language . . . what did you say, for instance, when you talked to your father's dog?"

"Well . . . I said, We're going to get to hell out of here, it ain't no life, we ain't like other people, we're going to the big city of Montreal and have fun. I didn't know I'd be scrubbing down trains, I didn't know a damn thing . . ."

"What else did you say to your dog?"

"Nothing, you don't have to say much to a critter. And that dog was like me, a lone guy . . ."

"Haven't you any friends in town?"

"I ain't got nothing, I tell you."

"What about your brothers and sisters?"

"Still at home, nobody can talk to them creeps, all they can do is pester my mother, they all holler and shit in the same room. I had to breathe the air of the world, I couldn't suffocate with them fleabags forever! Okay, but now I want to talk to you like a man . . ."

Vincent was getting impatient. "Then talk like a man," he says. "I'm listening, speak up. Maybe I could help if I knew what was eating you, what was tearing at your soul; but this way . . . you just sit there like a clod . . ."

At that exact moment Ti-Foin falls on the floor like a load of bricks. You don't hear sobs like that very often, they were like a waterfall. "I ain't got no words," the guy kept saying, "thass my trouble, I ain't got no words . . ." Vincent and me put ice on his head to change the record, but he went on saying, "I ain't got no words, they didn't give me none . . ." And Vincent says to me, "We'll need two wet towels, we'll be nurses tonight, Ti-Pit, but it goes to show you how long people can suffer without being able to tell anybody about it . . ."

I'M STILL deep in my memories of Ti-Foin and Vincent when Papillon starts telling us about the times they let him take his chum Oscar out of the loony bin for a twenty-four-hour visit to the sane world, as some people call it . . . "It was a ticklish business," says Papillon. "Once we stopped at a bar for a sandwich. Oscar started right in on the barmaid. 'Betrothed of pole and prairie,' he said. 'Have you any sunflower salad? It grows in the sun of night, during the callaloon, ah yes, in the season of wet sand.'

" 'With or without pickles?' says the barmaid.

" 'With.'

" 'Vinegar?'

" 'I recognize you,' says Oscar. 'Wilting on your stem, but fragrant as a broiled rattlesnake on a hot morning . . . What's your name?'

" 'Fanny Dutremble.'

" 'I can't see if your fanny is trembling,' says the

imperturbable Oscar, 'but your blouse is staggering. Put in a few walnuts, if you please.'

" 'We don't usually put walnuts in an egg salad.'

" 'Sunflower salad, I said.'

" 'I never heard of sunflowers, but I suppose that's what you mean, because you look educated.'

" 'So much so, Fanny Dutremble, that you'll trip over the crack in the top of my head if you don't watch out.'

" 'French fried or boiled?'

" 'No matter, provided they were planted under the pole star, I am herbivorous by nature.'

" 'I see . . .'

" 'Have you any asparagus? I only like it, listen carefully now, when the foxes bring it to me between their teeth . . .'

" 'We have no asparagus, monsieur, only a tomcat.'

" 'Bring me the cat, Fanny, I'll marry you tonight with your hair rolling on the brink of the precipice, it's near the Lovlavla Peninsula, you know, if you like Siberia, come . . .' "

The girl came back with the sunflower salad and the big tom and Papillon said to his chum, "Eat the sunflowers, but the cat is to pet, understand?" "No, my friend," says Oscar, "it's the opposite. Cabbage with cat is more digestible than sunflower seeds, which becloud the left intestine with clarity."

"Yes," says Papillon, "when those lyrical pearls of his fell to the ground, they made quite a clatter. And he didn't care who he spoke to, cop, priest, or lady. One time he sees a priest with his crucifix on his way to somebody's death bed. He goes up to him and says, 'How lovely to see you, Monsieur le Curé! Whom are you going to succor today, great castrator of the light?'

" 'Let me pass, my son, an unfortunate is expecting me for his last rites . . . Let me pass, I say, what's the matter with you, my good man?'

"But Oscar didn't crack so easy. He went right on 'The sacrament of death! You mustn't do it, Monsieur le Curé, The Lord said, "Thou shalt catch the star as it falls upon the wave." I hear your dead fish weeping in your coffers laden with the fruits of avarice.'

" 'What! Go away! Go away!'

" 'The Lord said, "And the fruits of desolation are bald and odorless . . ." '

" 'He never said any such thing. Get thee behind me, Satan!' "

Papillon wanted to apologize to the priest, but he couldn't say straight out, "I beg your pardon, my friend is mad." "No, I had to choose my words carefully. When I'd run out of smiles and gestures, I said, 'You must forgive my friend . . . he's a little . . . a little . . . hmm . . .' But Oscar came right back at me with: 'What! are you suggesting that I'm slightly cracked? Is that what you mean to intimate with your smirks and signs?' 'No, not at all, nothing of the kind . . . I wouldn't dare, you're an artist, hence slightly eccentric, that's all I meant to say.' That mollified him. 'Oh,' he says. 'It's just that sometimes you seem to think I'm crazy. But of course you'd tell me if I were, wouldn't you? You'd be frank with me, Papillon, wouldn't you?' 'Of course I would, Oscar.' 'Oh, thank you, you're a real friend. Because, you see, it would be dreadful if I began to lose my mind . . .' But a minute later he saw a gang of schoolboys coming out of school and he started right in again. 'Good afternoon, my little friends, what have you eaten today on the benches of sorrow?'

" 'The alphabet. We wrote our names all by ourselves.'

" 'Really?'

" 'What about you? What have you been eating?'

" 'Cat, with my friend Papillon. An alley cat by the name of Tommy, a rare species. I wanted to be like Puss in Boots, the better to understand you.'

" 'Who's Puss in Boots?'

" 'Me,' says Oscar. 'See my wispy mustache . . .'

" 'Go on! You're nuts . . . cat's indigestible . . . if you're all that hungry, try little kittens. I've got some, you can have them. One has yellow stripes, the other's all gray. But they won't like it if you eat them.'

" 'You can keep your kittens, there's a whole family of them in the tree of my head. Puss in Boots always has cats in his stocking, that's a proverb.'

" 'Do you like mice too? We've got some in our ice-box.'

" 'No, because their backs are shaped like bows . . . and I feel sorry for them. When the mouse nibbles at the wall, the cold will soon set in, says the proverb.'

" 'What about birds? Do you eat birds?'

" 'Without wings they'd get dizzy, don't forget that. Puss in Boots eats only leather. Birds are not for my stomach but for my aviary, which is in heaven. Good-bye, little friends . . .' "

Maybe, I said to myself, Papillon's Oscar is awake and the rest of us are asleep, walking under a vault of dreams. He saw his phantoms and climbed the stairs of delirium in broad daylight; it happened to me at night. I saw the ghost of Ti-Cul, swimming in the blue cove at Percé. We were diving off an enormous blood-colored rock, the sky was sharp and clear. Ti-Cul yelled at me, "Hey, look, Ti-Pit, you damn yellow-belly, look how high I'm diving from, I'm not afraid." He dove all right, but he didn't come up out of the black water. "Ti-Cul!" I yelled. "You coming?"

No, he wasn't coming, he'd escaped down below, it was all over, nothing there but water gurgling its way to the ocean. And sometimes the lousy hypocrite would appear in his first-Communion armband; all in white from top to toe, he'd be waiting for me at the street corner. "You got me wrong, Ti-Pit," he'd say with a sneaky smile, "look at me, I'm as white as snow, I'm even going to Communion just to please you . . ." "Where? In what church? It's closed at this time of night . . ." Then we'd be inside the church, in the dim light, Ti-Cul would be down on his knees praying, the bastard, but all of a sudden he'd get up and I'd see him stealing the lamps and gold vessels. "So now you come here to steal," I'd say. "Sure thing, it's food for my soul!" "Ti-Cul, you're a monster. And say, where'd you leave the Langloises, are they still lying in the mud and snow?"

"Don't you worry, Ti-Pit, they'll rise again someday, I promise."

Then I'd ask Ti-Cul, "While those poor bastards

were bleeding their lives out, did you comfort them at least?"

"Sure," says Ti-Cul. "I know my duties, I comforted them, I told them stories, I'm not a monster, Ti-Pit, you got me wrong."

"What did you tell them?"

"Everything the brothers taught me, Ti-Pit, I told them the angels and archangels would keep them company forever, I did my best to cheer them up, they needed it, do you think those big bruisers wanted to fade away quiet, without any back talk, hell no! One of them watched the blood trickling down his legs and said to me, 'Save me, Ti-Cul, save me, I'll treat you better, I promise, I'll give you everything I have, don't finish me off, if I've offended you, brother, forgive me!' Then he starts laughing, he explodes, the laughs come out of him like a thundering torrent. 'Did you hear that, Ti-Pit, the Langloises begging me for forgiveness, wasn't that something? Too bad you missed it . . . and all to save their no-good stinking lives.'"

Then I remembered I was champagning with Papillon and his lawyer from Quebec, and Ti-Cul crumbled away like a ragged marionette. After the third glass the subway passage was all red and the passing shapes were floating in liquid. We left the Queen of Clubs, and Papillon burbled, "Patriots of Joualonie, arise!" We see some ladies bent under the yoke of their Christmas shopping, breathless and flushed in their beaver-skin hats, and Papillon goes up to them. "Beg your pardon, Madame Whatever, permit me to draw attention to this manifesto summoning us one and all to participate in jubilation and revolt."

"What! Another demonstration?"

"An appeal, madame, to you and all the assholes of Joualonie, that is, I mean, to our whole valiant and industrious people . . ."

"I am not an asshole," says the lady.

"Of course not, I can see that, I beg your pardon, madame, but will you come?"

"Never!" said Madame Whatever, mortally offended.

She left us, and the lawyer from Quebec says to Papillon, "You see, Papillon, you don't know how to talk to people, you don't understand them. That woman's only thought is to go home and pop her Christmas ham in the oven, and you in your boorishness assault her with your leaflet, that's moral rape."

Who do we run into next, painting stars on the subway wall in an ecstasy of artistic creation, but Ti-Guy himself in his rainbow outfit, with strings of beads around his neck and joy in his heart.

"Hey, Ti-Guy! Good to see you out! Given up your medicine?"

"No, but I'm well now, no more body. Night of peace, night of love . . . I'm happy . . ."

"Did you get permission from the mayor of Joualonie to decorate the subway so flamboyantly?" the lawyer from Quebec asks him.

"No," says Ti-Guy. "I forgot. But our mayor is a good man, I'm sure he'd have given me permission . . ."

"I can't stomach the man," says Papillon. "I dislike him intensely."

"You don't like anybody," says the lawyer from Quebec. "That's common knowledge."

"What can I do? It's a question of character. I don't like his character and he doesn't like mine."

"The poet and the tyrant are seldom good bedfellows. Nevertheless, I maintain that the mayor of Joualonie loves the arts and that you, Papillon, are being unjust."

"Night of peace, night of love," says Ti-Guy. "We must all love each other. Ah, my friends, let me embrace you . . ."

"Gladly," says Papillon, and quick he pours himself into Ti-Guy's arms. The lawyer from Quebec was more reserved, he shakes Ti-Guy's hand and says in a fatherly tone, "You're a little too high, my friend. You won't feel so good when you wake up."

"I'll never wake up," says Ti-Guy, "except very soon in the bosom of Jesus Christ."

"Aren't you afraid his bosom might be cold and hard?" asks the lawyer from Quebec.

"They say it's as soft as swan's-down," says Ti-Guy, fixing his bleary eyes on the celestial bosom.

"Lucky for you," says the lawyer from Quebec.

"I have a confession to make," says Papillon to Ti-Guy. "I have a weakness for lambs. Couldn't you put a few lambkins in your fresco for me?"

"Of course," says Ti-Guy and draws a mess of triangles. He draws, he erases, he corrects, he ties himself up in his mysteries, but no sign of a lamb.

"There you are!" says Ti-Guy. "Do you see them? There behind the hedge, three black sheep and one white one."

"I don't see them," says the lawyer from Quebec.

"Of course you do," says Ti-Guy, "right there next to the three kings, but, you see, the form is secret. I'm an abstract painter, because that's how I see life . . . Or rather, I don't see it, it sees me, it transfixes me . . . I feel it . . . the unbounded totality . . . ah, if you only knew . . . it's wonderful!"

"I don't see any kings either," says Papillon sadly.

"But they're there," says Ti-Guy. "It's because you haven't got the eye . . ."

"Possibly," says Papillon humbly, "but ordinarily, being a Sunday painter myself, I see more than I am . . ."

"You need the diaphanous eye," says Ti-Guy. "It's hidden under the forehead" (he touched Papillon's bulging forehead), "you see, monsieur, that's your sixth eye, through that eye the wound passes and in it time stops."

"I usually keep it closed," says Papillon. "Don't you?"

"No," says Ti-Guy. "I have to keep it open, because that's where death enters."

In that case, says Papillon, who had a thing about life, he preferred to keep it closed. He was shaken. But then he pulls himself together and says to Ti-Guy in a tone of manly vigor, "How about it, brother? Coming to the demonstration? Every intelligent young man and woman in Joualonie will be there, all those who have a sense of beauty and justice like you, all those who aspire to live in an independent Joualonie, do you hear me, brother? Will you be there?"

"I don't think so," says Ti-Guy.

"Why not? At your age a man is like the wind, he

goes everywhere, proudly singing the song of his ideal. You've got to come."

"He's all ideal, that's the whole trouble," says the lawyer from Quebec. "You understand nothing, Papillon."

"Shut up, Lordship of Quebec. We know all about your infinite wisdom." Then, tapping Ti-Guy on his hollow shoulder, "Tell me, brother. Is it a girl friend who detains you in her bed? That I understand. But otherwise you'd be with us, wouldn't you?"

"I don't think so," says Ti-Guy. "My ties are not here."

"What do you mean, not here? Go on, it's not normal to talk like that. You can be your own master someday like every other Joualonese, master of your fate. Ah, what a dream we are on the point of fulfilling!"

"I have no ties anywhere," says Ti-Guy, "and soon I shall be walking the pathways of humility and meekness . . ."

"Look here, brother, you're not going to bury your fine young manhood in a seminary? You can't!"

"It's something like that," says Ti-Guy.

"But don't you realize that it isn't done any more . . . The seminarians are on strike . . . are you sick or what? Believe me, that stuff is pure crap, you break my heart!"

"But Jesus said: Blessed are they that mourn," says Ti-Guy. "Once the threshold of infinity is behind us, everything is all right . . ."

He's still painting away with his twinkling palette and his brushes, barely touching the cement floor with the tips of his toes. Papillon was getting discouraged, how could you talk to a bird like that? "Oh well," he says, "it's up to you, brother, to decide whether you love your people or not, but I thought this festival of Joualonese love and solidarity would attract you. I didn't realize that your ties were elsewhere . . . So long, brother. Merry Christmas all the same!"

"Embrace me!" says Ti-Guy. "Who knows? Maybe we won't be seeing each other again . . . maybe not for several years . . . and the years are dark . . . darker and darker . . ."

This time it was the lawyer from Quebec who bent his frame to embrace Ti-Guy and whisper in his ear, "This will end in tragedy, my friend . . ." but Ti-Guy didn't get his point.

Then all of a sudden we hear a woman's voice fluttering with frivolity. "Embrace me too!"

"Eglantine!" cries Papillon. "I sensed your presence, my true and eminently bourgeois friend, you have lifted the dark cloud that was beginning to weigh on us all. Have you been shopping?"

"For my mother and my aunt in Quebec," says Eglantine. "I never forget my aunt."

"Because of herself or the money you hope to inherit?"

"Both, my love, both."

"Is your aunt well?"

"She's failing," says Eglantine. "The burden of the years . . ."

"Don't tell me you've bought her another rosary, Eglantine."

"That's what she always asks for, Eloi, what can I do? But this time the beads are pure ivory. I think she'll be touched. Poor auntie, she's sinking fast . . ."

So now Papillon had Eglantine around his neck like a fur collar; it looked like he'd be buying her some more champagne at the Queen of Clubs. The lawyer from Quebec was looking down at his fur-lined boots, deep in thought; suddenly he starts walking fast, he's got his train to catch, the brats and their mummy were waiting for him, he was caught like a fish hook. So I trim my sails for Mère Fontaine and our crowd, Mimi, Ti-Paul, etc., it made my brains tingle just to think of them. I figured that Ti-Paul had set up the tree in the kitchen and Mimi would be putting up the decorations. All the way back to my boardinghouse reunion I could hear Ti-Guy's mournful song behind me:

> Night of peace, night of love,
> Farewell my friends of the dark years.
> The dark years are coming,
> Night of peace . . . night of love . . .

6.

THE ARMIES of assholes had spread their sails. At first the procession moved quietly along under our windows, with measured tread. It was snowing softly, big flakes but no wind. Mère Fontaine opens the shutters and says, "Take a look at that, Monsieur Ti-Pit, at last the rue Jeanne-Mance is getting its due. What, putting on your overcoat? Are you going to join their ranks, Monsieur Ti-Pit?"

"Yeah," I tell her, "but I think I'll wait till they're down the street a way."

Mère Fontaine's scrumptious midnight supper was still on the table, Ti-Paul was still up to his ears in vittles, Mimi, Jean-François, and Danny were drinking white wine at a festive clip, when discordant sounds rose up from the street. Mimi, all primped and prettied by Father Christmas, flits over to the window to watch the wretched of the earth through the blinds.

"We're all going," he says, "me and Jean-François and Danny, but we haven't decided whether to march with Homos Amalgamated or the Liberated Sex crowd. What do you think, Ti-Pit?"

"I don't know, maybe you could just drift with the stream."

"You see, Homos Amalgamated and Liberated Sex aren't the same as us, they're so respectable . . . And the other drag queens from the Dear Boy, even a hardbitten auntie like Yvonne, refuse to march on Christmas Eve, on account of Christmas spirit and all that crap, they hand me a laugh . . . come over and look, Danny, it's beautiful . . ."

Danny comes over, his eyes are popping out and he's got a ferocious scowl on his face. "The first cop that chucks tear gas at the people . . . I'll give him something to remember me by!"

"I like peaceful demonstrations," says Mère Fontaine. "Don't talk like that; Monsieur Danny."

"It'll be a night of nightsticks," says Danny. "I know the Queen's Constabulary."

"We've got to have law and order, Monsieur Danny," says Mère Fontaine. Then she gets to work on a plum in brandy to keep Ti-Paul company, who was still eating, nothing could stop him. "Christmas is Christmas," he says.

The frothy foam of the assholes flowing down toward Old Montreal in the haze of the still-young storm didn't stop the bells from ringing. The chapel doors opened, bursting with Christians, I guess; in a second I thought I'd see the whole nation marching through the night together, all hearts beating in unison. But that was only a vision, before I'd stepped into the bath of experience . . .

"So long, I'll be going now . . ."

"You'll be careful, Monsieur Ti-Pit? Gracious, what a turbulent night! Are you all going to leave me alone?"

"No," says Jean-François. "Not me, I won't leave you, Mère Fontaine. My career is broken but I prefer to keep my skull intact."

"Thank you, my boy," says Mère Fontaine.

The best thing to do in this demonstration, it seemed to me, was to strike out in all directions and get a miscellaneous noseful, the whole seething migration was sure to end up at the waterfront, the St. Lawrence was there to stop it from going any further. But I didn't have much time to think, because the first ugly mug that comes my way is my damn ambulance driver, and he drags me along. "You here, son? I like that. Let me tell you a secret. The people that death claws at tonight, it'll be just too bad for them, they won't see our faithful ambulance."

"You were supposed to work, you bastard! That's crummy."

"I'll work in the morning. What do you expect? The nurses are walking out for twelve hours too, a shebang like this doesn't happen every day . . ."

"But, Christ, it's rotten for the sick people!"

"Can't be helped. Somebody's always got to pay,

that's my philosophy, you never get fun for nothing. You see this gang here? They're my private assholes. I sowed the seeds of rage in their noodles, I pulled them out of the hospitals and ambulances, to hell with everybody else! We're going to yell for our rights, we're a special class of assholes, Sickness, Death & Co., that's us, the whole world's blood and shit falls on us, that's why we hate the world, that's why we say to hell with everybody!"

"Then the leaflet is lying, the leaflet calls it a 'night of justice' . . . Then we're all a lot of liars!"

"That's right, son, and worse. Say, you're beginning to wise up, slow but sure. But there's something I wanted to tell you about. You missed something sweet this morning when you were puking about those little murders . . ."

"I was not! It's not true!"

"I saw you, son. You were puking in the toilet like a sick calf, you're too delicate, son, I see trouble ahead if you don't get over it. Anyway, you missed something nice, a sweet story, the kind you like . . ."

"All right, fire away."

"Well, you remember the kid that was on his way out with cancer, him and his sister? Well, he was just about to close his eyes, last rites, prayers for the dead and so on, when all of a sudden he sits up in bed and says, 'No, I don't want to die!' See, he'd been lying in bed for months, and now this joker decides to sit up and say, 'No, I don't want to die!' His big sister says, 'But you must, you must . . . I'd give ten years of my life for you to spend Christmas with Mama like last year, but I can't help you . . .' But the kid sticks to his guns. 'I don't want to die and that's that!' "

"I wonder who'll win out, the undertaker or the kid?"

"Bad question, kid, we know the answer. But all the same, a thing like that makes an impression. The hospital crowd get all excited, they trot out the life-saving machines, they think the wasted tissue will grow in again, there's nothing as diabolical as hope, son, you have no idea. But in the meantime, while the Big Boss is thinking it over, picking his time to finish him off, the kid is eating his pudding, moving his arms, and learning to live again. Isn't that cute? I knew you'd like that."

"I've had enough of your company!" I say, and beat it to another crowd. The firemen were in a turmoil. One of them buttonholes me and says, "All in all we're a peaceful lot, we're not looking for trouble, but some intellectuals have wormed their way in, and when those guys take a hand there's always hell to pay, it's none of their business in the first place, and in the second place, those jerks don't know what it's all about, they think they're connected with the class struggle, that's a laugh, with the profs making fifteen thousand a year. And look over there, even the police are wrangling, if the law-and-order specialists can't see eye to eye, what's to become of us?"

"Yeah, but this is a special bunch, they're demanding ten thousand a year. They think they're not getting paid enough for kicking us around."

"Say, the more I look at you, the more I'm beginning to think you're an artist or some kind of a smart aleck, you wouldn't be a Communist by any chance? The police are a public service, this is no time to go on strike, we need them. Four hundred of those loafers are cooling their heels on the curb over there, watching the snow come down, hell, that's an insult to us guys that stand for harmony and duty. You see what I mean, you damned artist?"

"I'm no more an artist than you are, you damned fireman, and shut your trap!"

"Come on, let's not fight, it's Christmas. We firemen have a tough job, the fires wear us out. Nobody appreciates us, we never see our wives and kids."

"And suppose there's a fire tonight, is anybody holding the fort?"

"Sure, we've got emergency teams, we love our fellow citizens and want to protect them. But nobody appreciates us. We've come here mostly to show ourselves, that's why we've got our helmets and raincoats on. You wouldn't have a drop of brandy, those white prickles are beginning to prickle . . ."

"No, but if I see a chum I'll get you some."

"You'll see that we're different. We'll be the only quiet ones in the crowd."

"Okay, I'll be seeing you."

"Don't get mixed up with the intellectuals, hear?"

You could see that the striking cops—their placard, signed POLICE FOR BROTHERHOOD, was full of demands —were sick of being public servants. They were standing on the curbstone like a row of monkeys. Some of them claimed to be assholes, but not very many, maybe thirty at the most. I thought that would be a good place to cadge some brandy for my fireman.

"Hey, you. Got some brandy?"

"Who do you think you're addressing anyway? I'm a policeman by profession, that calls for respect, even tonight. Who are you anyway? A bum? A crackpot?"

"I saw your sign where it says WE ARE FORSAKEN ASSHOLES. So I thought I'd come and take a look."

"There's assholes and assholes. I may be an asshole in my way, But I'm not a drunkard."

"Maybe not," I say. "Then why do you call yourselves assholes?"

"Because we're in sympathy with you guys. I personally joined the police because I wanted to help my fellow men, help schoolchildren cross the street, succor the blind and all that. I don't like to crack people over the head and torture them, but some of my colleagues have it in their blood, they're the ones who dishonor our calling. A man should go into the police as he goes into the Church. I'm proud to be what I am, you sot!"

"I'm not a sot."

"Then why are you asking me for liquor? Yes, I'm proud to be a police asshole, a man despised by his colleagues because he refuses to shoot his fellow men. That's the story. I guess you realize that I could arrest you for drunkenness?"

The guy was nuts, I dropped him right there, him and his group of thirty, Christ, those cops were big, they looked like thirty snow-covered pine trees. Then, rolling along in that wave of voices, that clutter of heads, legs, and arms (things were still pretty quiet, no rioting, no smashed shop windows or any of that stuff so far, but the streets were filling up), I remembered how Mimi

had told Jean-François he had "an okay chum in the
Ottawa police, no kidding, he's crazy about me, he's
so gentle he wouldn't kill a fly, a regular teddy bear!"
"What, you're sucking off cops now? You're just a
shameless hussy!" says Jean-François. "Not every day,"
says Mimi, "but my prejudices evaporate once the pants
are down . . ." I looked around me in the crowd, there
were plain-clothes men with guns in their pockets, you
could pick the bastards out by their Judas grins, even
the fireman had given me a dirty look, he'd taken me for
one of them, everybody was eyeing everybody else,
you couldn't get rid of the suspicion that a traitor was
hidden in the woodpile. Sometimes the green spots of
the neon Christmas garlands threw grimacing masks on
our faces, you couldn't tell who you were in with. Now
and then the flow of faces seemed to freeze in a sudden
whiff of nightmare. I remember passing in front of a
funeral parlor, in the white light behind the muslin
curtains I could see the hair of some kneeling women,
they were praying around the coffin, you saw it from
far away, the only one whose face you couldn't make out
was the departed, on account of the flowers that filled
the room, but I could imagine him, all made up with
pursed lips. Just then a gang of teenagers shot out of the
waxworks with their mother after them, screaming,
"Where are you going? Your place is with your father!" But the children didn't listen, they melted away
into different groups (it was all mixed up, there were
twenty students' organizations, all at loggerheads), and
their mother stood there all by herself, wailing. "They
haven't even got time to mourn for their father."

    You got the feeling that this was a night of conquer
or die, any minute the crowd could throw an epileptic
fit and then you'd be crushed, torn in little pieces, that's
the way it is when the guts of the people start rumbling. The snow seemed to cloak us all in majesty, the
whole mob, I think, had dreams of being great and
noble, that was the intention, but the outcome was in
the lap of the gods, one thing for sure, a barbarian up-
roar within earshot of the guns would be enough to start
them crackling, the populace would drop in their tracks
and soon all this white snow would be red. While I'm

mulling it all over like this, I bump into the fishermen's contingent, the deep-water assholes, they smelled of raw fish and buckets of gin. The head man's name was Emile Fournier, he'd brought along his kids, from five to seventeen, sometimes the eldest spoke for his old man, same intonation, same angry silences. "These fishermen," Fournier told me, "aren't all from my village, they're from all over. We live on unemployment insurance. Holy Mary, three months a year we live by the skin of our teeth, the rest of the time . . ." "We've come a long way," says young Fournier, "two nights in the train to say what we've got to say . . . see, we've written it all on our sign. Hey, it's getting cold, but take it from me, these storms of yours are nothing to what we get out in Gaspé."

"But, holy Mary, we wouldn't leave our village for anything in the world, if it weren't for the shortage of money and the damn government relief we don't get, we'd be as snug as a bug. And without the sea we'd die. Say, boy, give me a swig of gin."

"It's only for your bronchitis," says Fournier Jr., "but remember, Papa, the doctor's forbidden it."

"I want some too," says the ten-year-old.

"Just a drop to warm you up, but no more. Your mother wouldn't like it. And don't go telling her."

"I won't tell her."

These Fourniers looked like a united family. I said to Emile, the father, "That's a good fishing crew you got there. I bet you take in plenty."

"I wouldn't say that. These kids you're looking at are tough customers, they run their mother ragged, and they've got to be fed. No, they're not much use at that age."

"We catch our good dozen mackerel, Papa," says the ten-year-old.

"Sure, but you don't clean them. All you think about is riding around in the boat and having fun. I got to tan their backsides now and then."

"We're used to it, our backsides are tough."

"Shut your trap or you'll get a tanning right now. Insolent brats! Sometimes I wonder if they'll grow up to be fishermen. You know, chum, our part of the country's getting depopulated, this good-for-nothing generation is bored with fishing, but God gave them to us and we took them."

Then Fournier looks at me out of the corner of his eye. "Say, you wouldn't be from the government?"

"No, I work on an ambulance, the pay's not bad, but . . ."

"You see, chum, I'm suspicious. You never can tell. I don't want this Christing government skinning my fishermen."

"So long, Fournier. Maybe we'll meet again . . ."

"Not behind bars, I hope. On the high seas."

"Right you are, Fournier."

I began to wonder if maybe Ti-Cul was somewhere in the crowd, hidden under Jos Langlois's coat, his victim's skin that he'd put on. No, he was too scared of the police and the radio said they'd have dogs— dogs, horses, men with fangs like wolves, the whole works, the big shots stopped at nothing when the plebs got steamed up and started yelling, "I want what I want." In that crowd there were more demands than people, a hopeless muddle, the King of the Last Judgment couldn't have sorted it out, looked to me like hell without fire. Anyway, Ti-Cul wouldn't be there, maybe he was limping away to the States like he'd said, he'd be afraid to write me, or maybe he was hiding in the north woods, slowly freezing to death. There was always a chance he'd knock on my door and say, "It's me, Ti-Cul, you wouldn't go with me, but this time I'll make you . . ." He'd stick his knife in my solar plexus and the world would go black; maybe he'd come in the dead of night, maybe at the crack of dawn, no way of knowing. That guy was the walking specter of death, seen in profile.

One bunch of rebels I came across called themselves the League of White Collar Assholes, they took up practically a whole street. The guy I latched on to looks real solemn and dignified, he's even got a tie on under his skimpy overcoat collar. "In our ranks," he says to me, "we have thousands of bookkeepers, bank clerks, and office workers of every kind. Some of the stenographers prefer to march with the Women's Secretarial Front, they complain that they're not as well paid as we are, but that's an outrage when bookkeepers of thirty years' standing are starving. I'm chief bookkeeper in a boot factory, believe it or not, monsieur, even in the winter I refuse to wear boots, you can see for yourself, my actions keep pace with my words . . ." True enough, he was tramping through the snow and ice in thin, low-cut shoes—a chilly way of expressing his disgust, it seemed to me. "No," he says, "never again will I wear boots; count them, yes, because bookkeeping is eternal and indestructible like insects, sometimes I think that accounts will be kept when man has vanished from the face of the earth. I can't stand the sight of boots, I walk with my head in the air so as not to see people's feet, the cause of my eternal bookkeeping. But who are you, monsieur? One of our unkempt students? I'd better tell you right away, I detest students."

"What makes you think I'm a student? I'm a small-time worker like you, except my job is worse, I'm on the agony wagon . . ."

"I don't believe you. You a common worker? You're a student disguised as a worker, imitating our accent, mine must astonish you, I detest vulgarity. That's it, a disguised student, they do that nowadays. I detest you, our society coddles you. You are unworthy to understand my martyrdom: thirty years a bookkeeper in a boot factory. I am educated, self-educated, but I detest students like you. Pretentious, arrogant, sitting in lecture halls, driving around in motorcars at your fathers' expense, not to speak of government scholarships, yes, monsieur, I detest you!"

"I'm not a student, I tell you."

"Don't lie, it's obvious, that supercilious look, the look of a young whippersnapper who understands everything and can explain everything, and all those books you read without digesting them. I detest you!"

This bookkeeper seemed to get a kick out of chewing me out. I tried to run away but he kept after me. "I've read Proust too," he says. "You're not the only one. I've . . ." That was his hymn of hate. You never know, I thought, what depths of bitterness you'll sound when a guy starts shaking all his fleas at once.

The striking cops had a chance to show they meant what they said. When the procession was passing Samson's, some hoodlum steps up to the chief of the vacationing cops and says, "Tell me, monsieur, would you still be on strike if we cut a hole in one of these shop windows?"

The head cop answers, "You've seen our proclamation. The people are ungrateful and we're fed up. I can guarantee that we won't even bother to blow our whistles, we'll let you help yourselves to your hearts' content, but on one condition. The operation must take no more than ten minutes, we wouldn't have the self-control to watch you breaking the law any longer, and you'll have to be quiet. When a thief is quiet, we can always pretend not to see him; if you're noisy, the itch to pull out our guns might get the better of us."

"That's damn white of you, boss. All right, boys, let's cut that windowpane, and no noise . . ."

The four hundred cops on the curbstone still had their poster saying COME HELL OR HIGH WATER, WE ARE ON STRIKE! But you should have seen those pigs, their eyes were popping, it was beginning to look as if the whole emporium would be stripped bare in ten minutes. The hoodlum says to the head pig to smooth him down, "We'll toe the line, boss, we won't take advantage." But it was pretty hard on some of those flatfeet, they had a dreamy look on their faces and they were starting to fiddle with their nightsticks, some had the itch on the revolver side, they'd never seen crooks working so piously, in such religious silence, not a word, not a grunt, their hands and fingers did the talking on every shelf and counter, and meanwhile the sweat was popping out all over the chief pig's forehead. One thing for sure, Monsieur Sir Samson was going to pass out cold when he saw his store, some Christmas present, but hell, when you say you're on strike you got to prove it, words without deeds don't mean a thing. The chief pig looks at his watch. "Five minutes more," he sighs. "It's a long time, boys, but grit your teeth, it's the principle of the thing." The boys were squirming, they'd smothered the voice of duty, but now it was perking up. "This city doesn't deserve to be protected," says the chief pig. "This is what they get for their ingratitude, so keep a stiff upper lip. Three minutes more." Two minutes, one minute, then the time was up, the looters trooped out, the whole street was a festival, they all emptied their pockets under the hungry eyes of the police, night of peace, night of plenty: clocks, typewriters, one musician guy and a pal were even trying to haul a piano away, a lot of them shared their pickings with the crowd, never had Samson's shown such generosity, pouring out manna on the ragged and sick at heart. The looters were in ecstasy, and the chief pig couldn't help saying, "I've got to hand it to you, for a bunch of amateurs you've done a bang-up job."

That's when I saw Prunier, my Acadian cab driver, he'd specialized in liqueur chocolates at Samson's, he'd offer them to his bishops, so he said, wouldn't that be class? This guy only worked for the upper crust, common mortals could walk as far as he was concerned. "Hey, Prunier," I ask him, "still as mean as ever? Still want to smack everybody in the puss?"

"Ah, Merry Christmas, friend Lemieux, I've been waiting for you every morning at the Unemployment Bureau to sing the praises of taxi driving . . . How about a chocolate filled with cherry brandy, they melt in your mouth like a woman."

"Are all the taxi drivers out?" I ask him.

"Yeah, but those saps are afraid of getting their feet cold, they're all sitting in their cars with the heater and radio on. They've blocked up all the bridges, Christ, do you call that demonstrating? Hey, Lemieux, you seen all those immigrants with their federations, demanding the same rights as us, the lords of the city?"

"Still the same old racist, Prunier?"

"Not at all, but when I see signs like LEAGUE OF UN-LOVED AND DISILLUSIONED FRENCHMEN, I can't help it, it gives me a pain. What about us? Aren't we unloved? Aren't we disillusioned?"

"You're not the only pebble on the beach, you damn racist!"

"And that's not all. Even the perverts are out. I didn't even know they belonged to the human race. Some lady, all decked out in furs and feathers, comes up to me and asks for a light. You know me, always ready to is okay with me, it's like hunting, man lives by woman, oblige, I light her cigarette. 'Like to step into my Citroën for a few minutes?' she asks me. I'm willing, sex you know how it is, and there's nothing wrong with my balls. But then in the Citroën . . . I won't tell you what happened, you're too young and ignorant. Anyway, I gave him a good punch in the eye, I mussed him up good, the damn pervert!"

"I know you, Prunier, you'd kill a man for stepping on your corns."

"Are you crazy? Who wants to be fucked in the wrong direction? I only gave him a little lesson. He'll be kind of bleary in the morning, but tomorrow night he'll be as gay as ever. What I say, Lemieux, is that in every society you've got to root out the foreign elements, same with the queers, they're our native foreigners. I say load 'em all on a ship and send 'em out to the middle of the ocean. That's my idea, Lemieux!"

"Damn racist!"

"It's because I love my country! My country first and last, see?"

"Sure, you've said that before."

"Take it easy, you could be my nephew, you're still wet behind the ears, I've told you that before too. Don't get sore at old Prunier; if you decide to try your hand at taxiing, come and see me. I'll slip you some of my bishops . . ."

"I'm not sore at you, you monster!"

"If you want some venison, ask me. It won't be tough . . ."

In the ranks of the assholes there was also a gang of carefree, slightly wilted damsels that were prancing around with a sign saying RESPECT THE COURTESANS OF MONTREAL! The men were tagging after them, drawn by the aroma of love. Now and then one of

these overripe damsels would say to some rutting, com-
rade-in-arms, "If you're cold, monsieur, our little
hideaway is right around the corner on rue Sainte-
Catherine, we could tear off a fritter or two and hurry
back . . ." These girls went down like sugar candy with
the men, but the jealous wives in the vicinity didn't see
it that way; some of those old biddies had been hanging on to the same poor bastard for forty years, they
were supposed to be dozing behind lowered blinds, but
they were making their hatchet-faced rounds, like spies
in aprons, and they were quick to join the dance.
They'd grab their husbands by the hair, and the poor
guy, all shaken and jolted, would groan, "Hey, this is
our night of freedom, it's lover's choice tonight. Forty
years of your damn hair curlers is long enough."

"Husband, go home! A husband's place is in the
home!"

"We can't, we're fighting for the cause!"

The insults shot from group to group: "Whores of
Montreal, corrupters of husbands, plying your sinful
trade on Christmas, hellfire's too good for you! My
husband was as tame as a puppy, and now he's talking
back to his wife."

"Hey, you old bags, get back to your brooms, we'll
take care of your husbands, we'll gobble them up like
cream puffs . . ."

"Bitches! Scarlet women!"

There was some kind of battle on every square. On
the pedestal of a monument I saw Militant Youth, surrounded by hundreds of snotnosed school kids. The
budding revolutionaries were bellowing, "No, we don't
want to go to the docks! We want to invade the Île
Sainte-Hélène!"

"Christ, why not occupy the ski trails of Sainte
Agathe while we're at it. We haven't come here for the
sport!"

Papineau was there too, as delirious as ever. He
shook Militant Youth by the ears and said, "I want
serious Marxists in my ranks! What can I do with
infants who've never had a thought in their heads!"

"Thought comes with age," says Militant Youth,

"they're only schoolboys today, tomorrow they'll be the vanguard of the embattled working class. The great Mao . . ."

"Shut up!"

"Life can't help starting with childhood," says Militant Youth. "I can promise you one thing, my young militants won't grow up to be lousy bourg . . ."

"Shut up! I won't have you in my ranks!" says Papineau.

"That's foul injustice!" says Militant Youth. "Anyway, my young people are taking orders from me, not from you."

Papineau's wife wasn't far off. She'd know when it was time for baby's bottle, because little Maritain was right there on her back with his little woolen booties sticking out of his knapsack, and the twins, Karl and Blaise, were tugging at her coat. According to Papillon, all his kids had been "in the movement" as long as they'd been sucking their thumbs, so this outing under the white flakes that were spreading their mantle over our shoulders was no great change in their timetable. Lucily for us there wasn't any wind, but the radio said it was coming.

In one of the straggling groups, the Last Farmers of Quebec, I caught sight of Ti-Foin, he sure had changed, still built like a brick shithouse but not so down in the mouth, a new man was bursting into bloom. "Hi, Ti-Foin!" I sing out. "Remember that time at Vincent's? You better now? Sworn off the Molson beer?"

"Converted, I guess. Maybe politics done it, I don't know. I was in bad shape when you saw me last, I blubbered because I hadn't any words, but now I've learned, I go to school at night, I listen to educated guys that lean more to bombs than to turning the other cheek, I don't know yet which way I'll swing, I learn slow . . ."

"You seem to have plenty of words now . . ."

"Enough to get by with, but I'll never catch up, our leaders are elite guys, they say they're working for all mankind, but if you ask me, even those idealists look down on me, they think I'm a yokel who'll never shed his thick skin. If you haven't got the words it takes for the revolution, if you haven't got the intellectual spark, hell, what are you good for? You can plant bombs and shut up, or you can go back to your village and milk the cows."

"You've done a lot of thinking, Ti-Foin . . ."

"Sure, but what's the use? I still look as if I'd come straight out of the woods. Sure, I want to revolt, but I can't learn to hate . . . Before I blow up my English-speaking brothers, I've got to study why. That's why I'll always have frost on my tongue."

"So you're deep in your books?"

"Yeah, and meetings. But the other guys step on me, and they're not Anglos, they're patriots of my own race. But they don't respect me any more than the yarn they mend their socks with. Sometimes I feel like going back home . . ."

"Haven't you any friends?"

"No, there's no time, I've got to study after work. And I'm saving up to take my mother to Quebec, she's never been away from the shack, too busy feeding the kids."

"You working in a factory, Ti-Foin?"

"No, I've found something better, greasing cars in a garage. It's not so good, but it's hard for our kind to get ahead. Tonight I'm with our country assholes, guys that were driven off the farm. Hope to see you again, Ti-Pit. We had many a jug of Molson together, eh, Ti-Pit?"

"Merry Christmas, Ti-Foin, Merry Christmas!"

I HEARD that even the nuns were fighting that night. The Sisters of the Modern Rule were at daggers drawn with the Maria Goretti Congregation, hard-bitten hard-liners that hadn't changed in two centuries, they were WEDDED TO THE HAIR OF PENANCE as it said on their black-and-white poster, and still wore the old mortification uniform, no hair under their coifs and big heavy crosses that crushed their breasts. "We are the daughters of bitterness and courage," they said, "but we shall see God. You Sisters of the Modern Rule powder your faces and shave your mustaches, for you the face of God will be the face of the impure world, wretched

creatures who deny your faith! . . ." The Modern sisters
were stepping lively, waltzing around in their yellow
skirts. They had this Sister Clara who's even organized
a band, they jazzed it up with the flute and guitar, the
Divine Messiah they were singing was the hottest thing
I ever heard.

Sister Clara said to the people, "Sing with us, brothers and sisters, it's a night of hope, a night of joy for us
all . . . The convents have been opened to let in the
light, we are sweeping the dust out of the chapels. Let
us rejoice, my friends, let us sing . . ."

The Mother Superior of the Maria Goretti crew
snapped, "The Pope has forbidden it, you hussy!"

"Come, come, Mother, relax," said Sister Clara.
"Dance with us, sing with us in honor of the Christ
child . . ."

"Never! You and I don't serve the same God. Our
Lord is sober, He is the heavy burden of martydrom,
the sorrow of the heart . . ."

"Ours is light and gay, Mother, he turns water into
wine, he walks on the waves of the sea, at his side we
fear no peril . . . We possess nothing; your hospices,
your convents, your mountains of wealth weigh on you,
Mother, your bank is bursting with stolen goods, that's
why your soul is not at peace, Mother . . ."

I said to myself, Too bad those little yellow sisters
hadn't run my orphanage back there in the middle of
the slums, Christ, maybe today Ti-Pit would be something more than a crystallized hole in the ground, maybe he'd be in there with the happiness gang, blowing
the flute and looking like a king. But that's the way it
was, I was born too soon. Papillon had told me. There
was hardly anybody left in the orphanages these days.
"All those abodes of desolation are being turned into
whorehouses," he says. "Aren't you glad? And all
thanks to the anti-bastard pill. You missed the boat,
Lemieux . . ." So these modern little sisters had turned
to better things, no more nursery, they were plunging
into math and all that stuff instead. The times, I said
to myself, were changing faster than I was.

Raising my head as I marched, I felt the storm wind,
not very strong yet, but I could hear it growing in the

distance. The snow was beginning to bite, better not think about it. Then I see somebody throwing snowballs at me, and damned if it isn't Mimi and Danny. "Hi, Ti-Pit, how do you like the carnival?"

"Not bad. But where's the Dear Boy crowd?"

"Oh, our precious clientele didn't want to exhibit themselves in the normal world."

"Closet queens give me the shits," says Danny.

"That's because you're so strong and handsome," says Mimi. Then he tells me that Homos Amalgamated had snubbed him "because of my blond wig and my earrings and my big Lady-with-the-Camellias hat." "Yes," says Mimi, "I wanted to chant, 'Mimi is a happy and contented queen,' but they wouldn't let me. They said it was too bold, we should just march in silence, under their placard that said WE DEMAND EQUAL RIGHTS FOR OUR MINORITY. What do you think of that, Ti-Pit? Minority! That don't mean a thing. They're just a bunch of cowards."

"You said a mouthful," says Danny. "Cowards that hide their cocks in their prayer books, that's what they are, parlor masturbators!"

"How well you speak, Danny darling!" says Mimi. "And the Liberated Sex crowd wouldn't take me either. They asked me if I subscribed to their magazine, *The Mystery of the Masculine*. I said no. Or if I'd read their article, 'The Secret Beauty of the Male' in *Dawn*. I said no, I only read Tintin, the reader in our crowd was Jean-François, but he was only interested in the theater. They were sore because Danny and me refused to read their magazines. I told them I'd rather be raped than read their crap . . . 'Aha!' they said. 'So you're nothing but a vulgar little drag queen, there are thousands of your kind in this town, we hate you, you give the movement a bad name, your feminine appearance calls attention to what we don't like to recognize in ourselves . . .' In the same crowd there was a group that called themselves Keep Straight. They were psychiatrists, specialized in the reconversion of queens. 'With our disgust treatment,' they told us, 'you'll be cured and returned to normal life in six months.' Danny and me didn't want any damn doctors cutting our cocks off,

so we tried to join the Sapphic Power girls. 'No,' they
said. 'Go see the Sisters of Bilitis, they're more broad-
minded about borderline cases.' Sure, why not? But the
S.B.'s tell us, 'The Courtesans of Montreal might take
you in, nobody else will. Tell them we sent you.' Sure
enough, the ladies of the evening coddled us like newborn babes, especially Danny, because he's so beautiful
with his Chinese eyes and his Cossack boots, not to
mention the rest of him, which the ladies admire as
much as I do. The girls made quite a fuss over you,
didn't they, Danny? Did you enjoy their honey fritters?"
"Those girls are okay," says Danny. "Even my old man
doesn't mind when I go see them, he says it keeps me
in shape, we eat olives in bed, yes, they're real nice, a
damn sight better than those Liberated Sex creeps that
don't even know how to fuck . . ."

"But you do, don't you, Danny? My superman!"

So hand in hand with his Danny, Mimi goes tripping
through the ranks like a nymph on a picnic, and I went
down to the waterfront to see if Papillon had started
sounding off. He'd be there, I guessed, with his belly
bulging under his coat, bellowing, "My Joualonese
brothers, things must change, let us unite!" But then his
asthma would ring down a curtain of fog on his eloquence, the cold always made him cough, it was pitiful,
especially when he was addressing his countrymen, a
fit of coughing would shake him and fill his throat with
gook, but he'd keep on gassing all the same, he was a
gasbag by nature.

The procession was still on the quiet side, the pigs
weren't doing anything to break the ice, but wherever
I went I saw anxious looks, with all those cops around,
you never can tell . . . Down on the waterfront the
first thing I see is a whole gang of bigmouths on a platform with Papillon in the lead. Corneille, his guardian
angel, is right behind him, whispering, "Tonight, Papillon, you must address yourself to all mankind, to uni-
versal man, not just to the Joualonese . . ." "No,
Corneille, this is the night of the Joualonese . . . these
people here are Joualonese and for me, in the here and
now, my Joualonese brothers *are* mankind . . ." "Sometimes I wonder why I publish a bigoted nationalist like

you year after year," says Corneille, who was surrounded by a pathetic group of universalists, guys that
claimed to be above the parties. Naturally, the in-
transigent Papineau was there too. "Lukewarm neu-
tralists, go home!" shouts that knight of the merciless
tongue, no one was safe from its lash. "Our love goes
out to man alone," the universalists answered, "we
speak in the name of all mankind!" But again Papineau flapped his banner in their faces. "Down with
sterile humanitarianism! Long live the class struggle!"
Then Militant Youth introduces a schoolboy poet, who
starts strumming his lyre and chanting:

> *"Comrades and fellow sufferers*
> *In this evanescent America,*
> *Surfeited with bitterness . . ."*

and Papineau attacks on another front.

"Shut up!" he bellows.

"We have the floor," says Militant Youth.

"The floor, the floor!" the schoolboy chorus repeats.

> *"Our cold collective agony*
> *Burns on the white plain . . ."*

Strife was in the air, you could hear its muffled roar.
Papillon clears his throat into the mike and starts up.
"My Joualonese brothers, let there be harmony and
union among us, every group has a right to state its
demands . . . a little silence, my friends! . . ." But the
factory workers were closing in on the stand and fists
were raised. "Hey, you! Who do you think you are?
What do you know about our troubles, you overpaid
professor, get down off there and let one of our guys
talk . . ."

"If it's my place you desire, monsieur," says Papillon,
"you can have it. We are all equals, all brothers . . ."

"We're not your brothers, pal," says the worker.
"Hell, no!"

"Aren't we all Joualonese, united to repulse the
same aggressor? To demand the same rights? Tell me
that, my friend."

"I'm not your friend. Our demands have nothing to do with you. We work on the assembly line, a dollar an hour isn't a fair wage, we're fed up. And we're fed up with you too, you rich, snooty bastards!"

"I assure you we are neither rich nor snooty," says Papillon. "I give you my word as a Joualonese that your desires, oh my brothers, are our desires."

"That's a lie, get down off of there, we want your place, you stuffed clown, you big-shot American capitalist!"

"I'm only a humble Joualonese," says Papillon, "I love you with all my heart, and that's why I've come here to speak to you tonight. Listen, my friends . . ."

"Shut up and get down off of there!"

Then Papineau pushes Papillon off the stand and shouts, "This young man is right, he knows his Marxism. Go shoot your mouth off some place else, Papillon, let the comrades speak . . ."

"Christ!" says Papillon. He jumps down from his stand and Corneille gathers him to his bosom. "You see what man has become, Papillon? A creature incapable of being good and beautiful for as much as five minutes . . . A creature without generosity. Poor mankind, condemned to live with each other!"

"I've got to speak to the Joualonese people," Papillon whimpers. "It's urgent . . ."

"Yes, sometimes I'm ashamed of your Joualonese, my Joualonese, if you prefer. Why must they be so intolerant?"

"What's more," says Papillon, "there's a blizzard coming on. I can feel it in my asthma, it's twisting my bellows."

All of a sudden Papillon wanted to get out of there, he'd just caught sight of his better half, she was one of the generalissimos of the female contingent. The sailing was no smoother on the distaff side, because Secretarial Front was on the outs with Radical Womanhood, and the League of Wives and Mothers was on the scene too, trying to grab Papillon's Jacqueline by the hair. Jacqueline's crowd were saying, "What do we need men for? We can make babies without them . . ."

"Boo! Hiss! Criminals, robbing woman of her greatest pride and joy! Boo!" The wives and mothers had a mean tongue on them. Their placard said WE WILL DEFEND OUR OFFSPRING TO THE LAST DITCH! Some of their signs featured enormous boxes of Lux, showing a blissful mother with her blissful baby, and written underneath: WASH YOUR BABY'S CLOTHES WITH DEVOTION! Another gang had a giant box of Pablum, and a superasshole baby with pink gums, crying out, "Pablum! Yum yum!"

"Slaves!" shouts Jacqueline. "Every three minutes you change their diapers. You're not women, you're washing machines! When will you wake up?"

"We're proud of our babies. We love to wash them and wipe them. We love our babies! Hurrah for baby's Pablum! Baby is king! Baby is king!"

Papineau's wife was there listening with her two young militants and little Maritain in his knapsack, chirping and burbling. All of a sudden she turns around to little Skeezix. "Hey you," she says. "You're starting to smell like camembert . . ."

"It's because we've been here a long time," says Karl.

"He'd rather be home in the tent," says Blaise. "Do you think we'll be so cold again tonight, Mama?"

"Don't bother me," says Papineau's wife. "If your father had any sense of responsibility, you wouldn't be cold. I do the best I can. I've bought a heater and I've lined the tent, so stop complaining."

"Where is Papa?"

"Don't mention your father to me! He's not a good comrade to you. He's not worthy to call himself your father."

"Comrade Maritain stinks something terrible, Mama," says Karl.

"He can wait. I'll change him when I get a chance."

"But his ass itches," says Blaise.

"The comrade can wait, I said. Let's get on with the march."

Papineau's wife finally found an oasis to warm the brats and change the baby in at the Wives and Mothers' headquarters. A Madame Pablum was sitting there with a baby at her breast. She was aghast at the sight of

Karl and Blaise, she'd never seen such pale children. "My goodness, madame, those poor little boys, they don't get enough to eat, let me adopt them and take care of them properly. You're an incompetent mother, mademoiselle, I bet you're not even married, obviously you don't know the first thing about motherhood. Oh, it wrings my heart to see such neglected children . . . oh, the poor little things!"

"Skip it, comrade," says Karl. "It's a hard life, but we like it."

"She's just a big fat bourgeoise, that's what my papa would say," says Blaise.

The lady blushed and said, "They're so brilliant it's abnormal. My God, on top of everything else, her children are abnormal! Ah, mademoiselle, fate hasn't been kind to you."

Then Madame Nursing Mother turns to the children. "Do you say your prayers every night?"

"Oh yes," says Karl. "We've got a red missal."

"Red? Ah, splendid, then you're good little Catholics . . ."

"No. Papa says Catholics are a lot of shits."

"And what coarse language they use! Oh, the poor children!"

Meanwhile, Papillon, with Corneille at his heels, was looking for a vacant monument to climb up on and harangue the Joualonese people. But luckily he runs into his chum Oscar Joyeux, as happy as a lark, his ostrich head looking out over the crowd. He's on leave for twenty-four hours, he tells us.

That has Papillon worried. "What a pleasure to see you here tonight, dear unknown poet," he says, "but haven't you got some friend to" . . . (No, thinks Papillon, looking around, I mustn't say "to keep an eye on you") . . . "to keep you company in this splendid demonstration?"

"Oh yes, a young mendicant nun, but I lost her among the yellow carnations . . ."

"One of those charming sisters of the Modern Rule, I suppose?"

"Yes, on the fringe of the blue woods . . ."

"Ah, I see," says Papillon. "Let us then sail the seas together. Soon I shall address my people ..."

"And all my deceased of 1925 have come with me too," says Oscar Joyeux. "Do you see my dear friends, Papillon? There they are on the courthouse steps, each with a raven on his wrist, I'm afraid their lamps will go out because of this snow that's raining down ..."

"It's raining harder and harder," says Corneille.

HOW THE shooting started, nobody knew, in the gray of dawn I heard some guys say that a drunken cop, disguised as the common man, had started experimenting with his gun, but there was no way of knowing because somebody else said it was a motorcycle pig who'd been scooting around from group to group, with one hand on the handlebar and the other swinging his club, and there was still another story about the armed law threatening a gang of factory workers. "Hey, you assholes, stand back or we'll shoot ..." But that only made the assholes madder. "You can't scare us with your popguns!"

Anyway, the boiler was overheating, all around me I heard the breathing and shouting of the crowd. The cops headed for the biggest noise and dragged the speechmakers off their stands and monuments. "Vile aggressor, hands off!" Papineau shouted, "you're cracking my skull!" Papineau was a man of steel, hardened by a strict diet of dogma, but now, just as he was starting on his sermon, he crumpled under the nightstick, and it was Militant Youth, his enemy No. One, the guy that Papineau from the heights of his soapbox had just been calling a "jugheaded fink," that picked him up and rubbed his bleeding brow with snow. In a near faint Papineau murmured, "Thank you, comrade, you're a real Marxist ..." The billies seemed to have kissed hundreds of people's noggins in the peaceful crowd, with a look of surprise they were feeling their foreheads, eyes, ears, and noses to see if they were still in one piece. "Christ," says one, "there's blood running down my neck, I was just trying to park my car when this pig clouts me for no reason, it's an outrage . . ." The scene was looking blurred, we didn't realize those Judases had been squirting tear gas, the world around us was heaving and pitching, and we felt heavy and slow like we were walking on the bottom of the sea. In the distance I saw Papillon, still at his mike under the light, and Corneille, begging the people not to move, to wait for the taxi drivers to come and help them, the ambulance drivers were still on strike, but the cabbies had offered to cart the wounded to the hospital. "Yes, my friends, tonight . . . we . . . have encountered . . . all the cruelty . . . the injustice . . ." Papillon was choking with his asthma and Corneille finished his sentences, I couldn't hear too good because of the screaming crowd that didn't know which way to go to get away from the nightsticks. Police cars were moving in to scoop up the pigeons, and I was damned if I knew why that vast multitude, which a minute ago had been sailing on wings of joy, were all howling and cut to pieces now . . .

"No," said Papillon, "we will never forget this night of barbarism and humiliation."

His voice was choked with tears, this was "the end of the federations, the leagues, the end of our freedom," but his words were lost in the rising wind, the weather machine had speeded up and the flakes were coming down thick, the snow was littered with fallen placards. The storm and the nightsticks, the dogs and the sound of shooting had dispersed the crowd, and there was nothing for Papillon to do but come down off his platform and blow his nose. He had waited bravely for the nightstick to fall, but in vain. "Why do they hit other people and not me?" says Papillon. "It's unjust!"

"Sometimes God's imprint is bloody," says Oscar Joyeux. "Maybe someone will need you, Papillon, to put flowers on his grave."

"Look at that, Corneille, all my friends are going to jail, everybody but me. There they go, and I'm not with them. I must follow them . . . I must . . . this damned asthma! . . . I must . . ."

"And who's going to get your friends out of jail?" says Corneille, "if you get yourself locked up. Who's going to defend them?"

"Yes! Yes! I will defend the dignity of the downtrodden Joualonese people! Yes, Corneille, you're right."

Papillon's Oscar, that prophet of doom, had been right about God's imprint. There were so many wounded you couldn't count them, and death had passed that way too, a sixteen-year-old student. A bunch of cops were standing around, they said it wasn't his injuries but heart trouble. Christ, I said to myself, even with the victim of their crime staring them in the face, those murderers go on lying, I wouldn't put it past them to ask for a medal, everybody knew the kid's skull had been cracked, the blood was gushing out, but those pigs had to insult his departed spirit. Even when the students paraded their comrade's body to the cemetery, the cops were still saying, "The doctors have assured us that the young man was suffering from heart disease . . ."

So that was the score: one dead, plus all those guys piled up behind bars, and nobody knew yet if it was for the night or until Easter, some guys were agitating to storm the jails and get their comrades out, but they didn't get very far, the blizzard was putting a damper on the crowd, the police had stopped charging, and the striking asshole cops were picking up the wounded.

We the people were retracing our steps in rout and disorder, the snow that had only wettened us at first was all around us, sticky and prickling, whistling in the wind, it slowed us down, and so did fear.

Papineau was still sounding off in spite of his split eyelid, you couldn't get him down so easy. "Friends, no storm will defeat us, much less the violence of our tyrants. Onward to struggle . . ." As soon as he could see straight, he started in again on Militant Youth. "It's all your fault, you and your idiotic schoolboys. You've spoiled it all, everybody knows the revolution isn't for twelve-year-olds . . ."

"Remember what the great Mao had to say about children," Militant Youth starts in, but discouragement grabbed him by the windpipe and he couldn't finish his sentence with all that snow coming down on him and his disciples, you could hardly see their chins under their mufflers. "Comrade Papineau," he says after

a while. "Let's stop fighting, I need your help. A lot
of those kids of mine will be spending the night in jail,
and these here will get pneumonia, listen to them
cough . . ."

"That's nothing," says Papineau. "I too am suffering,
but I know it's for my cause. Say, have you got some
Kleenex? My wound is dripping." "Sorry," says Militant Youth, "my revolutionaries have taken it all for
their colds." "Never mind," says Papineau. "Where are
your wounded? I'll give you a hand. I'll help you for
the principle of the thing, but I still think you're a
bunch of sniveling infants and that it's all your fault . . ."

"That's a crummy thing to say," says Militant Youth.

"And the halfwit hasn't even got a piece of Kleenex.
Nasty little snotnoses, catching cold on a historic night
like this!"

The taxi drivers were coming in quick to help the
wounded, even my damn ambulance man was there,
he was in his element. "Yeah, son," he says, grabbing
me by the coat. "When they attack the innocent, I draw
the line. All over the place I see guys with their heads
cracked and women in tears, it's lunacy to attack our
downtrodden assholes like this. Believe me, son, I'm
going to make somebody pay for this . . ."

"I'll give you a hand in my free time. So long, pal!"

"Hey, come to think of it, son, any news about that
Langlois massacre?"

"It's got nothing to do with me."

"Maybe not, but you're so touchy about it, I only
wanted to say in case you knew anything, see what I
mean, if one of these days you get the urge to cough
up. My guess is that you weren't in the clink for nothing, chum."

"Shut up!"

"Okay, okay, see you tomorrow."

I had some brandy for my fireman friend, we drank
it together. His left arm was hanging limp, he'd gotten
his share of the general punishment. "It's all the fault of
you Communists. Damned artist, what has the class
struggle got to do with you?"

"You crazy?" I said. "I've told you I'm not an artist."

"We've always served the people, we save women

and children from the flames, and now they beat us up the same as you, I'll never forgive you for that, chum."

The Police for Brotherhood crowd, the only pigs that hadn't used their clubs, were trying to quench the fury of the crowd. "Murderers! Murderers!" the people were yelling, but those boys hadn't shot anybody, they were just peaceful-minded strikers, their chief was trying to explain. "We were on strike, my friends. Yes, our comrades lost their heads, it's a damn shame, I admit it, but we haven't moved off this sidewalk . . . Can't you see our sign?"

"Murderers! Murderers!"

"We even let you steal for ten minutes, don't you remember?"

"Criminals! Barbarians!"

Now it was their turn to harvest insults and snowballs in the face. The leader armed himself with patience and said to his men, "Grin and bear it . . . For ten minutes, men, to make up for the sins of our comrades . . . Courage, messieurs!"

Fournier the fisherman was still surrounded by his children, the whole family was warm with gin. "Yeah," Fournier tells me, "the kids are all right, but some of my fishermen are in the government's Christing paddy wagon, and that makes my blood boil!"

"Christ, P'pa," says one of the kids, "two nights in the train from the ends of Gaspé, and this is how they treat our people. Like mangy dogs!"

"We're better off at home than here," says the ten-year-old. "There we've got the ocean all to ourselves."

"Anyway, you guys don't seem to be frozen."

"You call this a storm?" says the father. "We call it a cool breeze!"

"Seems pretty cold to me."

"It's nothing," says the eldest son. "When we have a storm it blows the roofs of our houses out to sea . . . this is a joke . . . A good night for skating on the St. Lawrence . . ."

"Try it," I tell him. "You'll sink so deep you'll never see your skates again."

I was sorry to leave them so soon, but there was a job ahead. The taxis were taking the wounded to the hospital, but they weren't getting anywhere in the white soup, the wheels were spinning around in the void. "God Almighty, why didn't I put on my winter chains? Hey, you Wives and Mothers, how about giving us a push?"

"No, messieurs, because some of you have driven our enemies, the Courtesans of Montreal, in your cabs."

"C'mon, ladies, save the sermon. Give us a push . . ."

Like it or not, the ladies had to push. There was grumbling in the ranks, but in that howling blizzard there was no time to vote. The groups were all scattered and mixed. "You can hardly tell the universalists from the separatists," says Corneille. But there Papillon drew the line. "Maybe . . . you . . . can't . . . I . . . can," he gasps. High above the wave of miscellaneous faces you could see Oscar Joyeux's ostrich head, he looked to be the only sane man in the crowd, even if he did keep mumbling stuff like "it has been observed that when earthquake threatens all mice assemble and resemble each other" or "The impassive inquisitor strides beside us and flagellates our steps . . ."

"I can recognize my people anywhere," says Papillon.

"Yes, but they will not consent to walking stoop-shouldered forever," says Oscar Joyeux. "Ah! There's my little nun in among the yellow carnations . . ."

Then we were in for a surprise. The Maria Goretti sisters and the Courtesans of Montreal had both been clobbered by the police, and now the survivors, without regard for creed or morality, were helping the wounded. "Take my arm, madame." "Let me help you, my dear" —words of charity were flying through the air like hail in the springtime. That went straight to Corneille's heart. "If only this could happen more often," he sighed. "If only each one of us could be charitable at least once a day . . ."

"You stop moralizing," says Papillon, "or I'll deport you to the Capuchins . . ."

"Indolent love grows distraught when it lives in a hothouse," says Oscar Joyeux, "how are you, dear sister?"

Oscar Joyeux seemed to have the wrong chick, because this one answered, "Yes, monsieur, I'm a novice, but not in the same racket. I'm a lady of the evening . . ."

"But you too have a golden cross on your breast . . ."

"Yes, it's the locket where I keep a picture of the deceased creep who kept me. You see, sweetie, he was no good, he got killed robbing a bank, that was his mission on earth."

"I congratulate you," says Oscar Joyeux. "You have chosen the best calling. But where is my sister with the orange blossoms between her breasts?"

"Not with us," says a Sister of the Hair Shirt, who had teamed up with a laughing, curly-haired little floozy. "Here we are all virgins, I must ask you to respect our purity and modesty."

"Virgins under the skin," says the floozy.

"The Lord concerns himself not with past sins but with present repentance," says Sister Hair Shirt. "The look in your eyes is pure, my daughter, and you had the kindness to dress the wound in my forehead after my accident . . . I don't know exactly what happened, do you, my daughter? . . . I was talking to some Sisters of the Modern Rule, I do believe we were arguing as usual, and then suddenly I saw the moon hurtling down at me . . . it was very strange. Tell me, my child, has there been an accident? I can't find my mothers and sisters?"

"Your mothers and sisters are in the clink," says the floozy.

"But why, my child? What have they done? Why are they imprisoning our nuns? It reminds me of the French Revolution . . . ah, the times have changed, I only hope they won't be raped."

"Oh no . . . I wouldn't think so!"

"You've taken a weight off my mind, dear child, but I still don't understand where I am or why. Maybe I drank some wine unwittingly, one never knows, I accepted a glass of water from a young medical student . . ."

"Come, sister. I'll take you to my beauty parlor. We'll put you to bed."

"Ah, what kindness, I shall never forget you, dear child."

So Sister Hair Shirt went off to the bed of sin, the episode was a big comfort to Corneille, he couldn't get over it.

Papineau's wife was beating the trails looking for one of the twins. "I've lost Karl," she tells us. "All of a sudden I turn around and he's not there."

"But, Mama, I've told you, he's in the paddy wagon with the other guys . . . Papa's students . . ."

"That won't do," says Papineau's wife. "He's too young."

"Go on. He wants to be just like Papa. So do I. I want to go to jail too."

"Oh well," says Madame Papineau. "If he's in jail I won't worry about him. But are you sure, Blaise?"

"Sure I'm sure. He said he had as much right as Papa to go to jail."

"That's a relief."

"But I want to go too."

"Not this time," says Papineau's wife. "I need you to light the oil lamp in the tent."

At this point Madame Pablum of the Wives and Mothers outfit turns up.

"Where's your other little boy?"

"Oh, he's all right, he's in jail."

"What!" cries the Wife and Mother. "With all those brutes and degenerates? . . . he'll die . . . he's so pale already . . ."

"Cool it, comrade, cool it!" says Blaise. Maritain Papineau had a bad cold, it was all over his cheeks, but he was chirping all the same. The sight brought tears to the eyes of the Wife and Mother, her woman's heart was convulsed with pity . . .

It was almost dawn before I saw Mimi and Danny again. "I told you the Queen's Constabulary wouldn't take it lying down," says Danny. "Look at my ear, like they'd taken a knife to it . . . they're savages, and don't tell me that dictator in City Hall wasn't in the know . . ."

"Don't work yourself up, Danny darling," says Mimi. "You're all the handsomer with your ear hanging down, it makes you look like a gypsy, poor Jean-François, spending the night with the carcass of Mère Fontaine's turkey, won't *he* be jealous!"

"I don't like to have my head split open for nothing," says Danny.

"You shouldn't have made a pass at that policeman."

"I made a mistake, I thought he was one of the striking asshole cops, his sign was covered with snow, I couldn't read it . . ."

"But, Danny darling, some people just don't like to be called sweetie, they'll split your skull for less. They treat us worse than niggers. Take my brother, the doctor, hell, he'd cut your beautiful golden balls off and hang them on a tree. Just to prove that he's normal. You make too much noise, Danny darling, I don't want you to end up in a pinewood box like that student . . . They're going to bury him on New Year's Day, isn't it great for his family? Man!"

"Stinking rotten mess!" says Danny.

Mimi had kept out of club's way with nimble pirouettes. "But I wish they'd hit me instead of you, Danny darling," he said. "I don't like the pigs marring your beauty like that, my gypsy."

For Mimi and Danny the adventure was over, but the rest of us, grimacing into the damn wind, buckling under tons of snow, breathing clouds in each other's faces, didn't know how it would end. Like it or not, we had to move the wounded, lift the taxis out of snowbanks, and shovel and shovel some more. "The white tears of our fair nature," said Oscar Joyeux. And there we were, one people, one arm, one barricade to repulse that monstrous storm!

7.

THE LAWYER from Quebec trots up briskly in his furlined boots, clearing a path through the hundreds of captives that were still corralled at the gates. Papillon was hobbling along on the icy sidewalk. "We've got to get those people out before New Year's," he says, sniffing at the velvety sky, the color of ink mixed with water, you only get such a sky, that pale merciful blue, after a lousy hurricane that uproots trees and telegraph poles and damn near drives people out of their wits. It was colder than ever, the carpet of ice underfoot was as smooth as a skating rink. "Hey, Lordship of Quebec, don't walk so fast, my lamps aren't working right this morning. I know your heart cries out for justice in spite of your moneybags, you damn capitalist, but don't be too optimistic. It's not going to be easy to free our comrades."

It seemed the hardliners in Papineau's crowd were in no hurry to get out, they wanted to express their "righteous indignation" first. "Ah, Jacqueline," Papillon sighed, "Poor woman, how unhappy she must be!" But Corneille said that Papillon's Jacqueline was "the happiest of women," adding her voice to the revolutionary chorus. The nuns were singing too, Sister Clara was their star songbird. There was always a song or two coming out of the women's windows. The nuns' production was on the syrupy side:

> *"Not always will our path be strewn*
> *With nettles*
> *The Lord is waiting for us . . ."*

Jacqueline would respond, "We will be masters of the roost!" And in the next cell, Corneille told us, "the

Courtesans of Montreal would come in with the counter-point."

> "Come, lover, share my bed of moss.
> My pretty one, let's a have a toss.
> My eyes are sultry,
> Your beard is silky,
> Come, lover, share my bed of moss . . ."

From the men's wing you could hear the taxi drivers and all the other asshole groups, the tunes that filtered through those walls and bars were angry, it sounded as if all the cutthroats in the country had joined in some outlandish Kyrie, maybe this Devil's Island was short on words like Ti-Foin but they sure knew the language of the birds . . .

Papillon was disappointed. "But if our friends aren't sad, they won't want to come back to us. We'll have to beg them to accept their freedom . . ."

"The Joualonese are like that," says the lawyer from Quebec. "You never know what they'll do next . . ."

"The streets are deserted," says Papillon, "I can't live in a Joualonie without Joualonese! Christ, it's like a father of twelve who wakes up one morning in an empty kitchen, alone with his dog . . . Oh, my friends, where are you?"

So to take Papillon's mind off his sorrows we move on to the Café Erect. The waitress comes up kind of droopy with her breadcrumb sponge in one hand. "Will it be toast with bacon and eggs?"

Papillon was in a murderous humor. "Mademoiselle," he says, "I thought this was a French restaurant."

"I dunno, we're bilingual, I'll go get the boss if you wanna argue . . ."

"Christ," says Papillon. "Why isn't the menu written in our language? Where is the boss?"

"So what's it going to be: bacon and eggs?"

"No . . . oeufs et . . . bacon. I mean oeufs et . . . hey, Lordship, what do we call it? Christ, oeufs et poitrine fumée!"

"And coffee with rum," says the lawyer from Quebec.

"And the boss . . ."

"Maybe he's asleep, I'll see if he's woken up . . ."

"Wake him up. I want to have a word with him."

"Now, really," says the lawyer from Quebec. "You're not going to pick a fight with the poor man over bacon and eggs . . ."

"I'm going to wring his neck, *mon cher* . . ."

And bang, Papillon's fist comes down on the table and starts a tidal wave in our coffee cups. "Calm down, friend," says the lawyer from Quebec. "Why are you always so impulsive?"

"And why are you always so calm? You give me a pain."

"People take a long time to wake up. You can't make a revolution by browbeating a poor waitress . . ."

"Wrong again. Revolution, the dignity of our people, is a matter of details, of bacon and eggs."

"Here's your bacon and eggs," says the waitress, plunking a plate down in front of Papillon.

"How about the boss? Did you wake him up?"

"Yes, but he went back to sleep again. He don't want to talk to no froggies this morning, he says."

"Hmm, if that's how he feels about it, I'll wake him up myself!"

"He doesn't speak your language, monsieur, and besides he's an ugly customer. He'll hit you, monsieur . . ."

The lawyer from Quebec didn't want any carnage. He grabs Papillon by the sleeve and says, "Come on, Papillon, it's no use, let's get out of here." But Papillon was still fuming. He gives the tablecloth a good tug and sends the toast and coffee flying. "Okay," he says, "I feel better now. Let's go."

And in silence we go back to visit our friends in the house of penitence . . .

THEY WERE all out of the cooler in time for the student's funeral. Corneille was going to lead the procession, this was a silent march, without placards or speeches, only the blown-up photograph of a wild-eyed young man with blood all over his face, and the eyes and hearts of the masses glued to that face. That day I ditched my ambulance driver as quick as I could, I wanted to get back to my Jeanne Mance and wash up, but the bastard follows me with his stinking breath and abominations. "You going to pray for that student, son, is that it? I say it's time to celebrate when a papa's darling gets it for a change, the billy club made a mistake, usually death comes to some poor bastard and everybody thinks it's fine, just the medicine he needed. Get the drift, son? Suppose that club had come down on a nobody, son of nobody, like you, for instance, do you think the whole town would be in mourning? No, son, don't kid yourself, they'd chuck you in the ground like an apple core or a lemon peel. You wouldn't have all those students mourning for you, you'd only have your landlady, and she wouldn't be weeping for you but for your seven bucks a week. Ah, son, you're too young to go marching with people that aren't of your class, burying a kid born with a silver spoon in his mouth. An asshole like you, without a hope in this world, ought to be glad that gilded youth has croaked a little sooner."

"Someday I'm going to wring your neck, you damn hearse driver!"

"You're too damn innocent, I'd been thinking maybe you had a hand in that sweet little Langlois massacre, but I was wrong, you're just an idealistic jerk that believes the crap the bourgeoisie and the priests dish out. Praying for your enemies. Hell, kid, I don't like it!"

"Shut your trap or I'll knock your false teeth down your throat!"

Back at Mère Fontaine's, I step into the kitchen to wash my hair under the hot-water faucet, because Ti-Paul was hogging the shower, he'd stand there for hours soaping the hair on his chest and singing, "Hurrah for Ti-Paul, Ti-Paul's a good guy, he hates to feed tender little calves to nasty old cows . . ." Meanwhile, Mère Fontaine was helping Jean-François to learn his part in some play. "No, Monsieur Jean-François," she says. "It's not: I lie down on the sofa, all ready to start my trio with you . . . it's: I lie . . ." "Of course, Mère Fontaine," says Jean-François. "I must be out of my mind. It's not a trio, it's a duet . . . I must have been thinking of Danny, that horrid little fag, though rather handsome, I must admit, because Mimi insists on putting him to bed between us, isn't that the limit? He sleeps like a baby. When Mimi kisses me over his head, his only reaction is a soft snore . . . isn't that touching, Mère Fontaine?"

"Let's go over it again, child," says Mère Fontaine. "Repeat the last speech . . ."

"Some people," Jean-François recites, "go to bed at night as though descending into the tomb. The stifling sheets . . . the . . ."

"Don't make so much noise with that faucet, Monsieur Ti-Pit," says Mère Fontaine, "Monsieur Jean-François and I can't hear each other . . ."

Usually when I wash my hair, Mère Fontaine comes running with the towel, but now she was under the spell of Jean-François's charm, I'd just have to dry it myself and climb into my sweater that I saw on the clothesline in the court, frozen stiff and spangled with icicles, Mère Fontaine had forgotten to take it in.

I was all ready to go when Vincent turns up in the doorway. "No, Ti-Pit," he says. "I'm sorry, you can't go to our friend's funeral . . . I'm taking you to the hospital, Ti-Guy is dying . . ."

"Ti-Guy? I don't believe it!"

"You must have known it would happen one of these days . . . Come on, the little social worker . . . you remember? . . . she's driving us in her car . . ."

"Isn't there anything they can do?"

"No, he's poisoned himself. We might have saved him a few months ago, but the drugs have weakened him and he hasn't been eating. Come on, we can talk later."

That charity hospital was a public flophouse, nobody asked for your checkbook or identification papers at the door, people went there to die if they hadn't any place else. Most of those derelicts didn't even remember their families, they'd groan their last words all to themselves. The beds were as far gone as the patients, bandages and dressings were lying all over the place, the water in the pitchers was gray. The doctor, who was only an intern, mopped his forehead and said, "I know it's inhuman here, but the modern hospitals are overcrowded, these poor devils were picked up during the night . . . Most of them are bums, they chose this way of living and dying, respectable people won't lift a finger for them, they fear them like the plague."

A nurse was trying to make Ti-Guy vomit up his poison. The poor guy was so thin you could see all his veins, his skin was like tissue paper. For the first time, I heard Vincent swear, I thought I was dreaming. "Jesus Christ!" he says. "They've left the window open!" his big hand he slammed it shut as if he'd wanted to punish it. Then he took some cotton and wiped Ti-Guy's lips. "So this is the end," says Ti-Guy. "Why is it taking so long? Why am I keeping you waiting, my friends? Where's Papa?"

"He'll be here soon," says Vincent. "I've phoned him, don't worry."

Vincent had told me that Père Baptiste had refused to come, so had Mère Baptiste. "Your friends are family too," Vincent tells him.

"I hope it doesn't take too long," says Ti-Guy. "It's not the pain, but my fix is wearing off and the monsters are coming back . . . I wanted beauty till the end . . . yes . . . beauty . . . that's all I wanted . . ."

"Go to sleep, don't worry," says Vincent. "We won't leave you, and your parents will be here soon. Are you thirsty? Is there anything you want?"

"Why do I have to die with this weight, Vincent, with this thing you call a soul? If only I weren't so lucid . . . these awful things that weigh on me . . . life . . . it's terrible . . . I never knew these things before . . . until you told me that Jesus . . . that suffering . . . I don't remember what you told me . . . Why don't you leave the window open? The snow . . . Do you hear the little boy crying next door? What's the matter with him? They're torturing him . . . like the camel I saw . . . in the desert . . ."

"No," says Vincent. "Nobody's torturing him. He's crying because his mother has just gone away. But no one is torturing him, I assure you. And you've never tortured anyone. Why won't you sleep a little?"

"Do you remember the poem? It's ringing in my ears . . .

"The poor old tramp, they ran him over,
Him and his dog Rover,
Murdered them by running over.

They dug a great big hole
And prayed there for their soul
And chucked them in the hole!"

I called Père Baptiste. "You heartless bastard," I said, "aren't you coming to see your kid before the Lord takes him away?" "No," he says, "I'm not coming. The little stinker's only pretending. He wants me to come, does he? Okay, just for that I won't. Let him croak!" He and that bitch thought I was making it up when I told them about Ti-Guy. I went back to the deathbed, Ti-Guy was still fighting with his ghosts, in a big hurry to beat it out of this world. I didn't want him to die groaning like that. He pulled up his blanket as if he was cold.

I turned away and said to Vincent, "Can't you do something to relieve him?"

"It's strange, his drugs don't help him now. Suddenly what he feared most has happened, he's alone with himself and his tormented soul, he's defenseless . . ."

"There are certain words you could say," I suggested to Vincent reproachfully. "You priests usually . . ."

"Stop right there! . . . words . . . such words would be a mockery! words to this child . . . what do you take me for?"

I hated myself for reproaching Vincent, it wasn't his fault that Ti-Guy was suffering. "I know you're not to blame," I said. "Ti-Guy isn't really your problem, you damn priest, but, Christ, it gives me a pain. Why can't you make it a little easier for him? And why is Père Baptiste so damn mean?"

Vincent lights two cigarettes. "Come on," he said, "let's leave him for a few minutes, I'm afraid of tormenting him with my presence. We priests have done grave wrongs at the bedsides of the dying. You're right in a way, but this isn't the time to tell me . . ."

"Do you have to wait so long? He's fighting snakes that you and I can't see. Why does it have to drag on like this? It's taking so long it seems as if we'd made a mistake and were waiting for somebody to be born. And we just look on like a couple of helpless slobs . . ."

Vincent said nothing for a minute or two. Then he sighed, "Leave me alone a little while, Ti-Pit, I need to get my courage back. Go sit with your friend . . ."

I go back to Ti-Guy's bed and he takes my hand. "Vincent, where were you?" he says. "I've got some questions to ask you . . ."

"It's only your chum Ti-Pit. Lemieux, don't you remember?"

"Lemieux who?"

"Abraham Lemieux, Ti-Pit for short, come on, you know me . . ."

"Ti-Pit . . . no, never heard of him . . ."

"I used to work at the Rubber Company with Baptiste, your father, we used to eat lunch together . . . we'd pick up extra change shoveling snow . . . anything to make ends meet . . ."

"I don't know you," says Ti-Guy. "You see that Papa's forgotten me. So has Vincent . . . All alone in the hour of death . . . you see how it is . . . day follows day without meaning. Do you understand, Vincent?"

"I'm not Vincent. I'm Ti-Pit."

"After all, where were we before we we born? In the pallor of death . . . isn't that true, Vincent? Don't lie, I'm telling the truth . . . mornings without light . . . and think of my bicycle, it's going to be all alone, Gyslaine doesn't know . . . We have a bird, a canary in a cage, he'll be all alone too . . ."

"Don't worry, I'll take care of your canary, I've never had a bird, and my landlady likes animals."

"One step from being to nothingness. 'Here he walked, here he laughed . . .' That's what they say about the dead, they pick up a book, a paragraph is underlined . . . 'He did this with his pen . . .' But you know, Vincent, what worries me most is that my parents won't be able to afford a plot in the cemetery. What will happen then? Will they drown them? When people are drowned . . ."

While Ti-Guy was rambling, I thought to myself that death was no joke for people's belongings, take Ti-Guy's bicycle, already the snows of the past were falling on all those things, his books, his paintbrushes, even his bed, there was a good chance that Gyslaine would soon be sleeping in it with somebody else, Ti-Guy's caresses were dead and buried. And yet he too had had his hour of joy: "Daybreak in the streets, on my way to her bed, and there she lay, heavy with sleep. Ah, in those days, in the beginning, life was so delicious, so good to me . . ." But it seems the flowers had soon faded, because he said to me, "One little doubt destroyed it all." Even a degenerate like Ti-Cul, I said to myself, had known times when the savor of life had gone to the marrow of his bones, like when we were sitting by the stove, warming our feet, with black night and owls and pine trees all around us, before his second face, his criminal's face, hid the first like a black moon that darkens the whole sky. I didn't know that when I opened my paper that same night I'd see pictures of the five escaped convicts who were suspected of the Langlois murders, they'd none of them been caught yet. The heads of Ti-Cul and his Cri-Cri and the rest of the gang were each worth a thousand bucks to anyone interested in blood money, it was sickening to think that Ti-Cul's death could be bought with treachery, but that's the way it was, all over the country and even in the States, those thousand-dollar mugs would be hung up in every post office, with the word REWARD staring people in the face like temptation. On the sardonic faces of Ti-Cul and Cri-Cri I saw in black and white what could happen to me someday, and a shudder ran through me. A different kind of shudder ran through Ti-Guy. "I'm hot," he said. And a minute later, "I'm cold." His whole life, from start to finish, was seeping away. "We don't know," he says. "We forget . . . we don't realize . . . but the suffering never ends. That's why we hybrids . . . it's only natural, Vincent, . . . that's why we look for deliverance . . . an emergency exit."

"Would you like me to open the window?"

"No, please close it . . . thank you for coming, Vincent . . ."

"It's only Ti-Pit, I tell you . . ."

"Why does God drag out our death like this? Wouldn't it be terrible if He did it to mock us ... to the very end ... it's been going on so long ... Oh, God! ... I'm cold ... I'm so cold ..."

"Don't forget, Ti-Guy, that our sufferings come from other people ..."

"No, they come from God, you told me He was our father, you spoke of His mercy ... lies, lies!"

I remembered how Ti-Cul had once said that if he were ever caught in the net, "yes, if ever there's a big roundup and the Mounties get me, you'll see me climbing the stairs of glory with a gala smile, yes, friend, you seldom see a man smiling on the gallows, well, when they string me up, you'll see one ..." In the newspaper photo I saw that festering bitterness, I knew Ti-Cul would keep his black laughter to the end and I'd never forget him as long as I lived ...

"Go outside and smoke a cigarette," says Vincent. "You're looking green, my boy ..."

"It's awful," I said. "I can't answer Ti-Guy's questions, I'm too ignorant for those kinds of questions ..."

"I'm here now, try and call up his parents again."

That damn Père Baptiste wouldn't even come to the phone. I paced the side walk with my butt, thinking that meanwhile the masses were marching in silence behind the student's coffin. There's always got to be a sacrificial beast, I said to myself, the old nightmare was still tearing at my eyelids, the memory of the beautiful white ox that Jos Langlois had killed with a blow on the head, and Ti-Cul's voice saying, "Someday you'll suffer like your ox, they'll cut up your meat and eat it for pleasure, do you hear me, Langlois?" Ti-Cul was only a kid then, a touch of the whip on the seat of his pants and he'd run off into the woods, yelling, "I'll get even, I'll get even someday ..." Now the papers were saying: "A gratuitous, fiendish, inexplicable murder ..." because of the bloody trails where the victims had been dragged through the snow. He hadn't contented himself with butchering the ox. Langlois used to say, "Once you're dead, you don't know a thing." The meat was shipped to the city, but they kept the flayed heads with their enormous innocent teeth that had never chewed

anything but grass, not people, those teeth screamed in
agony and supplication, but nobody heard them, and
we slaves, no better than Langlois the master (because
when we threw those heads all naked into the truck, we
didn't hear their screams), ate murdered flesh just like
everybody else. We'd go sell those heads to the flea-
bitten rabble that couldn't afford chops, the big glassy
eyes didn't faze them, those scarlet skulls were fine for
soup, we'd unload those heads as fast as we could
and bury the money in the ground, we thought we'd
dig it up someday when we wanted to fly the coop,
death was our business. A woman too poor to wear
stockings in the winter would welcome our heads like
a boon, to the poorest of the poor Ti-Cul handed out
innards, his hands on the wheel were sticky with blood.
I'd look at him and say to myself, Christ, will we always
live like jackals? I remember when Ti-Cul passed me
the bottle of Molson I had to wipe off the blood where
he'd held it. Thinking about the sacrificial beast, I saw
Langlois's white ox hovering over the city like a big
sheet, it had soaked up all the sorrow in the world,
same as the student's picture towering over the crowd,
they were one and the same sacrificial beast.

Then I chucked my cigarette into the gutter and
went back up to Ti-Guy. I heard Vincent reciting in an
undertone:

> *"Thou shalt not be afraid for the terror by night;*
> *Nor for the arrow that flieth by day;*
> *Nor for the pestilence that walketh in darkness;*
> *Nor for the destruction that wasteth at nooday . . ."*

"The destruction . . . at noonday . . ." Ti-Guy murmured. "I've seen it . . . it was the sun coming down
on us . . . Anne and me, in the desert . . . we've got
to close the tent . . . an orange light, Vincent! . . . it's
terrifying . . . and the thirst . . . the thirst . . . do you
remember, Vincent: 'Restore unto me the sound . . . of
. . . of joy . . . of feasting . . .' Bah! there's no sense
in all that, Vincent . . . I thought about it in the midst
of my pleasures . . . I thought, and now I understand
. . . those words were cruel mockery . . . 'The sound of

joy . . . of feasting . . .' And these words too, I thought
they were full of love . . . listen . . . how cruel they
are. 'And may the bones that thou hast crushed rise
and dance!' My bones! Rise and dance! That's what
God . . . has to say to me . . . and you talk of divine
mercy . . . Oh, God! Oh, Vincent, that sun! And my
Arab friends have fled forever . . . I see the orange sun
on the horizon . . . coming closer . . ."

"Sleep . . . sleep," said Vincent, same as two minutes
before, no, he didn't say a thing, his lips were tight. He
wiped Ti-Guy's forehead with a damp cloth, Ti-Guy
leans over to one side as if he was going to vomit,
Vincent takes him under the armpits to keep him from
falling. He was so light, all skin and bones, he looked
at us, the sudden flame of consciousness in his eyes was
intolerable . . . "Don't leave me in this bed! . . ." he
says, "no . . . no . . . if someone takes me in his arms
. . . I think . . . I think I'll live . . ." Then he falls back
and it's all over. Vincent closed his eyes . . . the nurse
covered him with the gray sheet he'd been hugging half
a minute before, and they carried him away on a
stretcher, that's the way it is when somebody dies,
there was nothing for Vincent and me to do but beat it,
the living are only in the way. We looked at each other
like two murderers, but don't worry, next day we'd be
back in our piddling little lives, him praying at the top
of his spiral stairway, me at the Unemployment
Bureau waiting for a job, but in that minute of hard
grief I wasn't in my own skin, I saw Ti-Guy on his bike,
waving at me like a scarecrow, I saw him painting the
subway, I heard the lawyer from Quebec saying to him,
"But why don't you love life, my boy? You'll miss it
later on . . ." and in the tavern, before the student had
his head bashed in, Papillon was saying to his chum,
"Yes, Lordship of Quebec, I'm expecting a Cadillac
from you before New Year's Day." While we're waiting
for the bus, Vincent says to me, "You at least will be at
Ti-Guy's funeral, Ti-Pit . . ." "And so will you," I said,
and then we didn't say anything, we didn't look at each
other, we both had to get away, each in his own direction, and not think too much. My idea was to sop
up ten or twelve beers in a dark corner, in some bar

where I wouldn't meet anybody; he was meaning to visit Ti-Guy's parents and give them a piece of his mind, and then he'd be going to comfort this country priest he knew, who was doing three years in the clink for deflowering little girls (Vincent spoke of him more kindly. "A sick man, a lecher to be sure, but that's not unusual among priests, the poor chap seems to be paying for all the rest of them").

Ti-Cul haunted me as bad as the white ox's head. Through the vapors of my beer, I saw him and his hateful crooked smile. If ever his neck found its way into the noose, I said to myself, he'd make a good show of his death. "At least, Ti-Pit," he used to say, "justice has the same chopper for everybody, we all got to die, don't we? So we might as well bow out in pomp and circumstance." Vincent, who'd always had a keen eye, had said to me, "I saw Ti-Cul's picture in the papers, that's the face of a man who has always chosen the path of darkness . . ."

"You don't know anything about him. He's just a bum that was sick of rotting in jail. That makes sense, doesn't it? He wanted his freedom . . ."

"It's not so simple . . . For him freedom is dangerous madness . . ."

"What do you know about it? You've spent your life with your nose in a missal, you've never been locked in a cell, you've never known prison and hunger. Sure, sure, you've fasted, but take it from me, that's not the same. Ti-Cul's life is *his* business, he forged it for himself, he's fought his way through brambles, what would you know about that?"

Vincent shrugs his shoulders and says, "Sometimes I think that even for all the evil deeds of a lifetime death is too big a punishment."

"If you're thinking of Ti-Guy, you're right," I say, "but there are some specks of humanity that aren't worth the crate to bury them in."

"Are you thinking of anyone in particular?"

But I didn't answer, I changed the subject to Luc, the crook who'd gone off with Vincent's stove and books, even his bookcase. "I'd told him he could take anything except my books, but no, he wouldn't listen . . ."

Flanked by silent drunks that could hardly stand on their feet, I downed my ten or twelve beers. All the while the television was growling that the world and me and everybody else was all "one big lump of shit" like Ti-Cul had written in his letter. Then I went home to brush my suit for Ti-Guy's funeral. Mère Fontaine, who always had her eyes open, followed me to my room. "I see you've been drinking, Monsieur Ti-Pit. I suppose it's because Mademoiselle Lison doesn't come to see you any more. Is that it?"

"No, it's on account of a chum that's just died, that bastard Baptiste's kid. Can you press my suit for to-morrow, Mère Fontaine?"

Mimi was in the doorway, powdering her face for the Dear Boy. "We'll all be dust soon enough," he sighs, "so we may as well hurry up and live. Ah, Ti-Pit, I know how you feel, I watched a young queenie die once, from hour to hour you could see her wasting away, and such a pretty little thing, still in her teens. Everybody said that vice had done her in. It was true, but that's no argument against pity, I went to see her every day, I massaged her legs and made her up to look her best. Titouche (that was her name) made me promise not to let her die without a little finery, I asked all the queens in my intimate circle, which was quite a crowd even then, to pay their respects to her when the end came and deck her out like a bride. It was lovely. Ah, Ti-Pit, I know how you feel, could you hook me up in back, I'm in a hurry . . ."

"One thing, Mimi, you certainly don't take very good care of yourself, aren't you afraid of being cut off be-fore your time? You're always at it . . . sometimes I wonder if you ever sleep . . ."

"When the lover-boys aren't too keen, I sleep like a baby, it's better to ball than to bitch is my motto. Keep moving and you won't have time for tears. So long, chum."

Mimi slipped away to his grotto of love and music. I shut my eyes because I didn't want to look at that crack in the wallpaper, I'd be getting a bucket of snow in the face if Ti-Paul didn't fix the roof. Just then he was passing the time of day with Monique and Josée in room 9, he was promising to smash the windows at police headquarters, he'd show them who was the real Goliath. But Monique said, "We were with the prostitutes and they treated us fine. We had everything, security and affection. The rosiest days of our life, weren't they, Josée?"

"Yeah, not bad. They can take me back any day."

I was holding a letter from Pierrot the lumberjack. "I'm like a new man out here in the mountains," he wrote. "It's paradise, Ti-Pit. I'm so happy it's turning me inside out." Then sleep came along and Ti-Guy's eyes were watching me through the crack in the wallpaper, his voice was like a ray of hope, I couldn't bear it. "I've changed my mind," he said. "The crisis is over . . . now I can live. Why don't they let me go?" I said to the ghost, "Sleep, Ti-Guy, sleep like everybody else." Then I went to see Pierrot in his mountains, we climbed with axes over our shoulders, the sun was so soft and bright it made us giddy. I said to Pierrot, "Anybody'd think we were drunk, my goodness, the more we climb, do you think we're drunk, my goodness, do you think we'll find the beavers?" "Oh yes," says Pierrot, "we'll meet them on that hill of black pines up ahead." His teeth were like pearls in the cloud of his cold breath. It knocked the wind out of me when he said, "I'll let you go on by yourself, my boss is waiting for me down below, gotta cut timber, I'll join you at noon, you'll see a cross at the end, that's where the beavers are sleeping . . ." I climbed and climbed, it was a high, steep peak, I was panting, I wasn't so cheerful since Pierrot had left me, running down the hill with snowballs rolling from under his boots, but it was too late for me to stop. It was true, there really was a big naked cross up there, I lay down beside it and dozed off for a while, then all of a sudden I notice that I've got Ti-Cul's clothes on, the coat and the felt hat and gloves he'd stolen from Langlois, and there's blood all over them. I shout into the glacial emptiness, "Hey, Ti-Cul, that's a slimy trick, passing your loot on to me. Come back, you damn murderer, come back . . ."

"I'm right here," says a voice that has all the softness and sweetness of hypocrisy . . ."

"Where? Where are you hiding?"

"Up here, on the cross."

True enough, I look up at the cross and there he is, grinning. Then he jumps down on me and his feet trample my guts. "In that coat you're my double, you can't deny it. You're my prisoner, I've captured you, tell the truth, Ti-Pit, admit it . . ." And then I wake up from my horrible nightmare, I'm all in a sweat and Ti-Guy's eyes are shining in the crack in the wallpaper. Now it's his turn to say, "Sleep, Ti-Pit, sleep like everybody else." Good advice. After that I lay awake till daybreak . . .

Then I was on my way to bury Ti-Guy. Never fear, Baptiste and his old bag turned up for the ceremony, it took a load off their minds to see the black sheep of the brood lowered into the ground, they licked the snot from under their noses and sniveled, "Poor little fella, why have they taken him from us?" But their main worry was: "How are we going to pay for burying the damn kid?" The truth was like a bad smell done up in lace. Vincent said to Baptiste, "Let's not talk about that. I'll take care of it . . ." If Vincent hadn't thought of giving Ti-Guy a Christian burial, Baptiste and his old bag would probably have let him rot in the suicides' icebox at the morgue, but this way all Ti-Guy's slobbering brothers, Baptiste's whole stinking tribe, trooped along in the wake of the coffin, praying and bawling. Everybody was weeping except Gyslaine and Vincent and me, we were as stiff as pokers, that shovelful of snow at the cemetery turned our stomachs. But then Vincent had the gall to bellow the Antiphon for the Dead into the gaping hole where Ti-Guy was disappearing like a tin can, and recite, "My mortified body shall rise again in joy." I expected Gyslaine to kick him into the hole and give him something to think about. "Do you remember?" she said. "Do you remember, Monsieur l'Abbé? When he was very unhappy, you sang for him. Why don't you sing now instead of dishing up formulas?" And Vincent answered, "You asked me then if I was a priest. Now you see that at certain times I am nothing else . . ." "I slept with him," said Gyslaine. "When I remember him, that's all I'll think about, not his resurrection, only the sexual pleasure that made him happy before he chose this awful death, this rot that has nothing to do with love. I'll never take him in my arms again, that's what I'll think . . ."

"You're probably right, because that's the way you loved him," said Vincent. Right after the requiem he beat it, he wasn't at all pleased with himself. He always walked off like that, with big long steps, burying his chin in his sweater, when somebody touched him too close. He was afraid, I thought as I watched him go, that the flaw in his charity had rubbed us the wrong way. Old man Baptiste was all mealy-mouthed. "Thank you, Monsieur l'Abbé," he said, "thank you very much . . . we're poor folk . . . we've done all we could . . . but death is expensive and that little bum . . ."

"Don't insult your son," says Vincent. "He wasn't a bum. You'd do better to pray for him . . ."

Then Baptiste comes over to me and brings up the past, the times at the Rubber Company when we were still chums and shoveled snow together. "Skip it, Baptiste," I said. "We're not friends now . . . I'm through with you!" "Aw, Ti-Pit, don't you remember the lunch box we shared? And shoveling snow at Upper-Nose? Hell, why all this sermon now? Is it my fault if that no-good Ti-Guy has slipped the harness of life . . ."

"So long, Baptiste. You and me are through!"

I saw Ti-Guy again in my dreams. Vincent was dragging his coffin the whole length of rue Sainte-Catherine, and me and Gyslaine were there too. Then suddenly, at nightfall, the crowd poured in from all sides, same as they'd done for the student, from all the boulevards and back alleys, everybody holding a candle for the Hallelujah. I recognized all the faces from the demonstration, Mimi and his gang were there, as frisky as usual, Mimi was singing and the whole crowd was keeping time with him. "My mortified body shall rise again in joy . . . hey, come on, Ti-Guy, come on out of there, don't let death hem you in . . . come on, Ti-Guy, get up! . . ."

Little by little the voices of the chorus died down, I was alone, heading back to my boardinghouse, but then I heard a voice calling me in the night. "Hey, Ti-Pit. Hey, Ti-Pit, damn you! It's me, Papillon . . . I'm coming . . . can't you hear the bellows? That's my asthma . . ." And Papillon grabbed my arm in his big paw. "Come on to the Cat, Ti-Pit, I've got some things to tell you . . ."

I turned to Papillon and said, "Ti-Pit, never heard of him . . . you've got it wrong, Papillon, my name is Abraham, Abraham Lemieux."

"Abraham Lemieux, my chum! Christ, how about a beer?"

It was only a dream . . .

SELECTED NEW CANADIAN LIBRARY TITLES

Asterisks (*) denote titles of New Canadian Library Classics

McCLELLAND AND STEWART LIMITED
publishers of The New Canadian Library
would like to keep you informed about
new additions to this unique series.

For a complete listing of titles and
current prices – or if you wish to be added
to our mailing list to receive future catalogues
and other new book information – write:

BOOKNEWS
McClelland and Stewart Limited
25 Hollinger Road
Toronto, Canada M4B 3G2

McClelland and Stewart books are
available at all good bookstores.

Booksellers should be happy to order from our catalogues
any titles which they do not regularly stock.